Kanti
Born of Shadows Book 3

J.R. Erickson

Copyright © 2018 J.R. Erickson

All rights reserved.

This is a work of fiction. Names, characters, places, and incidents either are the products of the author's imagination or are used fictitiously. Any resemblance to actual persons, living or dead, businesses, companies, events, or locales is entirely coincidental.

ISBN-10: 1983651842
ISBN-13: 978-1983651847

DEDICATION

For Pat-who continues to inspire me from the other side of life.

ACKNOWLEDGMENTS

Thank you to all of my family and friends, who have been my avid beta readers, and to my wonderful husband who has supported this re-commitment to my writing. Thank you to my ARC Team and the amazing indie author community that has taught me so much. Finally my gratitude to Rena at Cover Quill who designed my beautiful covers for the Born of Shadow's Series. And lastly, thank you to my little honey beast who keeps the wonder of the world always at the forefront of my life.

CHAPTER 1

Abby watched the fire grow and then ebb away. It spoke to her. In the flames, she saw Kanti's dark eyes observing her and the girl, more like a woman, whispered things that Abby could not hear, but the life inside her stirred in response. She shook her head to banish the strange images that often came unbidden to her mind.

"How's my beautiful goddess?" Sebastian asked, startling her as he approached from behind. He wrapped his arms around her and kissed her neck.

Abby sat, with her legs tucked beneath her, on their living room floor. Outside snow fell in gusts.

"I got you a present," he whispered and moved around and knelt before her on the lush burgundy carpet.

He wore a heavy wool sweater and torn blue jeans and his hair, now shoulder length, fell into his eyes. Abby brushed the hair away from his face and leaned into him. She pressed her face into his chest and felt a bit of the pressure inside her subside. She had been lying to everyone. No one knew of the child within her and in two days, they would go to the Coven of Ula, and she feared that the elder witches would immediately sense the baby.

Sebastian reached into a small purple bag and pulled out a tiny, intricately carved wooden jewelry box. He lifted the lid to reveal a glowing moonstone ring embedded in red velvet.

Abby's eyes grew wide and she looked at Sebastian, who watched her intently.

"I asked Helena before the ball to find it for me. I needed a little magic for the perfect ring."

Abby reached out and ran her index finger along the shining stone. It felt cold to the touch, and the coolness rose through her arm and into her body.

"I had a dream at Sydney's house, before all of this really began," he continued. "I dreamed of giving you this ring and asking you to marry me. In my dream, I knew that the moonstone was a source of power for you and that it would protect us."

Abby's breath caught in her throat and a flood of emotion rose from her diaphragm. Tears filled her eyes and spilled over and Sebastian shuddered, hard, as her energy coursed through him.

"Will you marry me?"

Abby wanted to blurt out the truth or run from the room. More than all of that, she wanted to say yes, but she could not open her mouth. She pressed her lips together and nodded.

Sebastian laughed and pulled out the ring.

"Whew, you scared me for a minute there."

He slid the gothic silver band onto her finger. The delicate twists and ridges fit her finger perfectly, and she threw her arms around him and cried into his shoulder.

He rubbed her back and then pulled away, looking into her face. He wiped the streaks of tears from her cheeks.

"What is it, Abby?" He looked unsure.

Finally, her lips obeyed her, and she spoke.

"I'm happy and it scares me. I just love you so much and I believed I had lost you and now..." She gestured to the room, but meant to encapsulate everything, the new house and the new life they had been given.

"It's okay to be happy, but I understand, I do. Sometimes feeling happy has seemed a bit like tempting fate. The gods will seek to balance the universe by destroying our happiness, but that's superstitious, right?"

"Elda would say that the universe finds balance through love and more love raises the consciousness of the world. You deserve to be happy, Sebastian. I want that for you."

"You deserve that too, Abby. You realize that, right?"

"Of course." Abby kissed him. It felt like a little white lie, the kind that everyone tells. Did she deserve to be happy when so many people in the world suffered?

Sebastian pulled her into him and Abby wrapped her legs around him, hugging him with every piece of her body.

"Marriage, huh?" She laughed, settling back into the sofa and admiring the beautiful ring. "You know we only met a few months ago. You sure you want to sign up for a whole lifetime with me?"

"Yep, not a doubt. My dad proposed to my mom after three weeks, so we're way behind the game." Sebastian smiled, his eyes dancing over her. "Plus, I want the whole world to know that I'm devoted beyond forever to you."

"Beyond forever? How long is that exactly?" She laughed and tugged at his curls. He kissed her again.

"We can't even fathom it," he whispered against her cheek, and then he scooped her up and carried her to their bedroom.

Kanti

****

Lydie sat on the end of the dock and stared into the rivulets of slate-gray water. The cold had stopped having an impact. Enough time in any environment and the body adjusted. Max had taught her that, but she couldn't think about Max. Max made her cry. But, of course, it was too late, and she started to cry; her tears caused the cold to touch her face and she wiped them away angrily.

She and Oliver had been staying at Abby and Sebastian's new house. They had gone there after Sorciére, after the day in the Vepar's lair when the whole world flipped upside down and never got righted. The day that Lydie realized why her parents, both witches, chose life outside the coven. It wasn't their fault, the witches of Ula, but tragedy seemed to follow them. Now Max lay dead in the ground and an evil spirit haunted them all.

"Kanti," Lydie said the name angrily. Kanti had killed Max and the others. Lydie hadn't known Adora or Thomas or even Rod, the two witches and the human who'd died that day. But Max, she'd known Max, and she'd loved him. Max had treated her like a daughter, a granddaughter and his friend. He had loved her unconditionally.

Kanti hadn't killed them directly, of course. Evil spirits couldn't kill on their own, but she acted through the Vepars. She helped them create the walking dead who had attacked her and Oliver and Sebastian. The fire that burned the lair came at the request of Kanti. Lydie knew it did. She hated Kanti. She didn't care what had happened to her as a young woman that made her mean, that inspired her to curse generations of witches after her. She wanted to hurt the spirit, but how do you hurt someone who's already dead?

****

"Do you think she's going to be okay?" Abby asked, startling Oliver, who stood in the kitchen watching Lydie on the dock. He had watched her for more than an hour, second-guessing himself every time he considered going to her.

He shook his head and sighed, leaning into the one-armed hug that Abby offered him.

Since Sebastian's return, Oliver's time with Abby had grown less frequent, and he dared not admit that he missed the weeks while Sebastian was missing and they were solving the mystery of the curse. He had also started to entertain another vision of him and Abby, but that too had begun to disappear. When Lydie returned to Ula, Oliver would no longer be able to stay in Abby and Sebastian's new home. They would never cast him out, but it was common sense. Lovers wanted their privacy, and he abhorred the thought of playing third wheel.

"What are you thinking about?" Abby asked, hoisting herself onto the counter and sitting cross-legged.

"Ula," he sighed. "I can't seem to put myself back there. I keep trying to imagine waking up in that bedroom again." He shook his head and shrugged. "I really don't get it, but there it is."

Abby nodded her agreement.

"You can stay here with us, Oliver, I mean it. I know you think that you have to go back, but this house is huge."

He smiled and patted her knee.

"I'd love to stay wherever you are, but the truth is that you guys need your alone time right now. You know it as well as I do. I also can't leave Lydie behind."

They both turned their gazes back to the young witch who sat motionless on the dock beyond.

"I just can't believe we only have two days. These last few weeks have flown."

Abby too had noticed how quickly the previous several weeks had passed. Though busyness could do that. From searching for and then buying the new house, to assembling all the materials from the curse, and adjusting to the mostly sleepless nights where all four of them regularly woke from nightmares, the days passed in a blur.

In addition, Abby's fear surrounding the secret she harbored accelerated time all on its own. She felt like the universe was rushing her toward some big unveiling and she was helpless to stop it.

"Are you scared?" Oliver asked, noticing her silence.

"Yes. I'm scared of this curse and I'm scared for all our recovery and I'm scared when I think about Tobias and Alva and where they are right now. I want to be strong and fierce and ready to fight, but most of me is just plain scared."

She laughed and rolled her eyes.

"Who knew this witch stuff would get so complicated."

"Not me," Oliver added. "But I know now that I was living in the dark. I think Faustine and Elda preferred it that way, maybe believed the old adage that what we don't know can't hurt us. Guess the joke's on them."

"Not a very funny joke."

"Nope." Oliver shook his head sadly and thought of Max. He still couldn't imagine sitting around the dinner table at Ula and not seeing Max's jovial face at the other end.

"Where's your partner in crime?" he asked, needing to change the subject.

"Buying a snowblower." Abby laughed. I'm sure there's some spell I could learn to wash the snow into the lake, but I'd rather let him do it. We need normal, and if blowing snow helps Sebastian feel human again, then so be it."

"Ha," Oliver chuckled, "well I don't blame him there. I had the most intense dream last night about changing a tire on my Jeep. Mind you I haven't had to change a tire in ten years, but in the dream, it felt like the most natural thing. I woke up wishing I had a flat tire."

****

"I want this space to reflect Lydie's dreams," Helena insisted. "This sand feels too gritty."

Demetrius rolled his eyes in exasperation and looked at Elda, who only grinned and shook her head.

"Here, let me try something," Bridget offered.

Since returning to Ula, Bridget's previously restrained demeanor had shifted. Eager to take the initiative, she participated in nearly every new spell placed on the coven. Additionally, she offered her suggestions to Elda and Faustine about how to rebuild the coven as a thriving community and refused to return to the status quo.

Bridget took a handful of the sand and whispered into it. Then she went to the case of elixirs sitting on the floor and pulled out a large bottle filled with dark green powder. She sprinkled the powder into the sand and then flung it into the dune that ascended to the ceiling of one of the tower rooms. Previously the vacuous space had held only stone slabs and crystals for purification and divining. Faustine had offered it as a special place for Lydie.

Demetrius had enchanted the tower to mimic Lydie's childhood home. The sand dune was real sand that Lydie could run up and down and sink her toes into. Holographic trees, like those at the Coven of Sorciére, rained colorful flowers onto the floor. A huge, living oak tree grew out of the stone floor. The branches extended and disappeared into the ceiling and the castle walls. Nestled within the branches was a duplicate of Lydie's childhood home as it had been before the forest took it back. Except this version was a tree house with a wooden spiral staircase for entrance. The room's floor was enchanted with real grass and hordes of tiny yellow flowers.

"Yes, perfect," Helena chimed, sinking her hands into the sand.

Helena had not made a full recovery from the attack at Ula more than three weeks before. Her body still ached and she had strange ghoulish visions that sometimes made her woozy and filled with panic. She often used a tall wooden cane that Faustine had carved for her. He had formed the top into a beautiful wolf with two shimmering emerald eyes. Though Helena loved the beautiful cane, it upset her every time she wrapped her fingers around it, and more so when she had to put her weight against it because her legs could not seem to hold her up.

Elda pushed open the heavy castle door and gasped when she saw the room.

"Oh my." She took her hand to her throat and shook her head in disbelief. "It's amazing."

"Isn't it?" Demetrius asked, grinning. "And that cloud up there is a door."

He pointed to the space above the sand dune where the wall looked like a blue summer sky.

They had cast a spell so that the ceiling reflected the weather outside the castle. A fluffy white cloud was placed exactly at a door that opened out of the castle, where they had continued the sand dune all the way to the lagoon. Helena imagined Lydie flinging open the door and tumbling to the lagoon edge to swim in the summer.

"It's absolutely breathtaking," Elda continued. She laughed as Garfield, Lydie's fuzzy orange cat, poked his head from a bushel of leaves far up in the oak tree.

"We thought it might be time to bring more animals into the castle," Bridget said, calling to the cat who immediately began a laborious descent to get his ears scratched. "They sense things after all, and frankly, I miss them."

Helena nodded vigorously. "I fully intend to move from this wolf," she held up the cane, "to a real one very soon."

"Of course," Elda replied. "It is not as though I banished pets from Ula."

And that was true. After the great tragedy of 1908, which they now understood as part of the curse linking Dafne and the Vepar Tobias, many of their pets were dead. Some of the animals were killed the night of the attack, and others had died of old age long after the incident occurred. However, no one at the coven had brought another animal in since Kissy, the fat gray tabby that Oliver had found abandoned during a Vepar hunt.

"Animals are powerful," Demetrius agreed. "Galla's parrot foretold of a sinister stranger visiting Sorciére and less than a month later, a dark witch from Galla's past appeared on our doorstep."

"Yes, animals have also communicated great dangers to us here at Ula," Elda agreed and Helena gave her a sad smile, both remembering another time.

As if on cue, the fat orange kitten dove from the tree and sailed right through a holographic butterfly at Helena's elbow.

****

"Back to Ula," Lydie commented absently as they walked the enchanted dock into the icy waters of Lake Superior.

The witches of Ula had built the dock a week before, bewitched so that it only appeared if a witch of the Coven of Ula called for it. Oliver had spoken to the lake and the dock had gradually materialized.

"Just think, Lyds, Bridget has probably whipped up some crazy chocolate thing that will give us a stomachache for days," Oliver teased, hugging her.

"Hey, there's Victor and Kendra," Abby announced as they stepped from the woods where they had parked their car. Abby waved at them.

"Damn it's cold," Victor bellowed, walking down the dock and blowing into his gloved hands.

"Victor and Kendra, this is Lydie and Sebastian," Abby told them.

"The infamous Sebastian." Victor grinned, shaking his hand.

"Good to meet you, man," Sebastian offered. He gave Kendra a quick hug. "Abby has said you're her new best friends."

"Excuse me?" Oliver joked, poking Abby in the sides.

"I have many best friends," Abby promised.

"Nice to meet you," Lydie told them, watching the distant form of a boat moving toward them.

Faustine picked the six of them up in a large steel, military-style boat. He ushered them into the cockpit where the glass was reinforced, and an array of weapons hung from one wall. Abby introduced him to Victor and Kendra.

"A corvette, huh?" Oliver asked.

"Yes," Faustine said seriously. "Can't be too careful."

"Isn't a corvette a car?" Lydie asked, settling onto a wooden bench and hugging an orange life preserver against her chest.

"Yes," Faustine told her. "But a corvette is also a fast military warship, and that's what you're riding in now."

"A warship?" she asked, and her voice trembled.

Oliver sat next to her and pulled her against him.

"Just for extra safeness, Lyds, but those Vepars aren't stupid enough to attack us out here. We're way better swimmers."

Lydie didn't respond, but her eyes darted back toward the trees as they pulled away from the mainland.

In the sleek and fast ship, the trip, to the island, passed in a blur.

As they entered the black tunnel that bore them into the lagoon outside the castle, Abby noticed that the passage seemed quite a bit larger than the first time she had sailed through it.

"We had to blast it out," Faustine commented, "make it larger for the new boats, but don't worry, we have a whole new security system at Ula. The devil himself couldn't get past our cliffs."

CHAPTER 2

The castle had changed. The main hallway held new rugs in bright reds and yellows. The candle sconces were gone, replaced by huge orbs with stained glass reflecting the light within. Garlands, twisted with tiny white lights, weaved down the walls and along the floor perimeter, and pictures hung where previously the walls had been bare. Abby saw images of rainbows and huge, heavy flowers in full bloom. She saw watercolor fantasies depicting spring rains and lovers dancing beneath the full moon.

The library too boasted new, plush white carpeting and pillows strewn in enormous piles, surrounded by soft, sunken chairs and giant round ottomans. Bohemian tapestries in a hundred different colors bundled together in the center of the ceiling and cascaded out and down to the floor. The astrological mural was hidden beneath the fabric. Only the books remained the same, but those too appeared brighter, as if the dust and age had been blown off them. The fireplace roared and on the mantel, the old pictures of Ula were gone. The space now held vases of fresh flowers and animal figures carved from rose quartz.

"Wow, how could you possibly do this in four weeks?" Sebastian asked Faustine, marveling at the room.

"With a lot of help and lot of magic," Helena broke in, appearing from behind a golden tapestry and carrying a giant tray of pastries and teacups.

"Give me that," Oliver snapped, taking the tray quickly from Helena and pecking her on the cheek.

"Well hello to you too," she said, smiling. She settled into one of the overstuffed chairs and exhaustion showed in her eyes. "Come give me a hug, Lydie."

She beckoned to Lydie, who went and hugged her and then pulled up a pillow near her feet.

"It's all so different," Lydie whispered.

"We thought we were due for a big change," Faustine told them. Though something betrayed another emotion behind his words, sadness perhaps. Faustine was largely a creature of habit, and changing the castle so dramatically had left him slightly uneasy.

"I think it looks great," Abby said and sat on a pile of pillows next to Sebastian. She rested her hands on her belly and then quickly moved them to her knees. For the previous two weeks, she had worked on concealment spells around the baby. It had taken much of her energy and garnered more than a few awkward questions from Sebastian, but she appeased him by claiming she merely created protection spells for their new home.

****

"Well it sure has been lonely without you and Lydie Bug," Bridget told Oliver, giving him a big hug and a kiss on the cheek. "But I don't blame you for needing a break from this place." She winked at him and returned to the stove to stir one of the seven steaming pots. Two of the pots stirred themselves and another made a sound like giggling as it boiled.

"That's dessert," she told him. "I thought we all needed a little mirth with our meal tonight."

Oliver grinned and surveyed the kitchen.

"No big remodel in here, Bridget?"

She looked at him sideways.

"It has taken me fifty years to get this kitchen just the way I like it. I'm not starting over now."

"Good point."

Oliver went to the oven and peeked in at the roasting turkey and glass baking dishes filled with yams and green beans.

"Are we feeding an army?"

"You could say that," Bridget said slyly, but Oliver heard the serious edge in her voice.

"All the change doesn't make it go away, does it? These last few months have left their mark."

"Yes, and I admit, I'm racked with guilt that I wasn't here when Helena and Lydie were attacked. What bad timing I chose for a trip south. But the truth is Ula feels unsafe right now. I know that it shouldn't. The most powerful witches of Sorciére combined with our own have rebuilt the spells and created new ones that are a thousand times stronger than those we used before. But still..."

"Yeah, I feel it," Oliver admitted. "I knew I would, and I won't pretend that our minds aren't part of the enemy here. We're all scared in a way that we weren't before. I almost thought Lydie would refuse to get on the boat to come back. She was so tense in the car on our drive up, I thought she might light the car engine on fire."

Bridget shook her head sadly and walked to the window that looked out on Lake Superior far below.

"Lydie will never be the same, and what's really sad is she's already been here before. Lydie faced death earlier than any of us and I'd like to say she made it out unscathed, but we all know better. Losing Max is going to stay with her."

"Do you think it's wrong for us to come back here, Bridget? I've wondered about that. If maybe I shouldn't buy a little house on the mainland too and keep Lydie with me."

"I don't think so, Oliver. The truth is that we're all afraid for Abby and Sebastian over there. They're alone, there's no fortress protecting them from an evil that has clearly grown in strength. When this is all over, that might be nice for you and Lydie, but right now...I think right now you both belong here at Ula."

****

Faustine stood at the head of the table. His cheeks glowed rosy from the wine and he was in rare form, with a smile on his face that went all the way to his eyes.

"Gratitude, my friends. I am grateful for this table filled with food and surrounded by witches and friends. I am grateful for our lives, for our health, for the intelligent universe that strives always to support us. I am grateful for each of you."

They held their glasses high and drank. Sweet cherry wine, spiced cider and the dark craft beer that Oliver insisted on bringing from the mainland. They drank and ate and talked.

Abby had second helpings of mashed yams and baked cauliflower. She watched Sebastian and Bridget excitedly discussing his new kitchen. Abby looked around the room at the smiling faces awash in candlelight.

I want to remember this moment, she thought and touched her fingers to the moonstone on her ring finger.

"You did it?" Helena suddenly gushed, grabbing Sebastian in a hug.

He laughed, and a blush rose up his face as the din in the room quieted and the other witches turned toward him.

Abby gave him a questioning look and he nodded toward her hand.

"Oh, I'm sorry," Helena gasped, covering her face. "My big mouth."

"No, it's okay," Sebastian reassured her.

He moved to Abby and took her hand. She stood with him.

"I asked Abby to marry me," he announced, and Abby felt a stiffness in his body as if he expected the witches of Ula to disapprove.

Instead, Elda began to clap and Lydie hooted. Helena did a little twirl and then looked sick and quickly took her chair. Abby glanced at Oliver, who gave her a forced smile. The other witches clapped as well and offered their congratulations. As Sebastian relaxed beside her, Abby returned to her earlier reverie. She wanted to stay in the moment forever, hearing the laughter of the witches and watching the moon rise, slow and white, into the dark sky.

Faustine cleared his throat.

"I am sorry to turn our attention to darker pursuits, but I believe it is time that we talk about the curse."

****

They gathered in the library after dinner, the witches of Ula and the small coven of Chicago. Everyone talked excitedly, drunk on food and wine and wanting to share their own secrets and adventures.

Abby chose a sunken red love seat next to the fireplace and pulled her legs to her chest, resting her head against the cushion behind her. The warmth dulled her senses and soon she felt her eyelids grow heavy.

Kanti had fought hard the day she was taken. Her fingers were bloodied, and her fingernails mostly ripped away. The giant had pulled out a hunk of her hair. Her skull, at the base of her neck, throbbed. She lay on the bed of dirty blankets and refused the tears and the panic that swirled in her abdomen. She could hear the giant and the white man outside the tent whispering together in their language that she did not speak. The white man scared her more than the giant. Though half his size, his eyes were black like a devil's eyes and when he looked at her, she felt lust and violence pour out of him. He had slapped her once, hard in the face, and made her mouth bleed. Then he had licked the blood off and cast her into the tent with no food or drink. Only a pile of soiled blankets awaited her, and she shivered in the frigid night air.

She could see the crackling flames through the opening in the tent and she wanted to go to the fire. The fire meant warmth, but more, she could communicate with Rowtag, the shaman of her tribe and her own teacher. Rowtag heard messages in the flames, and he had begun to teach listening to Kanti and her brother Nepi. Kanti took to the flames faster than Nepi, who was a spirit of the water and would likely seek his visions through the streams and lakes.

She moved onto her hands and knees, wondering instead if she might simply run. Break out of the tent as a whisper and steal into the dark forest at night. Before she could stand, the white man pulled back the flap in the tent. He walked inside and growled something in his language and then he laughed. She tried to stand anyway, and he shoved her back and pointed his finger in her face. He removed the leather strap from his pants and she thought he meant to hit her with it, but he merely cast it aside. She started to cry as she understood what he meant to do. He took his pants down and moved toward her.

Abby woke with a gasp and returned to the buzz of the library. She feared all the witches' eyes had cast toward her, but they continued to talk, lost in their individual conversations. Only Sebastian had tuned in to her. He sat on the love seat beside her, holding her hand and, she realized, pinching her skin slightly.

"I'm sorry," he said, patting the tiny red welt he'd left behind. "I could tell it was a bad dream."

Abby blinked a few times to clear the images.

"It was," she sighed, continuing to feel Kanti's fear as she realized the horrors in store for her. Abby had been having the dreams for weeks. Sometimes she saw new visions, such as the one she'd just had, and other times snippets of Kanti's original abduction. Each one left her sick and scared.

"Okay everyone," Faustine's voice boomed over the chatter. "Though I'm sure we could spend all evening idly socializing, I think it is time we get down to business."

He walked to the fireplace and stood before the flames, creating a long ghoulish shadow on the floor before him. Abby shuddered as the man from her dream drifted into her thoughts.

"I first would like to formally welcome Victor and Kendra to the Coven of Ula. We are honored to have you here to celebrate, and we are grateful for all you have done to help Abby and Oliver."

Victor held up his glass of wine and nodded in response.

"I wish we'd met under more pleasant circumstances. But we are here because the Vepars, our mortal enemy, have stumbled upon some demonic power that they are harnessing in a rather terrifying way. Somehow they are using this curse to their own advantage, and it seems we are woven into this curse in some meaningful way."

From what I have read so far of the documents gathered by the Asemaa, it is obvious that they believed the curse originated with the Native American girl Kanti. There is an overwhelming amount of material and we've had other business," he gestured to the changes in the room, "so we have only scratched the surface. "And we must consider that Sydney was only human." He looked apologetically at Abby. "And thus, her theories are more fallible than a witch who knows and understands our world. Still, she makes a compelling argument for this woman Kanti somehow cursing her own bloodline."

"How do you create a curse?" Sebastian asked.

"It's not easy," Elda answered him. "I've been doing a bit of research into curses and it's strange, and dark, magic. Though I doubt this girl had access to any such information. It seems obvious to me that it was born of anger, pain and intention."

"So, she was a witch?" Sebastian asked. "Because a human intention is not going to curse people for hundreds of years."

"Something powerful, yes," Faustine answered, looking pointedly at Sebastian, who himself had recently exhibited powers beyond the scope of a regular human. "In a tribe, she may have become a medicine woman, a seer perhaps. We don't know."

"Maybe that's why they kidnapped her," Lydie piped in. "To steal her power."

Faustine nodded.

"I tend to lean toward that idea. She was special, and that made her a target for the man who took her. Victor, did you want to get us started on the findings?" Faustine asked.

Victor stood and took Faustine's place in front of the fireplace.

"After Abby contacted us about Dafne and Tobias and the issue of the bloodline, we started digging into genealogy. Finding Dafne's maiden name was easy enough. The problem arose when we tried to find evidence of a child. Dafne didn't even use her first name, let alone her given last name when she had the baby. We searched for adoptions and abandonments within one hundred miles of your Lake Superior mainland, primarily because we felt confident that she waited until close to labor. She knew it would look suspicious if she disappeared for a long time and probably did not feel safe venturing too far away. We also found it really hard to believe that she wouldn't have traced her own bloodline, but since we don't have access to Dafne, we couldn't exactly ask her."

Abby noticed a subtle shift in all the Ula witches at the mention of Dafne's name. Helena looked ready to cry.

"We traced all the adoptions through hospitals that we found, but didn't discover any promising leads, and then we started to search for midwives. This was obviously a lot more complicated, but we got lucky. A group of northern Michigan midwives created an online scrapbook of births in Michigan dating as far back as 1878. We tracked every single midwife in the upper peninsula. They're all dead at this point, but midwifery is interesting. Many daughters follow their mothers into the field, and their work is the storytelling kind. Kendra found information on a midwife named Agatha Brinson. She spoke to Agatha's daughter, Julia, who is now seventy-two, but remembered her mom telling of an especially mysterious birth by a woman with long black hair whose eyes seemed to light on fire when her child was born. What's interesting is that a centuries-old oak tree outside the midwife's home burst into flames during the birth, and there was no lightning storm or strange activity except the young woman in labor."

"I can't believe Dafne had a baby," Helena whispered sadly. "Why didn't she tell us?"

"That's something we cannot possibly fathom," Faustine said, encouraging Victor to continue.

"Fortunately for us, Agatha kept a very detailed record of her births. Dates, times, names and adoptive parents. This woman with the fiery eyes demanded that her birth be anonymous, but the midwife refused and I'm sure Dafne, in her exhaustion, just let it go, assuming her false name would be enough."

"What name did she use?" Elda asked.

"Aubrey Blake."

"Wait, Aubrey Blake?" Abby interrupted. "As in Devin's cousin Aubrey?"

"Yes."

"Why would she do that?" Helena asked. "If she wanted the baby to be a secret?"

"To pay homage to her cousin," Elda said, understanding. "To atone for her guilt. I'm sure she believed that she caused Aubrey's death."

"From what we've found," Victor continued, "Aubrey and Dafne were like sisters, very close. It was their grandmother who had the fiery red hair, which only Aubrey acquired. Devin, the witch whose body Abby found, ended up looking nearly identical to Aubrey, amazing really, when you think about it."

"Yeah, I remember the newspaper article I found about the burning." Abby shuddered. The image of Devin's dead body returned, and she closed her eyes against the memory. Devin had looked nearly identical to the witch burned one hundred years earlier.

"Dafne's child's name was Sylvia. Dafne did not name her. She left the child with the midwife, who placed her with a family, and they named her. As far as I could find out, Sylvia did not have powers. She gave birth to three children."

"Sylvia was the name of my great-grandmother," Abby said.

"Yes, and they are one and the same. Which makes Dafne your great-great-grandmother."

Abby spit out the cider she'd been sipping. Sebastian grimaced and wiped his face.

"Sorry," she said, using her sleeve to wipe his cheek.

"Could it be true?" Helena asked. The dismay on her face mirrored every expression in the room.

"She obviously didn't know," Elda countered.

"Maybe not," Victor agreed. "Without speaking to her, we can't know for sure. She could have tracked the bloodlines herself, of course."

"But she didn't," Julian argued. "I believe after Tobias murdered her friends, she cast the child away out of pain. I don't think she knew about the curse."

"Then who told her? Why did she hate us?" Sebastian demanded. "She obviously started to investigate the curse at some point, and by the time we arrived…"

"She was expecting us," Abby finished.

Faustine held up his hand.

"We don't know that. Before you arrived, she may have gotten wind of the curse, but didn't fully believe it. Perhaps your arrival brought the possibility back to reality."

"Let's not speculate," Julian said, bringing the conversation back to Victor. "Tell us more about the genealogy."

I'm trying to understand where Devin came from," Abby added. "My great-grandmother Sylvia had two daughters. One was my grandmother Arlene and the other was named Hannah, but I never knew her. I didn't think she had any children."

"Well according to hospital records Sylvia had three children. However, she birthed the first child when she was only seventeen, and her parents forced her to give the baby up for adoption. That daughter's name was Denise, and she would die during childbirth with Devin. Devin's father, Denise's husband, did not want a child alone. He put Devin up for adoption. When Devin started to search for her biological family, she must have stumbled upon the photos of Aubrey. Obviously, she saw the physical resemblance, so she chose to call herself Blake."

"So, Devin was my second cousin?" Abby asked, incredulous. "And Sydney didn't know this? Despite her research with the Asemaa?"

"From what I can gather, the Asemaa discovered the curse and knew it affected Dafne; however, I don't think they tracked down her baby."

"Gwen thought Dafne died in the fire," Abby said suddenly. "She didn't realize that Dafne had survived."

"Why didn't they assume the curse died out with Dafne then?" Helena asked.

Abby shrugged.

"I'll contact Gwen soon and try to find out. I got the feeling they didn't have a strong grasp on the curse. The journalist Stephen seemed to know more, but now he's…"

"Dead," Sebastian said, frowning.

"The connections get even funkier," Victor continued. "Sylvia's daughter Hannah did in fact have a child. His name is Louis, and he's my father."

"I'm sorry, what?" Abby asked, wondering if he was joking.

"No way," Lydie murmured, and she looked toward Elda and Faustine as if they might return the world to sense.

Victor nodded. "I know. You can imagine my surprise when I realized the truth. My dad's mom lived as a recluse. I only met her a few times and she died years ago. My dad didn't know her family. Apparently she suffered from psychological problems. I never probed beyond that."

"A lot of secrets in your family tree," Galla mentioned, appraising Abby and Victor.

"I guess so," Abby agreed, tempted to apologize for generations of people she never knew.

"How is this all possible?" she asked. "The few times I heard my aunt Sydney or my mom talk about their aunt Hannah, they referred to her as the kooky aunt."

"Yeah, she was an odd duck. She died when I was ten and I never once saw her leave the house," Victor explained.

"And that pretty much sums up what we know about the bloodlines. Unfortunately, information about Kanti is virtually nonexistent. However," Victor quickly added, "that only means her existence hasn't been uploaded to the Internet. Some Native American tribes are very protective of their history, and they did a much better job of sharing their stories through generations verbally. We need only to connect with the right people to find her, I'm sure of it."

"What about your dreams, Abby?" Elda asked. "Have there been more? It's as though she wants us to know her story and though I am surely one for research, if we can get it direct from the horse's mouth, well..."

"Yes," Abby sighed, strangely reluctant to share. "I have dreamed of a white man whom Kanti was delivered to by the giant. I'm pretty sure that he raped her."

Elda shook her head sadly, and Helena closed her eyes as if warding off the images. Abby did not want to look at Lydie. She found it difficult enough to look into those haunted eyes without adding to their despair.

"Any inkling of who the man was? If she knew him?" Julian asked from a balcony high up in the books. He was sitting with his legs dangling over the edge.

"No, they're both strangers to her."

Sebastian stared at her, and she realized he was wondering why she hadn't shared the dream with him.

"I had it just now," she whispered and squeezed his hand. He smiled and lifted her palm to his lips.

"What about you, Julian? I know that you've amassed a pretty good history on this curse."

"Yes, Adora and I both," he responded grimly. "She went to Abby's aunt and collected information. She didn't take anything, only asked them for the Asemaa's interpretation of the curse."

"The Asemaa?" Bridget asked, still trying to get caught up on all that she had missed.

"Yes, they're a secret society of sorts that began researching witches in the early 1800s. They spent a lot of time focusing on the curse because they were located right in its midst."

"In Trager City?" Galla asked.

"Exactly."

CHAPTER 3

"Tell us about the room beneath the earth, Sebastian. The one with all the tubes?" Julian asked, after he finished summing up what he knew of the curse.

Sebastian stayed with Abby, not in the mood for standing in front of the fire, like he was giving a speech.

"It felt like a morgue, for lack of a better comparison," he started. "Steel floor, gurneys with black sheets and bodies..." He realized that his hands had begun to shake, and Abby took them in her own, steadying him.

"The people hanging from the walls were held by big black straps. Tubes went into their skin and electrodes into their heads. The tubes ran some kind of clear liquid out of their bodies and into this huge basin. It reminded me of those wishing wells that you drop a penny into and it circles around and around until disappearing into that little black hole."

"A coin funnel?" Helena said.

"Yes, exactly."

Sebastian noticed that Lydie had begun to squirm uncomfortably, and he offered her an understanding smile.

"The walls and the ceiling were drywalled, which seemed strange to me, but I think now they wanted to keep it sanitary."

"Because they were extracting something...," Julian said, thinking out loud.

"They were in my head," Oliver added. "The electrodes must have given them access to my mind."

"The room was gone when we went back," Julian offered, knowing that the Chicago witches likely hadn't heard about Julian and Faustine's return to the lair. "Everything was destroyed. The fire that came at us in that cavern must have traveled through all their tunnels. I'm sure they set it up that way. It killed everyone, and everything, in its path."

"Is anyone going to talk about the dead people?" Lydie suddenly asked, in a high-pitched voice that startled everyone in the room.

Oliver smoothed her hair back and hugged her.

"Yes, Lydie," Elda soothed her. "I promise we'll talk about them tonight too."

In the weeks since the experience in the lair, the witches had all carefully avoided the topic of that day. Lydie's heartbreak over Max, and all their trauma, left them wanting a bit more time.

****

"So we're all related then. It just seems unreal," Abby said later, as she and Victor sat in Lydie's dream room, sneaking a few moments alone to talk.

"But that's just it, right? We're not part of ordinary reality at all. We never were, and in truth, neither is anyone else, we just buy into it. That is until we can't anymore because fire is shooting out of our ass."

Abby laughed and settled back into the beanbag chair. She watched stars darting across the ceiling and decided she liked the changes at Ula.

"Tell me something, long-lost cousin…" Victor said, looking at her seriously.

"Hmmm?"

"Why doesn't anyone else at this party seem to know about the baby you're growing?"

Abby gasped and sat up, wondering for a moment if she should lie.

She could see in Victor's face that he knew the truth; there was no point avoiding it.

"I honestly don't know," she sighed finally. "I've considered telling Sebastian a hundred times, but then the words just won't come out."

"So even Sebastian doesn't know? He is the father, right?"

"Of course," Abby snapped, but she knew why Victor asked. She had, after all, shown up in Chicago with Oliver.

"No offense intended," he countered, holding up his hands. "And no judgment."

"No, nothing like that ever happened between Oliver and me. I adore him, but Sebastian has my heart." As she spoke, she realized how terrible it was that she had not told him about the baby. "I have to tell him tonight."

Victor nodded.

"I think so too and, what's more, I think you're keeping this secret because Kanti wants you to."

Abby pursed her lips and realized Victor knew way more than he let on. She hadn't even allowed the thought to fully penetrate her own mind.

"That's even more reason to expose the truth, Abby. She does not have your best interest at heart. I haven't figured out where she is, but she does not rest peacefully."

Almost in response to his words, a crack of thunder lit the magical sky overhead.

"I'm happy they didn't bewitch this room to rain on us," Victor laughed.

****

"Helena is calling it the Honeymoon Suite," Sebastian told Abby, leading her down a small stone corridor and across an open-air veranda that was quite frigid in the mounting darkness. He opened a set of French doors.

The circular room held an enormous round bed piled with a white, velvety comforter and sprinkled with yellow roses. The dome ceiling was glass and revealed the night sky. Carved into the curving stone wall stood an enormous fireplace, flames dancing in its hearth. Vases of white roses decorated the mantle. Two silk robes were draped over a velvet-lined bench, one cream and the other black.

"Did she set this up tonight?" Abby asked, amazed.

"Oh, to be a witch," Sebastian teased.

Sebastian turned Abby to face him. He lifted her, carrying her to the bed, and kissed her hard on the mouth. She fell back into the feathery pillows and held out her arms. As he began to kiss her face and her neck, she leaned close to his ear.

"We're having a baby," she told him. She tried to stay soft in his arms, but the moment she uttered the words, her body tensed.

He continued to kiss her and then he stopped, pulling away. He looked at her, bewildered. Slowly understanding dawned, but something more: fear.

"A baby?" He touched her stomach. "But how, when?"

"The night in the woods at the cabin."

He frowned and she grabbed his arms, squeezing to reassure him.

"I'm okay. The injury didn't hurt the baby or at least, didn't change the pregnancy. Don't ask me how I know. I haven't taken a test. I just know, okay?"

Sebastian nodded, looking serious, but then the hint of a smile touched his lips.

"A baby?"

He grinned and picked her up, spinning her around the room. He kissed her and then set her, gently, back on the bed.

"I don't want to tell the other witches yet. Our little secret, okay?"

"Whatever you want," he told her, still coming to terms with the news.

He pulled up her shirt and kissed her belly and then her breasts. He stripped her completely and between kisses, he marveled at her body as if seeing it for the first time.

Abby lay back on the pillows and surrendered to the pleasure of his touch. She felt as if an enormous weight had been lifted.

****

"Happy Birthday," Abby whispered, nuzzling into Sebastian's back. He stirred and rolled toward her. Sleepy eyed, he smiled.

"How did you know it was my birthday?"

"Helena told me. Remember when we first came to Ula? She said that you and she were both Scorpios. At Sorciére, she told me you had a birthday coming up, so I dug through your wallet to find the date."

"Quite the little spy."

"Why didn't you tell me?"

Sebastian shrugged.

"I haven't celebrated my birthday since Claire died. She used to make a big deal out of it and after her death, I just couldn't."

Abby leaned her head on his chest and sighed.

"I'm sorry, Sebastian. Sometimes I wonder why this witch stuff doesn't come with a power to take away grief."

"You have," he told her, seriously. "You've transformed my life, Abby. I should say it more, I know. I can't tell you how much knowing you and loving you has drawn me out of that darkness."

Abby scooted to the edge of the bed and reached over the side, shuffling through her backpack. She returned with a small gift, wrapped in black and silver paper.

"What's this?" He took the package and sniffed it. He shook it and held it to his ear. "Hmm, obviously not a puppy or a meatloaf."

"Or a bottle of tequila," she laughed. "In my state, I thought booze might be inappropriate."

He chuckled and pulled Abby against him, kissing her for a long time. She pushed her hands into his silky curls and cupped his head in her hands.

"Thank you." His face turned serious. "Before I found you, I was lost."

"You and me both," she told him, kissing his nose. "Now open your present."

He sat up and traced his finger along the edges of the box. He opened it slowly, as if savoring the experience. He took off the paper and looked at the small wooden box. On the cover of the box, a heart with the inscription A + S was burned into the wood. He lifted the lid and Abby watched his face. A wide platinum ring, set with an emerald stone, was nestled in the black velvet.

He touched the ring and smiled.

"Emerald," she told him.

"Claire's birthstone."

"Yes. I figured if we're getting married, you would need a ring too and…"

Before she could finish, he pulled her into a bone-crushing hug.

"I love it, you know that, right?" he told the top of her head.

"It's becoming apparent," she laughed.

He put the ring on.

"Have you seen my ring?" he gushed, in a high feminine voice. He held his hand out, wiggling his fingers.

****

"It scans the documents on its own and then searches for the names Kanti, Dafne, Tobias, Alva or Milda. It also searches for the word curse. It automatically stores all of those documents in this folder here." Victor pointed to the huge touch-screen computer that depicted images of a dozen folders. The label on the folder said "Important."

"Seems simple enough," Julian said, scratching his chin.

Julian, Bridget and Helena had gathered in the room that Julian had coined The Vault. It used to contain a series of inventions, many created by Max, that Faustine moved to the dungeon. The Vault was near the library, which made for easier investigating. The witches, mostly Victor and Kendra, had installed three state-of-the-art computers. One entire wall was a touch-screen that revealed scanned images of letters, photographs and articles taken from the boxes Abby had brought. They were calling those the Kanti Files. Abby kept the originals, but the witches at Ula and those in Chicago had copies.

In the corner of the room, Victor had set up an elaborate scanning system.

"Is there magic involved here or just computer wizardry?" Helena asked.

"Both," Victor told them. "The magic is the self-scanning aspect. Watch."

He went to the boxes of documents and set them in a metal bin next to the scanner. He hit the "on" button and the machine whirred to life.

The papers immediately began to levitate, and one by one the scanner lifted its lid, copied the document and then released it. Victor had arranged twenty cardboard boxes on the floor. After the documents were scanned, they floated to a box and settled into the bottom. Black words then appeared on the box, as if drawn by marker. "Trager Disappearances" materialized on one of the boxes. On the second box, the coven's name "Ula" emerged.

"All the documents that show up in the Important file on the computer will also get separated into the Important box."

"I think this will be very helpful, Victor," Bridget said, watching the papers lift and sort themselves. "Thank you."

"We're in this together," he replied. "Kanti's been contacting me for years. I want to know why."

****

Sebastian pulled his scarf up to cover his face as he walked with Elda and Faustine to the second lagoon. The wind lashed, causing the few dead leaves, still clinging to the trees, to swirl through the air around them. He glanced longingly at the mystical gardens that he knew lay further on. The garden where he and Abby had made love before everything started to come undone. He thought of her news from the previous night and smiled, shaking his head in disbelief, still reeling from the idea that he would be a father.

"Have a seat in the chair," Elda told him, squeezing his shoulder for encouragement.

He walked to the wooden chair, that sat on the stone slab, and settled into it. He watched the gently lapping water of the lagoon, but felt nothing. What did he want to happen? He honestly didn't know. The experience in the cavern had floored him. Shock and disbelief still clouded his thoughts when he remembered it. There had not been another moment like it since, and not for lack of trying. In secret, he had tried several times to tap into the power. Despite his attempts, nothing had happened.

Faustine and Elda watched him, their faces expressionless. He knew they didn't want him to feel any pressure to perform the magic again.

He closed his eyes and tried to concentrate. He imagined lightning streaking from the sky and rocks exploding on the beach. Nothing. The wind caused the trees to groan. The dune grass blew and rubbed together in a scratchy song. He heard Faustine's heavy breath and Elda's softer and slower. He felt the steady thud of his heart and the perspiration on his hands. His feet itched in the heavy wool socks that he had put on that morning.

Finally, he opened his eyes and looked at Elda and Faustine.

"I don't feel anything strange. I just don't think it's going to happen."

Faustine nodded and Elda gave him a warm, conciliatory smile.

"Sometimes that happens, even out here," Elda offered, wrapping her heavy black shawl tighter around her body.

"Go on back to the castle, dear," Faustine told her, kissing her on the forehead.

Elda smiled and gave Sebastian a pat on the arm before hurrying back to the warmth of the indoors.

"Let's go up the dune," Faustine said, beckoning Sebastian toward the sand dunes rising in the distance.

They plodded along slowly, the sand cumbersome beneath their boots. When they reached the top, Lake Superior stretched out in glorious abandon. The waves rose and crashed, creating a spray of white on the rocks below. The dune edges on the back of the island were windblown and packed hard, not the soft sand of the other side. They dropped with dizzying steepness and then gave way to the craggy rock sheath of the island.

"Mesmerizing, isn't it?" Faustine asked.

"It is," and before the words had left his lips, Faustine shoved him from behind.

Sebastian stumbled and sought to turn his body and reach back for Faustine, but he was already catapulting through the air. The wind whipped his face and his eyes bulged as he watched the water rushing to meet him. He closed his eyes and braced for the impact, sure that he would die instantly.

****

Abby left the castle and welcomed the biting February wind. She pulled her cloak tighter, but let the hood rest on her shoulders, savoring the cold on her face. Overheated after sitting in the library, she had told the others that she needed a walk. Sebastian was at the lagoon with Faustine and Elda, and she wanted the opportunity to slip away on her own.

She walked between the bare trees of the cherry orchard and wound her way through the forest until she came to the disintegrating steps that led to the floating garden. Lit with its own enchanted sun, the warmth of the garden startled Abby as she left the frigid hillside and moved into the dome. She sat among the flowers and removed her cloak and her shoes. Then she lay back in the soft-scented grass and allowed the vision to take her.

Kanti held the baby with exhausted arms. Every inch of her body ached. Her womb pulsed painfully as it shrunk within her body. The baby nursed hungrily on her tender, sore breasts. Beneath all the surface pains, beneath the sweat and gore that coated her slick and sticky body, she felt the bone-numbing cold. She shivered and clenched her chattering teeth. Through the single window in the cabin, the snow gusted and swirled. Night would come soon, and the temperature would drop. If she stayed as she was, she would die, and the baby would die. She considered it. She thought of fighting through the blizzard and flinging the baby into the icy waters of Lake Michigan.

As the baby, a girl, drifted into sleep, Kanti shuffled her onto a pile of blankets. She stood and braced both hands against the cabin wall to keep from collapsing as dizziness washed over her. The blood on the blankets had pooled and thickened. With numb fingers, she pulled the most saturated pieces away and threw them into a corner. She took the single wooden chair in the cabin and thumped it against the floor over and over. It took an eternity. She had to stop and rest every other minute, but finally a leg broke away. She took the leg and slowly beat it until it splintered. She piled the pieces of chair beneath the window. Remembering her teachings by Ehtamwa, she lit a fire by grinding one of the wood pillars into a groove in the chair base. It lit quickly, not due to method, but Kanti herself. Ehtamwa sometimes called her the Fire Dancer. It was the first time she had been alone with a fire since they'd taken her. She remembered that first night, how she longed to speak through the fire to Ehtamwa. More than a year had passed. As she watched the growing flames, she imagined calling him forth. They would come for her. They would take Kanti and the baby home. They would envelop her in the tribe. The men of her tribe would hunt for the white man and the giant; they would kill them both.

She didn't seek her people the flames. She stripped out of her soiled underclothes and wrapped the furs back around her body. She settled onto the straw with the baby and watched the billows of smoke sucked through the window. She began to plan her revenge.

Abby stirred in the garden. It took her a moment to readjust to the brilliant colors of the garden after the drab bitterness of Kanti's memory. Abby could not shake the image of the baby. Tiny and dark, she had watched Kanti, her mother, with riveting blue eyes. They were the eyes of the man who'd stolen Kanti, who'd raped her and impregnated her. Abby did not merely see Kanti's memories, she felt the spectrum of her emotions and she shared her thoughts. Kanti hated her child. She hated her innocent baby with an intensity that Abby had never felt for anything in her life. It was such a deep emotion that Abby struggled to reconcile its existence at all. Moreover, she struggled to to understand it in connection to the tiny, beautiful child who looked back at her mother with such adoration.

Abby pressed her hand against her belly. She would not begin to show for months, but her sense of the baby had already changed her. She no longer felt like a single being, but a creator, a mother. Would she feel the same if it were not Sebastian's baby that she carried, but instead the child of a monster?

****

The impact didn't happen. Sebastian opened his eyes and looked around wildly. He stood at the top of the sand dune, solid ground beneath his feet. Faustine watched him curiously.

"What just happened?" Sebastian sputtered, backing away from Faustine. "You pushed me!"

"You thought that I pushed you. It is true that I planted the experience in your mind, yes, but I did not actually push you."

"What the hell is wrong with you? Why?" Sebastian continued to back away from Faustine, feeling an odd mix of shame and relief.

"Because I wanted to see what your mind would do if I got you,

Sebastian, out of the way."

"Well, obviously my mind nearly fell to my death."

"No, you slowed and floated back to the cliff. Your body knew how to save you. Your greater mind knew how to save you. There is power in you, Sebastian. It was not a fluke in that cavern. Your ego is in the way."

Sebastian started to argue and then stopped. What good would it do anyway? Arguing with a witch who was hundreds of years old would likely end with him feeling an even bigger fool. He also wanted to know more. Had he really floated back up? Would that have happened if he'd actually fallen?

"Are you sure I wouldn't have just fallen and died?"

"Would you like to try a real push and find out?" Faustine asked, arching an eyebrow.

"Is it masochistic if I say yes?"

Faustine released a short bark that Sebastian recognized as laughter.

"I knew you had a sense of humor in there, somewhere."

"I save it for very special occasions," Faustine informed him. "There is no need for a real push. What is real in your mind is real-it is that simple. The task ahead will be to harness that power."

"Like Abby has been doing? A school of sorts?"

Faustine fixed his gaze on the distant horizon. A gathering of greenish looking storm clouds had assembled.

"With all that has happened, we cannot wait, but I must acknowledge that everyone needs a bit of adjustment time. Let's keep this between ourselves and I will form a plan for your training."

CHAPTER 4

Abby woke in the black room. In her disorientation, she nearly fell from the bed, but caught the side table and steadied herself, breathing heavily and gradually tuning in to the pressure on her bladder. As her eyes adjusted to the darkness, the alien landscapes of her dreams melted away and she saw the familiar outline of the bedroom that she shared with Sebastian in their new home. He slept deeply, his chest rising and falling with his breath. She edged along the bed and felt for the wall. The moonless night left their home cast in an inky darkness that unnerved her. She crept into the master bathroom, relieved when she successfully found the toilet.

Somewhere in the house a floorboard groaned. She assumed that her cat Baboon lurked the hallways, but her justification felt dismissive. She listened again. Another creak and this one louder. Baboon seemed hardly capable of such a sound.

She stood and walked to the Zen water fountain that sat atop the bathroom vanity. Closing her eyes, she placed her hand into the trickle of water. The tiny blue light pulsed at the base of her spine. She channeled the energy and directed it through the house. She could not literally see the rooms, but she could sense them and when she entered the nursery, her roaming stopped as if thrust against a brick wall. A big energy occupied the space, and it was not a benevolent spirit merely passing through. The tiny hairs on her arms prickled.

She sat down on the edge of the bathtub, suddenly dizzy, and pressed her hands into her forehead. She could still hear Sebastian's steady breath from their bed, but she wished they were not alone in the house. Well, actually, she felt quite sure they weren't alone, but she wished that Oliver and Lydie still slept nearby.

They had stayed behind at Ula, and Abby remembered the reluctance in Oliver's eyes. She'd almost considered inviting them to visit until the New Year, but knew he would say no. Helena and the other witches had worked hard on Lydie's dream room and the other changes to the castle. They wanted, maybe even needed, Oliver and Lydie to return to the Coven of Ula.

When her breathing slowed and the dizzy spell passed, she stood and walked down the hallway to the nursery. The door stood closed, though she always left it open. She touched the handle-ice-cold. Overcoming her fear, she pushed the door in. It swung into the empty room on creaking hinges.

She stepped into the room, wiggling her toes in the soft blue carpeting. The sheer white curtains trembled softly.

"Just a breeze from the door," she whispered, and walked to the center of the room, but it wasn't just a breeze.

As she stepped fully into the room, she felt her breath sucked from her lungs. The room seemed to spin and disappear. For an instant, she stared at the ghostly image of a woman clawing to escape some dark, tiny space.

Abby felt a wave of panic as the same heavy darkness closed around her. She fell to her knees and clutched her chest. She felt void of breath, like she was being suffocated.

Her breath came back in a rush and the room returned to focus.

She gasped and coughed, welcoming the sweet cold air. For a moment, she stayed kneeling on the floor and then carefully climbed to her feet.

"What do you want?" she asked the room.

Silence.

The woman had vanished and with her, the oppressive darkness, and the cold.

Abby plodded downstairs to the sitting room and dug out her cell phone. Victor had given phones to all the witches at Ula. He insisted on handing them out, despite Faustine's declaration that they would get no cell reception at Ula. The phones were untraceable and operated on a network that he and the Chicago witches had created.

She scrolled through her contacts. All the witches were listed, and she paused at Oliver's name, knowing he would likely be awake at two in the morning, but unreachable on the isolated island. She pressed Victor's name.

A self-proclaimed night owl, he answered on the first ring.

"Goddess of the North Woods, why have you called me during your hours of beauty rest?"

Abby laughed and immediately relaxed.

"I just wanted to get your input on Ula and everything we talked about."

"Ha, liar! I didn't mention it, but one of my witchy skills is detecting BS, and you're serving it up right now."

"Victor!"

"Abby, it's true, I heard it in your voice when I picked up the phone, and no way are you roaming around in the middle of the night without a reason better than What did you think of Ula?"

"Okay, I got spooked."

"Spooked how?"

"I woke up tonight to pee, which I'm starting to do at an uncommon frequency, might I add, and I sensed something in the house with Sebastian and me."

"Something or someone?"

"I don't know, both I guess. I feel like it used to be a someone, a woman, and now it's..."

"Dead?"

"Maybe, but it felt very much alive and it knew that I could feel it. What's more, it was in the nursery."

"You already have a nursery?"

"Well, not technically, no, but I knew it would be that before we even bought the house."

"Have you told anyone else that?"

"Yes. Sebastian. We talked about it yesterday."

"So, this thing may have overheard you rather than getting in your head?"

Abby shivered and scanned the room for a blanket. She found one and wrapped it around her, sinking lower into the couch.

"Maybe."

"Do you think it was Kanti?"

"I don't know. I saw a woman, maybe Kanti, but it was so dark and she seemed to be dying. The presence, the spirit, was not good."

"Not good, meaning evil?"

"I think so, yes."

Victor was silent for a moment.

"Kendra and I are coming your way in a couple of days. I'd like to get a feel for the area, energetically and all."

"For Trager?"

"Yes, I haven't been there in years. The curse obviously originated there so we'd like to do some research. I also want to visit the Ebony Woods. What I'm thinking is we could shack up with you guys and perhaps you and I could have ourselves a little ghost hunt?"

"Oh, that sounds like a fabulous time. After our last adventure into the Vepar's lair, I'm not sure we make the best team."

Victor laughed, but Abby wondered if she'd struck a nerve with that memory.

"No repeats of that disaster Abby. I promise."

****

"Any news on Dafne?" Oliver asked, walking into the Vault.

Julian and Faustine sat at computers. Oliver bit back a laugh at Faustine's laborious, single-finger typing.

"No news," Faustine grumbled, clearly frustrated by the task at hand.

"Not entirely true," Julian quipped. "Select the Dafne File up there." Julian pointed at the giant touch-screen.

Oliver touched the corner of the screen and it filled with manila folders, each labeled with names. He looked past the files labeled Tobias and Sebastian, The Curse, The Lourdes of Warning, Ebony Woods and dozens more. He clicked the file for Dafne and grimaced when a larger-than-life picture of the witch appeared on the screen.

He knew the picture. It showed Dafne as a young woman at the Coven of Ula. Her black hair hung long and shiny and her gaunt body was hidden beneath a heavy dark cloak. She stood on the stone slab near the second lagoon, and a dazzling ball of fire erupted from the ends of her fingertips.

"She was a force to be reckoned with in those days," Julian said, standing up from his computer and moving beside Oliver.

Faustine continued to stare fiercely at his compute,r and Oliver sensed that he could not stand to look at the picture. Not out of anger at the witch, but fear of what had become of her.

"I would have liked to have known her then," Oliver said.

"Ha," Julian laughed. "She was mean as hell. Now, at least, I understand why." Julian shook his head sadly. "If only she'd have told us. What difference a hundred years could have made in figuring all this out."

"She was traumatized," Faustine said sharply. "I almost wonder if she didn't block it all out for a couple of decades."

"She did a lot of good here," Oliver added, hoping to ease the tension between the two elder witches. "She was a brilliant hunter and she taught me a lot."

Julian ran his finger across the screen and a list of topics appeared. He clicked on Present Day.

"We know that she and Indra appeared in France right after we rescued Sebastian. We probably missed them by hours, if not minutes."

"And Sebastian said that he saw Isabelle's body in the charnel ground," Oliver added.

"Yes. We've been able to trace their journey to France. Dafne flew first class, chose not to use any magic, which seems odd. She rented a car and we haven't found a record for any stops, so we're assuming she went straight to Isabelle's apartment. We think that she and Indra had planned to take Sebastian to another location to perform additional magic, likely because Isabelle alerted them that his memory was returning."

"Was it?"

"Not exactly," Julian explained. "But he had met an American woman who owned a store and who also happened to be a very good friend of mine."

"A witch?" Oliver asked.

Julian shook his head.

"No, but the daughter of a witch. Her mother lives in a coven in Italy, and she is quite adept in the ways of the magical world. When she saw Sebastian's ring, she knew instantly that it contained a spell of some sort and as luck would have it, she called me."

"That is lucky."

"Luck has nothing to do with it," Faustine said crisply. "Our world does not rely on luck. Dafne went against the laws of nature, and nature merely set things right."

"We know that Dafne and Indra stopped into the coffee shop where Isabelle last saw Sebastian. We wonder now if that's where the Vepar Alva intercepted them."

"Because Sebastian was speaking with Alva when you guys found him?" Oliver asked Julian.

"Yes, when Adora and Rod found him. We don't know how he tracked Sebastian down. We're speculating a link between Dafne and Tobias. You see in 1908, when Dafne originally came to us, she was somehow still open energetically to Tobias. That is how he made it into Ula. Either the curse closed on its own or Dafne shut it down, but we think the connection disappeared. However, we wonder if triggering the curse again reopened it."

"How do we find that out?"

"By sifting through this material, for starters," Julian said.

"And by speaking with the Lourdes of Warning," Faustine added, still not looking up from his screen.

"Why the Lourdes? What does she have to do with this?" Oliver asked, knowing that the Lourdes of Warning was not a witch to meddle with. Only months earlier, she had attempted to send Abby directly into the hands of Vepars waiting to consume her.

"She's in this material. She was clearly the witch afflicted by the curse before Dafne."

"That doesn't make sense. I thought the Lourdes was in love with another witch who turned bad, not a mortal man."

"Well so did we," Faustine answered. "But it's not as though we have an accurate history book somewhere. These stories are word-of-mouth, they're passed through generations and like all things, they get distorted."

"Yes," Julian said thoughtfully. "Look at any of the great religions or histories for that matter. What story isn't rewritten to serve some other agenda-be it money or power or control? I doubt anyone got much of the story from the Lourdes herself anyway. She'd clearly gone mad by the time she knew the truth about her love, whatever that truth might have been."

"Who will go see her?" Oliver asked, eager to volunteer.

"I will," Faustine said shortly. "It has been many years, but I have had dealings with the afflicted witch before and she cannot deceive me. I can sense her lies."

Oliver didn't argue. He had far less experience than the elder witches and virtually no practice dealing with witches who had turned toward darkness.

"We feel sure that Dafne and Indra were not in the cavern with the other bodies," Julian continued, returning to their original discussion. "Partially because Galla from Sorciére can still sense that they are both alive. She cannot track them or even get any inklings to their state of being, but she knows that they live. We have all taken turns visiting the caves astrally, and none of us have been pulled to the Pool of Truth. We're confident that Dafne's death would trigger an unveiling for one of us."

"Maybe I should go too," Oliver said quickly, desperate to be of use. In the previous weeks with Abby, he had felt so involved, so alive, and back at Ula, he felt isolated and, honestly, trapped.

"That is a wise choice," Faustine said. "I believe that Helena is guiding Lydie toward that very end this afternoon if you want to join them."

"Lydie, is that a good idea? What about Max?" Oliver asked.

"Lydie witnessed Max's death. The Pool only reveals that which is unknown."

"How did they do it? Indra and Dafne? How did they manipulate The Pool of Truth?"

"It's been done," Julian answered. "It's old magic and the kind with heavy repercussions. When you take the energy of such a powerful entity, you repay threefold and it was not borrowed, but stolen for ill intent, regardless of what they believed when they did it. I fear for both of them having dabbled in such dark magic."

"As do I," Faustine agreed.

"But how they did it," Julian continued, "I couldn't say. I'm sure they exhausted a lot of texts to discover that kind of magic, and not likely the stuff on Ula's library shelves."

"So, they asked other witches?"

"We think they likely visited the L'Obscurite."

"In New Orleans?" Oliver asked.

He knew little of the witch community in New Orleans, though he'd heard talk of them over the years. Mostly complaints by Helena, who loved the city, but several run-ins with witches of the L'Obscurite had scared her away. She referred to them as lost souls and rarely offered more detail than that.

"Why would they go to them?"

"Their books," replied Julian. "They're collectors of the macabre and they're fascinated with dark magic."

"Is it only a fascination?"

"Not likely," Faustine answered simply.

"How do you know that Dafne went there?"

"Elda found Dafne's personal articles disturbed at the warehouse. While she was picking through, she stumbled across a little notebook that Dafne left behind. Most of the pages had been ripped out, but the L'Obscurite quarters were written down. We're sure that it's recent. Bridget recognized the notebook from the room of elixirs."

Oliver considered the warehouse and suddenly felt tempted to dig around there as well.

"Did she find anything else?"

"Not much. When we found Dafne, one hundred years ago, she had no possessions. Later, she did go to retrieve her things, though we realize now that is when she disappeared to have the baby," Faustine continued.

"And no one had a clue?"

"No, Oliver. I know it seems hard to believe, but Dafne was very secretive and clearly traumatized. We treaded carefully around her. We wanted her to feel welcome at Ula, so we didn't examine her too closely. You also must realize that we experienced an enormous tragedy during that period of time. When she disappeared for several months, it nearly went unnoticed in our state of grief."

"She just took off?"

"No, no," Julian corrected. "She offered an elaborate story about tying up loose ends at home and saying goodbye to her family. Some of us thought that she would not be back. The fear at Ula was palpable and it was easy to see why she would want to run away. I wanted to run away. The last thing on my mind during that time was where she had gone and why." Julian's tone had grown bitter.

"But then she returned," Faustine finished, trying to steer the conversation back to a less emotional space. "A little over two months and she was back with a few boxes of stuff and a new hardness. She was no longer weak; she was strong and fierce and wanted to be a hunter of Vepars."

****

"Hey, babe?" Sebastian said.

Abby looked up. Sebastian was making their morning French press of coffee. Their first morning French press, anyway; sometimes they drank two or three. He stared at her curiously.

"What's up?" she asked.

"Why didn't you want to tell the witches at Ula about the baby?"

Sebastian added milk to his coffee and set hers down, black and steaming hot. She watched the pattern of oils on the surface of the dark liquid, searching for any images, a form of divination that Helena had briefly taught her. She saw nothing curious.

"I'm just not ready for all of the excitement. With everything that's been happening, I thought it'd be nice to keep it between us at first."

"Doesn't it seem strange that they couldn't tell though?" Sebastian continued. "Several of them can read minds."

Abby sensed this was the real question that he wanted to ask.

"I've been performing magic to hide the baby," she told him calmly, fighting the urge to lie.

"For how long?"

"Sebastian." Abby stood and walked around the counter. She wrapped her arms around his waist and looked into his questioning blue eyes. "I love you so much and when I realized that I was pregnant, I sort of freaked. I got scared because the Vepar that attacked me tore open my stomach and honestly, because it's scary as hell just to think of pregnancy and motherhood and then being a witch on top of that. I wanted time to think and come to terms with everything."

He continued to look at her, waiting for an answer to his question.

"I knew I was pregnant the day of the attack in the Vepar's Lair. I felt the child inside of me."

"How is that possible? To know the day after we made love?"

Abby shrugged.

"A witch thing, I guess."

Sebastian unwrapped her arms and sat on one of the stools at the counter. He looked troubled, but seemed to come to a conclusion.

"Okay, it concerns me that you didn't tell me, but I trust you and I know that you had your reasons. What kind of magic conceals a pregnancy?"

Abby sighed, relieved that he didn't probe further.

"Nothing too complex. Herbs, a few rituals. I've been drinking some pretty bitter-tasting tonics for the last couple of weeks, but don't worry, they're actually good for the baby. They cloud the body so that once the nutrients are dispersed through the blood and across the placenta, the baby is basically undetectable. Some witches use it if they get a terminal illness. It's healthy for the body to consume, but it also hides what's going on inside."

"So that's the fungi-smelling stuff in the jar at the back of the refrigerator?"

Abby laughed. "Yes, it's pretty wicked."

"I'd say so. I nearly passed out when I opened it the other day."

"I'm sorry that I didn't tell you, Sebastian. I should have."

He stood and pulled her into a rough hug and then loosened immediately, looking at her belly.

"Sorry, I didn't...?"

"Nope, the baby's pretty well protected in there."
He kissed her and smoothed a curl away from her face.
"I love you, Abby. You've given me life again."

****

Sebastian rolled over and reached for Abby. His hand struck something hard and cold and he grunted in pain. Blinking in the darkness, he realized that he was not in his bed. He felt blindly. Concrete beneath him and his hands closed on something sharp. A screwdriver, he thought.

He shifted onto hands and knees and then struggled to standing. He stood in the garden shed. He could see the vague outline of a lawn mower and the wall of power tools. He touched his head, but felt no lump or blood. If he had fallen, he hadn't struck anything.

He realized that something must have attacked them. He ran out of the shed, leaving the door wide, and raced across snowy drifts to the porch. Inside the house, silence and more darkness greeted him. He ran up the stairs, three at a time, and burst into their bedroom.

Abby sat up, startled. She held the comforter bunched in her fists and blinked across the room at him.

"Sebastian?" she asked sleepily.

He stood in the doorway. His breath came in ragged gulps and his eyes swam with spots of light and dark. Too relieved to speak, he watched her for another moment.

"What is it?" she asked. She stepped out of bed, her nightgown ghostly pale in the moonlight.

She looked like an apparition with wild curls flying and her milky skin aglow.

He swallowed hard and moved into the room. He took her in his arms and lifted her, burying his face in her neck.

"You're so cold," she murmured, her voice thick.

"I went outside, and I thought I heard something. I came running back."

He told the lie easily and did not consider offering her the truth.

"Come to bed," she urged as he laid her down. He tucked her into the covers and kissed her mouth.

"I will soon," he promised.

Downstairs, he found a flashlight and returned to the shed. He scanned the floor and walls, but could find nothing amiss. How had he gotten there? Had he sleepwalked?

Outside, he found a set of his footprints that led from the house into the woods. He had not taken a walk in the woods in days, and any prints should have been long buried by the heavy snowfall. He followed them.

The trees groaned and whispered in the eerie night. They made a human sound, like mournful cries, and he wondered how many legends of forest creatures originated from the calling of the trees. He shivered and wondered why he had not thought to put on his heavy winter coat and scarf. He considered turning back, but knew if he returned to the house a second time, the call of Abby's warm body beneath the blankets would be too tempting to ignore.

    He followed the path further into largely unexplored forest. Though he and Abby had walked the woods before they bought the property, they had mostly traveled the shoreline without probing too deeply into the dense forest.

    He came to a crumbling rock wall, only a few feet high. He shone his light along the rocks, but saw nothing out of the ordinary. He scanned the snow around the wall and a spot of color caught his eye. It barely registered and had it not lay on a bed of stark white, he never would have noticed it. He bent down and plucked a long black hair from the snowy ground.

CHAPTER 5

Elda found Oliver in Lydie's dream room. He was draped across a fluffy mushroom-shaped pillow, a book open in his lap.
"No Lydie?" Elda asked, scanning the room.
"She went to raid the kitchen," Oliver told her. "She heard Bridget talking about making cupcakes earlier. It's a good sign, she's getting her appetite back."
"Yes," Elda agreed. "She does seem to be improving, a bit anyway."
Oliver set the book aside, sensing that Elda wanted to talk.
"What's up?"
"Well Faustine and I were speaking with Julian and we wonder if you shouldn't go back to Abby and Sebastian's house, after all."
Oliver stared at her, surprised. He had wanted to return to Abby's house, but feared that Elda and the other witches would be upset by the choice.
"Why?"
"Because we don't know how this curse works. I trust Abby, we all do, but she is a new witch and Sebastian is a new love. If something began to change, get weird, she might be too close to realize it was happening."
"So, you want me to spy on them?" Oliver asked, not liking the idea at all.
"Of course not," Elda replied, exasperated. "Oliver, I'm afraid for Abby. There is dormant power in Sebastian. Power that appeared in the cavern. It was…"
"Insane," Oliver finished. "And you think it came from the Vepars?"
Elda sighed and held up her palms.
"I have no idea. None of us do, but it wasn't there before they got him underground. Julian agrees. It's possible that they did something down there. Why wasn't he tied up like the rest of you? Why weren't they siphoning from him? In some regard, why did any of you escape at all?"
Oliver hated how much sense she made, but in truth, he'd had the same thoughts. Why would the Vepars have left them unprotected to escape? It had all been too easy.
"Okay," he said, resigned. "But I don't want to hone in on their alone time. They just got engaged and bought their new house."

"That's why you'll take Lydie."
"What? How can you think that's a good idea?"
"Because Lydie got kidnapped from here, she's still scared, and the truth is, she's pretending to be fine, but that's it, an act. She's miserable. I see it every time I look in her eyes. At Abby's house, she felt normal, safe."
"But you want to send Lydie into a home where a Vepar may be rising?" Elda shook her head no, hard.
"No, I want to send both of you and I want daily communication. I want reasons to drop by, any of us, at any time. I want eyes and ears on Sebastian and maybe on Abby too. There's something going on with her, and it scares me that she has access to this Kanti spirit. I'm afraid that both she and Sebastian are in the throes of something very powerful, and we need to be there to protect them if the need arises."
Oliver stood up, mobilized by Elda's theories, and suddenly concerned for Abby.
"I'll call her now and tell her Lydie is struggling to get adjusted. I'm sure that she'll welcome us back."
"So am I."

****

"Welcome," Sebastian called from the kitchen as Abby opened the front door and Victor and Kendra trudged through, kicking snow off their boots.

"Wow, it's a winter wonderland up here," Kendra breathed. "I feel like we should have driven up in a sleigh."

"We could have," Victor told her, winking at Abby and helping Kendra out of her heavy silver jacket.

"Well I'm happy you made it," Abby declared, hugging them briefly and leading them toward the kitchen where Sebastian was preparing a giant breakfast of omelets, potatoes and cinnamon rolls.

"Yum!" Kendra groaned. "It smells so good."

"Two minutes," Sebastian told her, taking a quick break to hug them.

Abby had already set the little table that occupied a light-filled alcove off the kitchen. It was surrounded by windows on three sides and looked out on the lake where snow continued to fall in heaps along the shoreline.

"This is beautiful," Kendra said, staring out the windows. "Does it get lonely though? All alone out on this peninsula?"

Kendra referred to the two hundred acres of woods that surrounded the huge house. Beyond their property, state forests stretched for miles. Their closest neighbor was located ten miles to the south. Kendra and Victor lived in a Chicago loft, surrounded twenty-four hours a day by hundreds of thousands of people; solitude was not their norm.

"Not lonely, really," Abby responded, considering. "Not yet anyway. It

doesn't get much more isolated than Ula."
She wondered if Victor had told Kendra about her late-night scare, but the witch seemed merely curious.

"Yeah, but you have all the other witches at Ula."

"The good and the bad ones, apparently," Sebastian quipped, walking to the table with a huge tray of food. He slid the tray onto the table and returned for two French presses. Abby spooned food onto everyone's plates, feeling her own stomach growl with hunger.

Victor winked at her, but didn't say anything. He had promised to keep her secret about the baby.

"So, what are the guerrillas up to while you guys are gone?" Abby asked, referring to the other witches Victor and Kendra lived with in Chicago. They called themselves Guerrilla Witches due to their endless array of grassroots projects.

"Ezra is working on a pretty elaborate self-defense school for women. She's calling it Fierce Femmes, and Dante and Marcus have been installing greenhouses all over the city. They talk about plants like they're their children."

"Yeah," Kendra laughed. "Marcus refers to all of the sprouts as Herbie."

****

"Hello, my love," Abby whispered to Sebastian, coming up behind him in the shed where he stood organizing his winter tools. He'd gone a bit haywire at the hardware store and bought three snow shovels, a snow blower, ten bags of salt, two generators and five survival suits–just in case.

"Mmmm, nice surprise," he murmured when she kissed his neck. "But it's cold out here, you should be inside."

He turned toward her and started to rub her arms vigorously through her heavy jacket.

"I just got off the phone with Oliver," Abby told him. "He's coming back with Lydie."

Sebastian cocked an eyebrow, genuinely surprised.

"Really? Even after all the changes at Ula? That makes me feel bad for Helena."

"It's not permanent," Abby continued, though she really didn't know. "Lydie is still pretty upset and Oliver said he's afraid they haven't given her enough time to recuperate."

"She did seem happy here," Sebastian agreed. "Why Oliver, though? Shouldn't he be staying at Ula to help protect them?" He tried to hide his annoyance, but knew that Abby sensed it.

"They've put a ton of new protection spells on Ula. Plus, it seems clear that the link between Dafne and Tobias is how the Vepars got in, so I'm sure they can spare Oliver."

Sebastian shrugged, but didn't argue.

Abby turned him to face her and pulled his head down to hers. His lips, hot, pushed hungrily against her. He felt her body start to respond to his touch. He slipped off his gloves and reached his hands inside her coat, pulling her hard into his body. He kissed her neck and collarbones, pulling at her layers.

Outside they heard the crunching of snow underfoot. Sebastian pulled away, breathing heavily and feeling a bit like a wild animal.

Abby giggled and kissed him again, lingering.

"We'll finish that later," she whispered.

He leaned his forehead against hers and sighed.

"Will Lydie and Oliver come today? I could make a big dinner tonight."

She laughed.

"You know, I'm the pregnant one and you think about food about five times more than I do. But yes, they're coming this afternoon, and I'm sure Lydie will be thrilled at the idea of a big dinner. I think her favorite part of the whole house was your cooking."

Sebastian grinned.
"Don't tell Bridget that."
"Our little secret."

"I'll run into town to stock up," he said. "We're low on cream and I'm thinking peanut butter curry for dinner."
Abby made a face.
"You'll love it, I swear."

"Do you want me to join you?" she asked. "If not, I'll probably go with Victor. He's dropping off Kendra at the library in Trager and then checking out the Ebony Woods."

Sebastian bit his tongue.

He didn't want her to go, but he also didn't want to treat her like a weakling because she was pregnant. He would have preferred she stay home by the fire and read, but Abby was a witch and their life would never be one of tranquil domesticity.

"No, go with Victor, it will be good for you."

****

Abby and Victor left Kendra at the library and continued out of town to the woods. The forest looked different in the winter. Bare branches, piled with snow, hung heavy over the white, padded ground. Abby directed him to Sydney's house, still vacant. Abby stared at it for a moment with longing. She wondered if there would ever come a day when she could look at the house and not see Sydney. A thousand memories pricked at the backs of her eyes and she shook them away.

Victor killed the engine and they walked to the woods by way of the beach. Both thick with coats, snow pants and winter boots, the walk was slow. Abby enjoyed the cold lake air filling her lungs and noticed how quickly her muscles grew warm and hard.

She squatted a few times.

"I feel like I could fly right now," she laughed, springing into the air.

"Well we are surrounded by your element."

Abby smiled; she hadn't made the connection.

She looked at a snow-laden branch overhead and flicked her fingers. The branch broke, but did not fall and a heap of snow landed on Victor's head.

"Hey," he laughed and shook his head back and forth like a dog. "Not fair play. The air in this cold feels impossible to manipulate."

"Okay, no more, I promise," she said, holding up her hands.

"How are you feeling?" he asked, pulling his scarf further up his chin.

"Really good, actually. I was gravely injured four weeks ago, I'm pregnant, the Vepars have become skin-walkers that can turn into flying monsters, the last time I saw my mother she was in the full throes of a nervous breakdown, and yet I feel, strangely, at peace with everything."

"Wow, just hearing all that made me anxious. Maybe it's part of the pregnancy? Happy hormones pumping through your witchy body?"

She directed a fluff of snow to float into the air and fall lightly over them.

"Possibly, though it's still so new. I'm barely five weeks along."

"Doesn't change the chemistry experiment currently underway in there." He gestured at her belly.

"Yeah, though I prefer to call her a divine experiment, thank you very much."

"Her?" he asked, cocking his head to the side.

Abby blushed and put a hand to her stomach.

"Her. Believe it or not, I know it's a girl."

"Believe it," he said.

"What do you think Kanti wants?" Abby asked, changing the subject with reluctance. She preferred to stay in the happy imaginings of her unborn child, but she and Victor rarely had time alone. They each had a special connection to the Native American girl's spirit. Abby felt she could talk to Victor about Kanti in a way that she could not discuss her with the others.

He stopped and kicked the snow, staring into the hard ground beneath. Not finding anything interesting, he moved on.

"I think she wants to tell her story. I keep hoping that she wants to help us, you know? But the curse makes that seem pretty unlikely."

Abby nodded.

"I know what you're saying. I have this mixed sense of her, like I'm afraid of her and yet connected to her in some magnificent way. Even though the dreams are disturbing, I want to have them. When I'm in her experience, I'm living an entirely different life in a different time. It's terrible, what happened to her feels impossibly painful, and yet I savor the moments. Afterward I can feel the huge love that she shared with her tribe. I feel her connection to the earth, the water, the sky, the air in a way that I have never known as Abby."

"And then she got stolen from it all," Victor said solemnly.

"Yes, stolen, raped and I don't even know what else. She was angry, she is angry. I'm just not sure where she's directing it."

"At everything, I think."

****

Sebastian surpassed Trager City and drove the winding forest roads that led to the more secluded spaces beyond the town. During his childhood summers in Northern Michigan, he and his father had made a point of regularly getting lost in the woods. They hiked in with their camping gear and spent days tracking deer, eating fish they caught in the river and forgetting about life in the city. Sebastian's dad worked as a mortgage broker, but his passion was the forests. Sebastian's mother joked that he should have been a forest ranger. He took Sebastian and his sister Claire along for most of his journeys. They camped beneath the stars, only climbing into their tents if it rained.

Sebastian turned down the ruddy dirt road that led him to the cabin where he had taken Abby less than five weeks before. It looked the same. Despite the remodel it had received in the years since he'd visited it with his father, he could still see it through his childhood mind. He remembered sitting on the porch, carefully assembling artificial flies with feathers they had found in the woods. His father was not much of a fly fisherman, or any kind of fisherman for that matter, but he loved it nevertheless. Anything that took him into nature, he delighted in. The weekends at the cabin were father-son trips only. Claire would stay home with their mother for girls' weekends.

Sebastian walked to the cabin steps and shuddered at the memory of the night the Vepar took him. The thing, Tobias or Alva, had bitten him and its venom had rendered him mostly unconscious. However, he still recalled the sensation of being hauled through the door into the darkness of the night. In his drugged state, he knew that death had come for him and it would not be a peaceful transition out of the world. Though the real terror had come later when he awoke in the Vepar's lair. He thought of the bodies hanging from the walls, something within them getting siphoned through tubes, and clenched his jaw to keep from howling his rage.

He sat down in an old rocking chair that squeaked and closed his eyes. He needed to return to a more peaceful place. His anger had led him for years and it had gotten him into trouble more than once. He took a deep breath and blew it out slowly. Opening his eyes, he scanned the snowy expanse before him. In the light of day, with drifts of snow sparkling, the cabin returned to the sanctuary that he remembered. He rubbed his hands together and blew a puff of warm air onto his fingers.

Abby was pregnant. He wanted to jump for joy. He wanted to buy cigars for his friends and send out postcards with little storks on the front. He wanted to do all the foolish, conventional things that normal people did when they learned a baby was on the way.

Most of all, he wanted to tell his mom. He wanted to see the looks on his parents' faces when he broke the news. He wanted to hear Claire's squeal of delight and watch her race to her bedroom to retrieve her favorite stuffed animal Lambert the Lion to give to the baby as a welcome gift.

He coughed and tried to clear the sob that had started to form in his throat. He thought of them less and less. He obsessed over Claire's death less and less. Since Dafne had used his love for Claire and his desire for vengeance as an opening into his mind, he worked hard to block Claire from his thoughts. Not because he wanted to forget his baby sister. He loved her. He would never forget any of them. But he knew he lived in another world now, and the doorways that led to the deepest parts of him had to remain closed at all times. Only in solitude, and perhaps with Abby, could he safely venture there.

He stood and left the porch, walking to the edge of the forest. Tall pines, already heavy with snow, scented the crisp air. He walked to a tree and pressed his palm against the grooves of bark.

He wondered how the Vepars had found them that night. When Sebastian came upon Abby near the stone cottages and he witnessed the creature that attacked her, his conscious mind seemed to shut down and something primal took over. He snatched a large rock from the dirt and fell upon the beast, intent on killing it and making the monster pay for all of the pain that had been visited upon him. Most of all he wanted to kill it for trying to take away Abby, the only person he had left in the world. When it flew away, he lifted Abby into his arms and raced back to her car, but he watched and he listened. He felt sure that the thing had fled, that it couldn't possibly have followed them. He was wrong.

Sebastian snapped a branch off the tree and flung it into the woods. He searched the forest floor and found a larger branch and beat it against the ground. He needed to channel the anger, and more so the guilt, that flooded his brain. He wanted to grab the huge trunk of a tree and shakes it until the roots tore free of the earth and he could fling it into the sky. He found a giant boulder and worked it free of the ground. He hefted it up and threw it. Rather than fumble heavily from his hands, it catapulted through the air like he'd merely thrown a pebble. It smashed into the earth with a spray of snow and dirt and rolled to a stop. He stared at it in wonder. He walked to it, lifted it again, threw it a second time. He hit another boulder, larger than the first, and it exploded.

He felt the burn of lactic acid as his muscles stretched and flexed. He turned to a pine tree, and wrapped his arms around the base, and pulled. For a moment it stayed rooted, held tight to the earth and then gradually the earth began to split as the roots tore away. He groaned with the tree as it pulled free. Awkwardly, he threw it into the forest. Branches and bark ruptured over the forest floor. He grasped another one and then another until he stood in a clearing that he had created with his bare hands.

He wanted to set fire to the trees. Instead of quelling his rage, the act of destruction had fueled it. He went to his car and found a lighter in the glove box. As he walked back toward the forest, he glanced at the cabin and stopped. For several minutes, he watched the cabin, blood pounding in his ears. He walked into the little cabin and gathered newspaper, logs and kindling. Carefully, he arranged every flammable item that he found throughout the cabin, and one by one he lit them on fire. It took time. He returned to the edge of the woods. He watched and waited. After an hour, he noticed the first snatches of fire catching the little white curtains. When the fire climbed to the roof, he got in his car and drove away.

CHAPTER 6

After dinner, Abby, Sebastian, Victor, Kendra and Oliver sat around the large square coffee table in the living room. Lydie, complaining of a headache, had gone to bed early. They looked through articles that Oliver had printed about the L'Obscurite.

"And they believe that Dafne found out how to manipulate the Pool of Truth from these witches?" Abby asked again.

"They didn't come right out and say that, but yes, I'm pretty sure Faustine believes that."

"Is a road trip totally out of the question?" Victor asked, looking at each of them separately.

Sebastian leaned closer to the printed picture before him, his expression dark.

"All of us?" Abby asked. "What about Lydie?"

"Shoot, Lydie would love it," Oliver said. "She's barely left Michigan. Not to mention, it's cold here and New Orleans is warmer. We'll call it a vacation."

"Keep her in the dark?" Victor asked.

"No," both Abby and Oliver spoke together.

"No, she has to know what we're up to. The secrets have gotten to her and I can sense she's finding it hard to trust the witches at Ula. I don't want that suspicion to include us," Oliver explained.

"So, what then? We drive to New Orleans and demand information?" Kendra asked, looking skeptical.

"Not demand," Victor appeased her. "We meet them, we tell them that we're curious—which we are—and then we sniff around. It's an adventure!"

Sebastian forced a smile, but Abby saw tension in his jaw.

"When will we go?" Oliver asked.

"We have to go back to Chicago in a couple of days. We do a lot of Christmas stuff that needs our attention," Victor explained.

"And you love it," Kendra teased, tickling him.

He batted her away.

"Yes, I do happen to enjoy playing Santa."

"Tell me you don't climb down people's chimneys?" Abby asked.

"Nope, a little magic and I'm in through the front door. I know, I know," he held up his hands defensively, "technically it is breaking and entering, but I'm giving, not taking."

"And no one freaks out?" Sebastian asked.

"We stick with the neighborhoods that are really in need," Kendra explained. "The truth is they tend to have a lot of faith, more so than the people with money. They want to believe in miracles so they do."

"That is awesome!" Oliver exclaimed.

"You're welcome to join us," Victor offered.

Oliver shook his head.

"Next year, I'll take you up on that. I think this Christmas needs to be nice and quiet for Lyds. We'll hang here with Abby and Sebastian and knit scarves and sing Christmas carols, that kind of thing."

"It's decided then? A road trip to New Orleans after Christmas?" Victor announced.

"I'm not sure that I've recovered from the last adventure," Sebastian said, taking Abby's fingers and tracing his thumb over her ring.

"None of us have," Oliver retorted. "But what's our alternative? Wait and see?"

"No," Abby declared, shaking her head furiously. "We're not going to wait for this thing to find us."

"What thing is that?" Kendra asked, brow furrowed.

"The curse."

****

Faustine stood and watched the flowing red weeping willow. Even in winter, its color smoldered amongst the stark white surrounding it. The branches continued to drip the sticky red pulp that they secreted onto the forest floor. Beneath the tree there was no snow. The red spongy earth lurked as ominously as the witch herself.

He walked to the base of the tree, careful to avoid the willow's branches and paused at the black hole that descended into the earth. He could feel the Lourdes beneath him and she too knew of his presence. In his jacket pocket, he had tucked the elixir that she so coveted. It lasted less than twenty-four hours and he was grateful. The witch's beauty, when under the spell, was mesmerizing, which made her a danger to anyone who stumbled into her path. Only with the potion's magic in her veins could she leave the sanctuary of her tree. He preferred to believe that she did not kill during her transformations, but he knew she had before.

Faustine descended into the hole. The Lourdes stood in the corner, her crooked body hunched over. She scraped her fingernails down the dirt walls. He saw blood and small pieces of flesh clinging to the wall. Her long hair looked dirty and unbrushed, hanging in knots down her back. Somehow she'd grown even more bony in the years since he last saw her. A mere skeleton wrapped in a leathery skin. She wore the same tattered pink dress she'd worn for decades, if not centuries, and it hung from her body in rags.

He knew that she sensed him, but she did not turn, merely continued her scraping.

"I have brought your potion, Lourdes, and I will need your help in return," he spoke matter-of-factly and without emotion. In his life, Faustine had experienced many horrors and, though the Lourdes repulsed him, he did not fear her.

She stopped scraping and tilted her head to the side like a cat following the sound of her prey.

Faustine took a step closer, taking the potion in his hand. He uncorked it knowing that the Lourdes would smell the contents. She breathed deeply and sighed, finally turning to face him.

"What good is it?" she hissed. "I'd rather you brought me death."

It took effort, but he did not cringe in the face of her ugliness. Her eyes had sunk further into her skull and through lips, too thin to distinguish from the skin around them, he could see her teeth. She smiled her sick, malevolent smile and let her gray tongue dart across her teeth.

"Have a seat, old friend, maybe a cup of tea." She cackled at the spread of decaying food on the table.

Faustine sat, setting the elixir on the threadbare cloth and willing away the smell of rancid food hanging in the air.

The Lourdes walked her hands down the wall and lay on the floor. She slithered and dragged herself to the table. Her wasted legs only worked properly when she drank her potion. She struggled back to her feet and swept the elixir into her yawning mouth. Faustine looked away, not interested in seeing any more than he must.

Bridget's concoction worked instantly, transforming the hideous monster into a beautiful young witch with glittering eyes and a throaty laugh that had lured many men to their deaths. Faustine could have made the potion himself, but he preferred not to bleed near the Lourdes. Her thirst for powerful blood and her hatred of men made him a temptation that might be hard to resist.

Faustine watched her, unaffected. He could see behind the shiny veneer to the dead thing that lived inside.

"You spoke with Dafne recently. I need to know why she came to you. I also need you to tell me about the curse of Trager City."

The Lourdes skittered to her vanity, the mirror cracked, and snatched up a black tube. She removed the cap and painted her now-blossoming lips a shade of crimson that Faustine recognized as Dafne's. The Lourdes watched him hungrily in the mirror.

He waited patiently. The longer he sat in the hole, the more time the Lourdes lost under her transformation. He had all the time in the world, while she had very little.

Finally, rolling her eyes like an insolent teenager, she spoke.

"Dafne has been a very bad witch and she had to be punished."

Faustine felt anger churn within him and he took a slow, careful breath, willing a sense of calm to return. He could not afford to get angry with the Lourdes. Once emotions took over, a witch's power was hard to direct.

"What did she do?" he asked.

"What didn't she do?" the Lourdes cackled, but she held no laughter in her eyes. "She lied to you, didn't she, Faustine? She lied to you and all of your superior witches. How did she do that, I wonder-are you really so easy to deceive?"

Faustine sighed and glanced at the watch he'd put on for the occasion.

"Already four minutes has elapsed, Lourdes. How much time until this magic," he waved his hand dismissively, "wears off?"

She sneered and he saw the dark chasm of her mouth. He sensed her restlessness.

"I'm flattered you think me so knowing," she flirted, moving closer to him and taking a chair. She sat on the edge like she might flee at any moment. "I last saw your deceptive witch at the half-moon. She cried and begged that I help her. How could I not?" The Lourdes cast her huge, shining eyes on Faustine. He saw the darker shadows twitching beneath their color.

"She had failed. The human's memories were returning and the young one, Abby, had fled Ula. Dafne knew her web grew tangled-there was another spider in the fray. I said go to the man, isolate him and begin the spells again. Stronger spells, the kind that wipe a memory forever, the kind that we don't come back from." The Lourdes held a faraway look, and Faustine wondered what tragic part of her past had resurfaced.

"So she went to France for Sebastian. And you told Tobias where she was going?" Faustine asked, the rage again bubbling at the thought that the Lourdes had betrayed Dafne.

The Lourdes laughed and touched her fingers to her dark lips.

"Tobias doesn't need me any more, you silly fool. He has Kanti."

****

Faustine slid behind the wheel of his car and cranked the heat high. He held his numb fingers in front of the vents. His head ached from the exertion of prying into the Lourdes's mind. Telepathy without his tower at Ula was never easy. He had brought a crystal and proximity helped, but even standing right next to the Lourdes, he struggled to sift through the jumbled contents of her mind.

It took all his energy to collect her memories while also staying present with her in the lair. Insane, yes, but a fool she was not. He believed that she had not detected his searching, but he could not know for sure.

He arrived back at Ula in time for supper. Bridget had prepared a quinoa casserole, but he left his plate mostly untouched. His brain pulsed and he longed to retreat to his private quarters to examine the Lourdes's thoughts.

"How did it go?" Elda asked as they left the dining room and moved toward the stairway that led to their rooms. They had begun to share a bed since the tragedies of the previous months, but Faustine still retired to the tower for work. He needed quietude and, as important, a space free of energetic entanglements.

He stopped at the base of the stairs.

"I think that I must go to the tower, my dear. These memories are important. I need to channel them appropriately."

"Of course," she agreed.

He kissed her good-night and held her for a long time, pressing her against him for comfort. He wanted to follow her to their room and allow the sound of her steady breaths to lull him to sleep. Instead, he turned and strode back down the hallway.

In the tower, he seated himself on the stone slab suspended far above the floor. Arranging his crystals in a semicircle, he lifted the mirror that would reflect the memories as he conjured them.

He watched the reflection as if a movie played out in the glass.

He saw the Lourdes as a child and then as a young woman. When he came to the memories of her lover, he slowed the reel in his mind and observed.

The Vepar, Alva, much younger and vibrant looking, courted the Lourdes. In those days, Alva was merely a man named Ira and the Lourdes was a witch named Milda. Faustine watched Milda's beautiful daughter Delphia swimming in Trager Bay. He watched as she rolled down sand dunes and chased after butterflies. He shuddered as the memory of her funeral crossed the glass. Milda threw herself upon the soft mound of earth. She screamed and thrashed and Ira, already plotting his betrayal, comforted her.

Then a moment that Faustine had not expected

Milda in the forest giving birth to a child, another daughter. She abandoned the child, left it beneath an enormous weeping willow tree. As Milda stumbled into the trees, falling and bleeding, the child wailed behind her.

"Of course," Faustine whispered. None of them had asked how the Lourdes could have been part of the curse. If her child had died, shouldn't the curse have ended with her? But no, there had been a second child, the daughter of Milda and Alva. Did she believe the child had died? So she banished herself to the forest? Turned the tree into a forever bleeding, forever weeping homage to the child she let die?

"But she didn't die," he said.

He wondered who had found the child. Clearly not the Lourdes herself, because the only memory of the second daughter included the birth.

Faustine skipped years of memories. He did not have the strength to watch the Lourdes in her full unraveling. He found the present day and when Dafne's face flashed through the memories, he honed his vision on that place. He watched Dafne move deftly through the forest to the Lourdes's burrow. He saw that she knew the way-she had been there before. He moved back in time and discovered Dafne, swollen with child, speaking to the Lourdes near the red weeping willow. The Lourdes stood above her, cackling in her diabolical way. She urged Dafne to birth the child in the woods and to kill it immediately.

"It is the only way to end the curse," the Lourdes screamed, and the murderous gleam in her eye caused Dafne to scramble to her feet and run. Through the Lourdes's eyes, Faustine watched Dafne's retreating form disappear into the trees.

Again he returned to the memories of the previous months. He watched as Dafne sought the Lourdes out. She begged for information. She took her potions, many of them, in exchange for tidbits about the curse. She confessed to the Lourdes that a young witch and her human lover had arrived at Ula, that they would surely sow the destruction of the coven that she so cherished.

Faustine felt something wet strike his hand. He blinked and looked away from the mirror. Tears fell in a steady stream from his eyes. He did not realize that he had been crying.

.

CHAPTER 7

Abby awoke on Christmas morning to find Sebastian hovering next to the bed.
"Did I wake you?" he asked, feigning concern, but grinning.
She yawned and stretched her arms overhead.
"No, were you trying to?"
He smiled mischievously and shook his shaggy curls from side to side.
"No, maybe, okay yes." He held out a shiny package wrapped in purple and silver. "Merry Christmas," he told her, leaning down and kissing her mouth.
He tasted like cinnamon and coffee.
"Mmmm, maybe I should give you your present first," she cooed, clutching at him as he pulled away.
"I have cinnamon rolls in the oven, but I'll be taking you up on that offer after breakfast." He started to back out of the room.
"After I'm full and feeling like a pregnant hippo?" she growled, laughing.
"I've always thought hippos were the sexiest of the jungle creatures."
She scowled and pretended she might fling his present back at him.
He blew her a kiss and backed out the door.
She shifted to sitting and fluffed the pillows behind her. Her clock said 6:24 a.m. Early for Sebastian. He wasn't a late sleeper per say, but generally liked to stay tucked beneath the covers until eight a.m. at least. Apparently the holidays had him excited too.
Despite having a moody mother who used Christmas to punish her daughter for any perceived transgressions, Abby still had fond memories of the Christmas holidays. Her Aunt Sydney had often visited Lansing over Christmas. She and Harold, or later Rod, would rent a hotel room downtown. They would pile into Abby's small family home in the evening to drink wine and play cards with her parents. When Abby got older, she and Nick joined the card games.
Sydney would get tipsy and tell stories from her childhood while Becky frowned and complained that she preferred to change the subject. In the

two Christmases that Rod joined the festivities, he showed up one year in black leather pants with a red turtleneck covered in jingle bells and the second year as a fully costumed Santa Claus. Sydney cracked endless jokes about going to bed with Kris Kringle, and Abby's mother made snide comments about exploiting a Christian holiday that was meant to be marked with reverence, not lust.

The holidays had never been easy with her mother. Nothing had ever been easy with her mother. Over the years, Abby had probed Sydney for reasons. She wanted to understand why her mother shifted from cold and cruel to warm and cuddly without batting an eye. Becky's only sister had provided few answers. Sydney mostly talked about Becky as quirky and moody, but Abby knew a much more sinister aspect to her mother.

She remembered walking down the stairs one Christmas morning when she was eight. There were presents under the tree, but they were crushed and misshapen. Her mother lay on the floor with a shovel, as if she had grown so exhausted destroying the beautifully wrapped gifts that she had just fallen down and gone to sleep. An hour later, Abby's father walked down the stairs. He saw Abby sitting on the floor quietly and her mother snoring nearby. He ushered her into a coat and shoes and took her to a pancake restaurant. When they returned home, the mess was gone and so were the presents. They had never spoken of it.

Abby wondered what her mother was doing in that moment and felt a crushing wave of guilt. Becky's parents and sister were now dead in the ground and her husband and daughter had abandoned her. Abby had no idea if her mother sat alone at that very instant, perhaps devastated by loneliness. She should know. She should have called her mother, checked on her. She should have taken the time to ensure that she was okay. Abby felt tears welling behind her eyes and she clenched them shut. She didn't want to think about her mother.

Sydney would have told her, "Don't should on yourself."

Abby smiled at the thought of her aunt and then felt the tears threatening a second time. Sydney would never hold Abby's baby. She wouldn't help teach her to swim or let her stay up late watching scary movies.

"I have to stop having these thoughts," Abby said out loud.

She shifted her attention back to Sebastian's present. No card accompanied the slim rectangular box. She carefully untied the silver bow and then slid her finger beneath the sharp edge of the paper. Nick used to call her a pack rat for her tendency to save beautiful wrapping paper. She pulled the paper off and folded it neatly on her bedside table. The box was cardboard and plain with no distinctive markings. She lifted the flaps and peered into a cloud of purple tissue paper. Gently, she pulled a framed picture out. She looked down at a charcoal drawing of herself, in profile, sitting in the floating garden at Ula. It looked very much like an image from the previous visit to the coven. Flowers and trees surrounded her. A sky marred with giant clouds drifted overhead. She looked at the signature on the bottom: Lydie Rose.

Tracing her finger along the polished black frame, she marveled at Lydie's talent. It was a magnificent drawing. Abby held the frame to her chest and smiled.

She would call her mother.

Abby slid out of bed and put on her robe and a pair of fuzzy slippers.

In the kitchen, Sebastian stood at the stove. Christmas music played from his laptop, which he had propped on the counter.

"Well look at that timing," he laughed as "I want a Hippopotamus for Christmas" started to play.

He swept her into a twirl and she laughed as he spun her to a chair.

"I'm going to let that one slide because of this beautiful gift," she told him as he kissed the top of her head.

"Decaf or regular?" he asked.

"Regular," she said. "It is Christmas after all."

"Anything for my girl," he told her and handed her a huge mug of steaming coffee. She leaned down and inhaled the scent. "Oh how I love thee," she told it.

"Moi?" Sebastian asked.

"Well you too, of course."

"Are we the only ones awake?" Abby asked.

"Yep. I wanted to get a jump start on Christmas breakfast and Oliver and Lydie had a pretty heated Monopoly game going at all hours of the night, so who knows when they'll get up."

"Lydie drew this?" Abby held up the lovely picture.

"She did. I saw her sketching a few weeks ago, so I commissioned a piece as an extra-special gift."

"Wow, thank you, Sebastian. This really means a lot to me."

"I knew it would," he told her, leaning down and pecking her nose.

"I put your presents under the tree," she told him. "And not very stealthily, I'm afraid. They've been sitting there for a week."

"Oh, I know, my love, I've already unwrapped and re-wrapped them twice."

"You have not!"

"Okay, true enough, but I may have noticed them there. No peeking though, I promise."

Abby smiled and took a sip of her coffee, nice and dark. She liked Sebastian this way. He bounced around the kitchen like he didn't have a care in the world. He reminded her a bit of the Sebastian she had first met at Sydney's, seemingly carefree. After she'd discovered Devin's body, his other side emerged. She loved his melancholy too, oddly enough. The bottom line was that she loved him, all of him, the light and the dark.

"Well I want you to open one of them before Oliver and Lydie join us. We can save the second one for the group."

"I'm down with that. Let me just mix up this quiche and pop it in the oven and I'll be ready to go."

They moved into the sitting room, and Abby took a gift bag decorated with superheroes wearing Santa hats from beneath the tree. She sat on the floor next to Sebastian and handed it to him.

He took out the red tissue paper and reached into the bag.

He lifted out a tall white candle inscribed with gold symbols.

"It's a memory candle," Abby told him, gently touching the inscriptions. "Helena helped me make it."

"A memory candle," Sebastian said thoughtfully. "Is there a manual here somewhere?"

He peeked in the bag.

"When you burn it, you can revisit the past. Not truly, of course, but in your mind. You can sort of relive moments."

Abby watched his face closely, suddenly concerned that the candle had been a mistake.

"Really?" he asked, blinking at the candle with a growing look of amazement and perhaps fear.

"Yes, it was Helena's idea actually. I wanted to give you a magical gift, but I'm so new, I didn't know of much."

"It's perfect, Abby, really. I can't wait to try it."

****

Lydie woke up first.

"I smelled frosting," she told them groggily, stumbling into the kitchen. She walked to the counter and looked down at the huge pan of cinnamon rolls. "Oh thank God it wasn't just a dream."

She shuffled to the kitchen table and eyed the previous night's Monopoly game.

"Oliver better not have moved my piece." She looked at them suspiciously. "Has he been down here?"

Abby laughed.

"Don't worry, if he'd been lurking around, we would be the first to snitch."

"Good," she grumbled and returned to staring at the cinnamon rolls.

Her stomach rumbled loudly.

"Better get those cut," Sebastian laughed. "I don't want your stomach to eat us all."

He scooped out three cinnamon rolls.

"Eating without me?" Oliver exclaimed, skipping into the room in adult-sized Yoda footie pajamas.

"There are no words," Abby said, trying to muffle her laughter.

"You like?" Oliver asked with a curtsy. "Lydie's present. She gave it to me early so that I could wear it on Christmas morning."

"It looks…cozy," Sebastian added, averting his eyes and winking at Lydie.

"I ordered it online," Lydie told them. "For witches with all kinds of crazy powers, it sure is a pain in the butt to use Amazon," she complained. "I had to row to the mainland where I had cell service and then get it shipped to the warehouse in Berkely and have Faustine make a special trip so that we could pick it up. You better love it," she told him.

"Love it, I do, my young Padawan."

"Lydie, this picture is amazing," Abby interrupted, holding up the framed charcoal drawing.

Lydie blushed and shrugged.

"I was happy to do it."

"Wow, Lyds, you are getting really good." Oliver picked up the frame and examined the picture. "This in the floating garden?"

"Yep, Sebastian hired me to be an artist and a spy that day."

Sebastian bent down to pull the quiche out.

"Hot, hot," he announced, sliding it onto the hot pad he'd set out on the counter. "I only hoped Abby wouldn't notice you," he explained. "It would have been okay if you'd been spotted."

Abby remembered back to that day. It made her feel a little funny that she had not sensed Lydie during her time in the floating garden. Of course, she had experienced a Kanti dream, which made noticing anything rather difficult. Not to mention the garden itself seemed to have a hypnotic effect on the senses.

They ate breakfast and then Sebastian ushered them into the living room. The giant sparkling tree nearly touched the ceiling, but somehow Oliver had still managed to cram a large glowing star that occasionally shot little bursts of green and red fireworks into the room.

They passed out their gifts.

Abby opened a set of fantasy books from Lydie. A purchase from the local bookstore because one adventure with Amazon had been plenty for this season, Lydie told her. From Oliver, she received a copper bracelet engraved with the phases of the moon.

Abby slipped it over her wrist.

"It's lovely," she told him, handing him her gift.

Oliver smiled, but avoided meeting her eyes.

"Sweet, CDs!"

"There's Coldplay and Kings of Leon and some other really good ones. I think you'll like them," Abby told him, feeling strange that her gift seemed so impersonal compared to his.

Oliver set the CDs aside and opened another gift from Lydie. He held a glass sphere with a flame glowing in its center.

"It's bewitched with an eternal flame, or that's what the spell said," Lydie told him. "But who knows, it might burn out next week."

She gave Sebastian a set of kitchen utensils that performed their task magically when you sang to them.

"Let me show you," she told him, running to the kitchen to retrieve a potato.

"Peel peel peel my potato, right into the sink!" she sang to the tune of "Row, Row Your Boat," and the peeler floated around the potato, quickly shaving off the skin. However, when it went to dump the skin into the sink, it started to spin madly through the air and then ricocheted off the wall, nearly taking Oliver's ear on its way.

"Maybe wear a helmet when you're peeling the potatoes," Oliver joked.

"Thank you," Lydie said shyly when she opened her gift from Abby and Sebastian. Abby had bought her a necklace with an intricate silver pentacle charm and a shining amber stone nestled in the center of the star.

"Here, put it on," Oliver told her, smiling at Abby. He clasped the necklace around Lydie's neck.

From Oliver, Lydie received a large acrylic paint set and canvas.

Sebastian opened Oliver's gift, a long, lethal-looking knife.

"Awesome, right?" Oliver asked, scooting by Sebastian.

"Yeah," Sebastian breathed, running his hand along the ivory handle. The handle was shaped like the head of a panther, the bone carved with a fierce eye and snarling teeth.

"Extra special too," Oliver said. "Better not show you in here though, we'll try it outside later."

****

"I have one secret gift," Sebastian told Abby after Lydie and Oliver returned to their Monopoly game. He led her up the stairs, pausing to tie a scarf over her eyes.

"Are you getting naked right now?" she whispered, reaching out for him.

"No peeking," he murmured, spinning her around twice.

He pushed open a door and she felt him guide her forward. When he removed the blindfold, they were in the nursery. In the center of the room stood a beautiful wooden bassinet. Half-moons were carved into the sides.

A mobile of tiny white birds, identical to those that Helena had made for Sydney's release ritual, hung above the baby bed.

"Wow," she breathed, walking to the bassinet. The smooth blond wood felt warm beneath her touch. She rubbed her fingers along the soft purple blanket tucked inside.

Sebastian moved behind her and wrapped his arms around her waist. She leaned into him.

"I can't believe we're having a baby," she whispered and felt her chest constrict with emotion.

There hadn't been time to talk about it. Between their trips back and forth to Ula, and having Oliver and Lydie in the house, they both skirted around the topic, but suddenly it felt absolutely necessary.

"Are you happy" she asked.

"More than that. I don't know how to describe the way I feel. I think about it constantly. What will the baby be like? Will he look like both of us? Will she have some forgotten trait of my sister or one of my parents?"

"Will she be a witch?"

"Yeah, I wonder that most of all."

"And what do you want?"

"I guess I hope that she will. If I thought we could escape danger by pretending you're not a witch, I might consider that. I'd do anything to protect you both, but I've learned that we can't escape our fate. Even if we tried to hide her from that aspect of our lives, she might come into her own power and resent us later."

"You are having some heavy thoughts."

"Now you know why I keep burning the bacon."

She laughed and turned into him.

"You're going to be an amazing father, Sebastian."

He looked into her face, seriously.

"Sometimes I wonder. I failed Claire, you know? I was her guardian."

Abby shook her head.

"No, you did amazing with Claire. I wasn't there, but I can feel her sometimes. She adored you."

"Sure, what sister doesn't adore their big brother, but I should have protected her. I should have known about Tobias. I've gone over it a thousand times in my head. How did he get into her life without my knowing it?"

Abby leaned her head against his chest.

"That's what he does, that's what his kind does. You never saw him coming; how could you possibly have prevented it?"

"That's what I'm afraid of. I never saw him coming. Will we see him, this time?"

****

"I have to call my mom," Abby sighed, crawling to the edge of the bed and nibbling Sebastian's neck. They had slipped off to their bedroom after their talk in the nursery. They both wanted an escape from thoughts of Tobias.

"Mmm, that tickles, in a good way." He kissed her.

He turned to look at her sideways.

"I wondered about that. I was going to bring it up, but didn't want to hit a sore spot."

Abby sat back and looked toward the window.

"I need to call and a part of me even wants to, but I'm also dreading it. I haven't been there for her. The last time I saw her, she was falling apart and I just took off."

"Why don't we go see her?"

"Go?"

"Yeah, let's pack up the car and drive down for Christmas evening. I want to meet her. We can take Oliver and Lydie. It will be like a portable Christmas party. I'll load up the steaks I was going to make for dinner."

Abby groaned.

"Now I feel like we have to."

"We don't have to, but this is going to torture you all day. Why don't we do something about it?"

"You're right," she agreed. "I'll go ask Oliver and Lydie if they can be torn away from their Monopoly rematch."

****

"Woo-hoo!" Sebastian called as he took the turn out of their driveway fast and they spun in a complete 360-degree turn.

"Donuts," Oliver howled. "Yes, do more."

"Not unless we want to drive three hours with the smell of puke wafting through the car," Abby told them grimly, her knuckles turning white as she clutched the armrest.

"I agree," Lydie chirped. "I don't have a spell to stop the car smashing into one of those trees."

They drove through a mostly deserted Trager City and got on the highway heading south.

Several hours later, they arrived in the industrial part of Lansing.

Lydie frowned out the window.

"This isn't what I was expecting," she said.

"Hoping for something more metropolitan?" Oliver teased.

"Well, yeah."

"Industrial wasteland," Abby said, watching the familiar landscape pass by.

She did not miss her hometown. Some people moved away and longed for home. They looked back with rose-colored glasses at the little ice cream shop downtown or the bookstore with the quirky old widow who smelled of lavender and mothballs.

Abby mostly remembered the confines of her childhood home. She remembered listening quietly to figure out where her mother was in the house so that she could avoid her. She loved her mother, but she never escaped her scrutiny. Becky couldn't stand a hair out of place on Abby's head. She micromanaged her like she was a full-time job.

"Turn here," Abby directed Sebastian as they came to her old road.

"This is pretty," Lydie added. The houses were mostly decorated with twinkling lights. One house boasted a giant glowing Santa, sleigh and reindeer.

"That one." Abby pointed to the saddest-looking house on the street. Dark windows had their shades drawn and there was not a decoration in sight. A pile of newspapers huddled beneath the mailbox, turning yellow and mushy.

"It's nice," Lydie lied.

"I better go in first," Abby told them.

Sebastian gave her a wounded look and she leaned over to kiss him.

"My mom will never forgive me if I introduce you while she's in her bathrobe."

Abby walked around the garage and tried the door. Locked, which was strange because Becky rarely locked her doors. She claimed a strange pride about living in a neighborhood where no one had to lock their doors.

Abby returned to the front door and rang the bell. She listened for sounds within, but heard nothing. She knocked and then called loudly.

"Mom, it's Abby."

She waited, turning to the car and holding her hands up.

Sebastian got out of the car and walked to the stoop.

"Do you feel okay? No weird vibes or anything?"

Abby stilled her thoughts. She pressed a hand on the door and searched for any feelings of misgiving. Nothing sinister greeted her.

She rang the doorbell again and this time it jerked open.

A man Abby did not recognize stared back at her.

"Who are you?" she asked.

"Who am I?" He looked surprised and annoyed. "Who are you?"

"I'm Abby Daniels. My mother lives here."

"Oh, sorry." He thrust a hand through the doorway. "I'm Cody. I think I'm renting your old room. Ha, who would have thunk it."

"My mother rented out my room? Abby asked, incredulous.

Sebastian shifted slightly so that he stood just in front of Abby.

Cody-who looked like a grungy teenager trapped in a man's body-seemed affronted.

"And you are?" he eyed Sebastian, critically.

"Sebastian. Is Abby's mother home?" he asked curtly, making it clear that he wasn't interested in warm greetings.

"Yeah, sure. Probably in her room talking to that psychic hotline. She seriously loves that lady. Kanti I think is her name."

"Wait, what?" Abby grabbed him by the shirt before he could turn away.

"Candy. That's her name, Candy Stevens. I've listened to her on speakerphone a couple times. What a hoot. She told me that my dead cousin wanted me to know he liked my new haircut. Wild, right?"

Abby frowned and nodded.

"Yeah, wild."

Cody shuffled back into the house, and they moved in behind him. He wore tattered red slippers. Abby recognized them as an old pair of her mother's. Above the slippers, a long gray robe hung just past his knees. Abby studied the robe, unnerved by the familiar fabric. Also her mother's, she realized, though she thought it had been pink before.

"I'll just go get your mom," Cody told them. He turned and smiled and Abby noticed missing teeth. His breath smelled. Even from several feet away, the scent made her recoil.

Her pregnant body reacted with double revulsion and she searched the room for a place to throw up.

"Are you okay?" Sebastian asked, startled as Abby pulled away from him.

She closed her eyes and gradually the nausea passed. She nodded and watched Cody, who had turned back to stare at her.

Finally, he broke his watery gaze and flapped up the stairs.

"Something is not right," Abby whispered to Sebastian, clutching his hand.

CHAPTER 8

The door banged open behind them and Oliver strode in.

He looked keyed up and ready for a battle. He seemed surprised to see Abby and Sebastian standing calmly by the door.

"What's happened?" he asked.

"Nothing," Sebastian reported, but looked at Abby. "Is it the guy? I mean he's pretty dodgy, but he hardly seems dangerous."

"I saw something outside," Oliver said. "Upstairs. A flash of red. It freaked me out."

Upstairs they all heard a scuffle, followed by a thud and then silence.

Abby ran toward the stairs with Oliver and Sebastian on her heels. She knew that she might be racing into a trap, but she didn't care. A vision of her mother, beaten, held captive flashed through her mind.

She burst through the master bedroom door to find her mother angrily batting Cody away from a heap of blankets on the floor.

"I said no, Cody," she shrieked as he leaned over and tried to pry her from the nest of comforters.

"Mom?" Abby asked, surprised.

Her mother, hair a halo of snarls, looking bedraggled to say the least, glared up at Abby.

She frowned and snatched away the blanket in Cody's hand. He stumbled back and landed on his butt with a loud thwack.

Oliver snorted and Abby saw that he was trying to keep his laughter at bay. Sebastian held out a hand and helped the disheveled, and annoyed, Cody from the floor.

"I told her you was here and that she ought to see her own daughter on Christmas Day. Didn't I?" Cody accused, looking pointedly at Becky.

Becky rolled her eyes and shooed him toward the door.

"Get out of here, all of you. I'm trying to sleep for God's sake."

"Mom, it's four in the afternoon."

"So, what's it to you, how I spend my time? You suddenly have a conscience because it's Christmas? No thank you, Abigail Daniels. I definitely won't be listening to a lecture from you today."

Exasperated, Abby turned to Sebastian and Oliver. She offered them a tight smile.

"Why don't you guys go back downstairs?"

Neither of them look thrilled at the prospect of leaving Abby alone with her apparently nutty mother. Sebastian stepped forward and leaned in to kiss Abby's cheek.

"I'll just wait in the hallway," he whispered.

The three left and Abby looked around the room. Near the heavily drawn curtains, Abby noticed a tall lamp that had fallen and smashed on the floor, likely the red light that Oliver had seen. Hundreds of porcelain dolls lay in heaps along the base of the wall, nearly stacked as high as the window ledge. Becky had collected the dolls all of Abby's life. Her mother insisted that Abby collect them as well. She remembered countless Friday and Saturday nights watching the Home Shopping Network and carefully gluing the doll parts together. She shuddered at their wide, vacant eyes watching her.

She sat on the floor next to her mother, pulling her knees up and wrapping her arms around them.

"I'm sorry I haven't been around, Mom."

Becky continued to stare fixedly at the opposite wall, refusing to meet Abby's eyes.

"So much has happened. I got caught up in it all and I should have checked in."

"Hmph, checked in? Why on earth would you do that? I only raised you, fed and clothed and cared for you. Ungrateful! You never appreciated all that I sacrificed for you."

Abby cringed and tried not to argue. She wanted to. She wanted to remind her mother of all that she had sacrificed. How she, Abby, lived those eighteen years in constant fear of her mother's emotional flux. Would her mother go on a rant and smash half the dishes because Abby forgot to empty the trash in her room? Or would it be a silent, brooding mood where Becky stared into nothingness and didn't speak for days?

"I'm grateful that you took care of me, Mom. I know it wasn't always easy."

"What do you know?" Becky sneered. "Living in some paradise now? Check out of reality?"

"Actually, Sebastian and I bought a house."

"Sebastian? One of those thugs you brought in here?"

Abby snorted. She couldn't help it. Thugs?

"Sebastian and I are getting married."

Becky blinked slowly at her daughter as if examining an alien life-form.

"So that's why you're here? For my blessing?"

Abby tried not to take the bait. Her mother knew just the things to say to send her teetering into an emotional meltdown. I am a different person now, she reminded herself.

"Mom I came here to try and bring you into my life. I know I've screwed up. I ran away, I left you behind and I'm truly, genuinely sorry. Let me make it up to you? At least a little. Come downstairs and meet my fiance and my friends."

Becky set her lips in a grim line and Abby knew that she wanted to take another jab at her daughter. Finally, she sighed and started to struggle out of the blankets. Abby stood and helped her up. Becky had put on a little weight. The last time Abby saw her, she looked like a skeleton wearing skin. Now she had a slight puffiness to her face and body. Abby wondered if she'd been drinking, but dared not ask.

"Let me get dressed."

Becky opened her closet and pulled out a dress and shuffled into the bathroom. Abby waited, growing impatient after more than thirty minutes had ticked by. She spotted an empty bottle of gin next to the bed and gazed around the room. Drawers hung haphazardly from the dresser with clothes sticking out. Several glasses cluttered around a remote control on her mother's nightstand. The Becky that Abby knew did not live like this.

She heard a light knock at the door and opened it.

"Everything okay?" Sebastian asked, peering beyond her into the room.

"Don't worry, I've tied her to the bed. We're all safe now."

He grinned and shook his head.

"I'm sorry that I pushed you to do this."

"No," she sighed. "It was the right thing. I want her to meet you and as hard as it is, I need to show up for her."

The door to the bathroom opened and Abby quickly closed the door in Sebastian's face. She didn't want her mother to think she was talking behind her back.

Becky strode into the room in a full face of makeup, her hair wound in a twist and wearing a long, sparkling blue dress.

"The stilettos or the silver sandals?' she asked Abby, holding up two pairs of shoes.

"The sandals?" Abby asked, fighting the urge to remind Becky that it was hardly a formal affair.

Abby's mother had always been unhinged. Her father called her sensitive, but Sydney's death appeared to have sparked a new fracture in Becky's personality. She had never been a woman who wore shiny, fancy things. In fact, she mocked Sydney incessantly for her clothes, jewelry and general beauty. Abby didn't quite know how to manage this new version of her mom.

"You could have gotten dressed up, you know?" she scolded Abby, looking at her jeans and sweater with disapproval.

"Don't you love this dress?" she asked, doing a girlish twirl and catching a sandaled foot on her blankets. She nearly went sprawling to the floor, but Abby caught her elbow and steadied her.

"It's great," Abby lied. The dress was pretty enough. The issue had more to do with Becky's overall demeanor. She looked like a woman on the verge of an internal catastrophe. Somehow when Abby had seen her mother the last time, chain-smoking and angry, she'd appeared more together. Now, Abby realized that her mother needed help, badly.

"Mom, please don't get upset, but where's Dad?"

"Dad?" Becky sneered. "You mean your father? He comes around every now and then. Tries to run Cody out of here and gives me a sermon about turning over a new leaf. What a hypocrite! I'm sure he's shacked up with some twenty-year-old. Always did have a wandering eye."

Abby frowned. Her father had never had a wandering eye-at least not toward other women. He avoided Becky during her moods, but he opted for work and golf, not pretty co-eds. Though Abby had never felt especially close to her father, she longed for him in that moment.

"I'd like to tell him Merry Christmas. Do you have his number or address?"

Becky narrowed her eyes at Abby.

"I'm sure it's somewhere." She waved a dismissive hand. "Are we going downstairs or should I get back into bed?"

Abby forced a smile and held open the door. Sebastian peeked around the frame and smiled.

"This is my fiance, Sebastian. Sebastian, this is my mom, Becky."

"Nice to meet you." Sebastian held out a hand and Becky took it, scanning him slowly. She paused on a rip in his jeans and cocked an eyebrow, but didn't say anything. "Beautiful dress," he added.

Becky offered a small smile and nodded.

"Thank you. Had I known you were coming, I might have prepared a meal."

"No worries at all," Sebastian assured her. "We brought the meal with us. I love to cook and we already had everything prepped."

Becky gave him another look as if reconsidering her first impression.

"A man who cooks? Now that's a rarity."

"Dad cooked," Abby argued, wishing she'd kept her mouth shut.

Her mother shot her a dark look and continued.

"If you consider fish sticks cooking, then you're right, darling, he did cook."

Becky teetered on the stairs and Sebastian crooked his arm through hers. Abby watched her mother as they descended. She swayed as she walked and her head bobbed loosely on her neck.

Cody sat in the living room flipping through the channels on an enormous flat-screen TV. Containers of takeout lay scattered across coffee tables and tucked into spaces on the bookshelf. Oliver and Lydie both stood by the front door looking like they wanted to make a quick getaway.

"Mom, these are my friends Oliver and Lydie," Abby introduced them as they moved into the foyer.

Becky curtsied awkwardly.

"What beautiful hair you have," she told Lydie, fingering a bouncy strawberry-blond curl. "Like Heidi."

"Heidi?" Lydie asked.

"You know, the little girl who lived on the mountain and yodeled or some such thing."

The expression on Lydie's face revealed that she clearly did not know Heidi, but she offered a polite smile.

"Smokin' hot dress," Oliver offered. "Looks like you're ready for a beauty pageant."

Sebastian rolled his eyes and continued into the kitchen.

Becky lit up and held out her hand for Oliver to kiss, which he did.

"I bought it online. You can get the very same dresses that movie stars wear on the Internet."

Abby followed Sebastian into the kitchen.

"Is everything okay with your mom?" he asked, keeping his voice low.

"No." Abby shook her head. "She's in a weird place. I'm not sure what to do."

Abby walked to the kitchen counter piled with dirty dishes.

"This is all so unlike her. She used to scream at me if I left a water glass in the sink. I don't even know how to wrap my head around this mess."

Sebastian's eyes drifted over the kitchen. Near the back door, stacked bags of garbage leaked an unpleasant rotted food smell. Several of the cupboards stood open with a mess of cups and dishes piled together.

Abby opened the silverware drawer and found several balled-up socks.

"She needs help," Sebastian agreed. "Where's your dad?"

Abby shrugged.

"Who knows, she gave me some delusion about another woman, but I highly doubt it's true."

She strode to the refrigerator and pulled off a large sheet of white paper with her dad's writing scrawled across the page.

"This is my number-call me if you need anything!" in large bold letters as if he went over the words several times to make them darker.

"Will she freak out if you call him?"

"I'll sneak out, say I'm running to the store. I'm sure we'll need to anyway," Abby added, scanning the room. "I don't think we're going to want to cook with any of the food in here."

"No, and first this place needs a good cleaning. I don't want to upset her though."

Abby considered. Old Becky would have balked at someone else cleaning her house. She would have taken it as a personal insult, but this new version seemed to be a wild card.

"Your mom had a great idea," Oliver called from the front room. "She said there's an awesome restaurant downtown that's open today. And," Oliver bounded into the kitchen, "they offer real live oysters!"

"Not live, you joker," Becky giggled.

"Sounds great," Sebastian volunteered. "Yes," he mouthed at Abby.

****

They arrived at Sophia's Lantern, an Irish-creole fusion restaurant that occupied an old train depot in downtown Lansing. Despite the holiday, cars packed the parking lot and most of the tables were occupied.

Their host, Georgina, led them to a large round booth on the second floor.

Abby pretended to have forgotten her wallet and ducked back out of the restaurant. She found an empty bench in the lobby and quickly dialed the number from the paper.

Her dad picked up on the first ring.

"Merry Christmas, Dad," Abby said, suddenly lost for things to say now that she had her dad on the line.

"Abby? Oh thank God. I've been trying to reach you for a month. I tried your old cell, but it was disconnected. Your mother kept telling me she didn't know your new number."

Abby sighed, relieved. A part of her had believed her father had abandoned her. Obviously, she had forgotten that she was the one who abandoned him.

"I'm sorry, Dad. I moved to the upper peninsula and my old cell service didn't work. I've just been so busy with school." She hated telling the lies, but couldn't imagine the truth would go much better. *Dad, I found out I'm a witch and moved to a coven on a secret island. Now I'm living with my non-witch boyfriend and I'm pregnant.*

"Sounds like a paranormal soap opera," she muttered.

"What, honey?"

"Oh nothing, sorry. I'm talking to myself. Listen, I'm in Lansing with friends. We picked up Mom and came to Sophia's Lantern for dinner."

"Your mom? You actually got her out of the house? I'm happy to hear that. Cody isn't there, is he?" Her dad asked grimly.

"No, he's not. Who is he anyway? And why did you move out?"

Her father sighed. Abby could picture him rubbing absently at his balding head.

"It's a long story, honey. One I'd rather not tell over the phone. Could you come by? After dinner? I can whip up a mean strawberry shortcake."

"Maybe you should join us here at Sophia's?"

"I don't think that would be a good idea. Your mother has not reacted favorably the last few times I've stopped by. I'd rather she enjoy her time out. She needs it."

Abby reluctantly agreed and hung up the phone. She felt lighter having talked to her dad, as if the life she used to know had not completely crumbled.

"Oliver ordered champagne," her mother exclaimed when Abby returned.

"Great," Abby mumbled, reminding herself to kick Oliver under the table. Her mother did not need more alcohol.

"I ordered you tea," Sebastian said, as she slid next to him. He tucked his hand under her and gave her bottom a little squeeze.

She jumped and elbowed him playfully.

"They have fried green tomatoes!" Lydie announced, pointing at her menu.

"You like those?" Oliver asked, surprised.

"My mom used to make them," she admitted shyly.

"I like them too." Sebastian winked at her.

"Well I think a toast is in order," Becky announced when the waiter returned with the bottle.

Oliver filled each of their glasses.

"To Abby's new friends, who I guess are better than her own family."

She beamed and gulped her entire glass of champagne. The rest of them took a sip and tried to make awkward conversation. Becky glared into her menu as if it had insulted her.

Sebastian wrapped his arm behind Abby and pulled her a little closer. Oliver gave her a questioning look and Abby shrugged. What could she say? As strange as her mother's behavior seemed, the sudden mood shifts did not surprise Abby. She'd spent the first eighteen years of her life navigating the cyclones of her mother's emotions.

They ordered and Oliver tried to make polite conversation. He asked Becky questions about her working life, but since she'd been a stay-at-home mom, a source of both pride and resentment, she soon lapsed into another lengthy silence.

Finally, Oliver shifted his attention to Lydie and they chatted amicably about their favorite Christmas movies.

"Scrooged," Lydie insisted. "I love Bill Murray. Why don't we have a TV at Ula?" she asked suddenly and then clapped a hand over her mouth.

Becky's head shot up and she stared at Lydie for a long time.

"What's Ula, honey?" The sticky sweet voice she used made Abby's skin crawl.

"It's a city in the U.P.," Abby said at the same moment that Oliver explained it was Lydie's boarding school.

Becky looked coolly between them.

"Do you all think that I'm stupid? Is that why you came here today? To share your little secrets and mock me?"

Becky's voice rose and Abby reached across the table, trying to clutch her mother's hand.

"Mom, it's okay, no one is trying to keep secrets."

"Ha," she laughed and stood, staring down at her daughter.

For an instant, she reminded Abby of Ursula-the sea witch from The Little Mermaid as she rose out of the ocean with Titan's trident blazing in her hand.

"I know what you are," she hissed at them. She looked triumphantly from one face to the next. "I've seen what you become. Slithering monsters that live in holes and feed on little girls."

She suddenly clambered onto the bench and then the table, kicking over their glasses in her sandaled feet. She jumped off the table and ran down the stairs.

CHAPTER 9

"Let me out, I have to go after her," Abby demanded, trying to push Sebastian out of the booth.

"No, let me go," he urged, pressing her back down.

Shamefaced, Lydie turned to Abby.

"I'm so sorry, Abby. I can't believe I said that."

"It wasn't your fault, Lydie," Abby promised.

She watched Sebastian trot down the stairs and out of sight.

"My mom is…"

"Cuckoo for cocoa puffs?" Oliver asked, but he smiled warmly and gave Abby's hand a squeeze across the table.

"Yeah, exactly. Now you know why visiting her on Christmas was a last minute, and obviously terrible, idea."

"She needs help," Oliver offered. "I'm sorry about the champagne. I thought she might feel more comfortable."

"She might if she hadn't already downed half a bottle of gin at home."

"She did?"

"I saw a bottle on the floor next to her bed. I could tell she'd been drinking, but don't let that fool you. She can launch into a complete rage totally sober."

"That must have been crazy to grow up with," Oliver added.

"Yeah, it was."

"What did she mean about slithering monsters that eat little girls?" Lydie asked, frowning.

"I don't have a clue," Abby admitted. "Creepy though."

Their waitress appeared and began to mop up their spilled drinks.

"Heard you guys had a bit of a showdown over here," she said lightly. "Is everything okay?"

"Yeah, we're okay," Abby said, wanting to leave and drive back up north without a backward glance. Every time she returned to her hometown, she received a thunderclap reminder of why she had fled.

"No luck," Sebastian apologized, returning to the table. A red welt showed across his cheek and Abby grimaced.

"She slapped you?" she asked, appalled.

Sebastian touched his cheek.

"To her credit, I tried to pick her up and carry her back from the bus stop."

Oliver snorted.

"Was she upset?" Lydie asked.

"More self-righteous than anything. Even after I confessed that I was a mere mortal, she still insisted on calling me a warlock and wagging her finger in my face. Fortunately the other patrons waiting for the bus looked equally unhinged, so I'm not sure anyone will be reporting the incident."

Abby moaned and put her head in her hands.

"I'm sorry, you guys," she told them. "I obviously didn't think this through."

"Why are you apologizing?" Sebastian asked, incredulous. "I'm the one who insisted on the family Christmas trip. At least now I can say, I've met your mother."

The waitress brought fresh drinks and a plate of appetizers.

"No live oysters, thank the Goddess," Lydie said, grabbing a piece of bruschetta from the plate.

****

"Abby!" Abby's dad wrenched open the door of his condo and pulled her into a hug.

The condo occupied one half of a small yellow building in Mason, a rural community south of Lansing.

"Hi Dad." She hugged him back.

He pulled away and looked her up and down.

"Your hair is longer, but I could have sworn it was short the last time I saw you?"

She smiled and touched a curl.

"Yeah, I found some miracle grow shampoo. Pretty amazing, huh?"

"Sure is. Could use some myself." He touched his mostly bald head and smiled.

"Hi, I'm Sebastian." Sebastian thrust his hand forward and Abby's dad shook it vigorously.

"Nice to meet you, young man. Is this your fella, then?" he asked. "Or that one there?" He cocked his head toward Oliver, who stood next to the car with Lydie.

"This is the one," Abby said, wrapping her arm around Sebastian's waist. "We're engaged."

"Whoa, engaged? Well congratulations then. Come on in. Dessert's all ready, and I think I have a bottle of wine floating around here somewhere."

They followed him inside.

"This is Oliver and Lydie, Dad," Abby told him as they walked through the door.

"A pleasure." He smiled at them. "You look a bit young for college though, little lady. Are you one of those super geniuses who becomes a doctor when she's thirteen?"

Lydie laughed and blushed.

"Oliver is my brother. I'm just tagging along."

They had made up the lie on their drive down.

"Well that's an awfully nice brother to let you do that."

Abby surveyed the condo. Very plain with neutral colors. It revealed that Abby's dad still hadn't accepted that he could pick his own decor. Not that he was a decorator. Though she imagined if he truly tapped into his secret interior designer, they'd be looking at blown-up photos of golf courses and not much else.

Becky had not allowed Jim much space to have anything of his own. The one time he tried to bring a reclining chair home, she marched him right back to the store and returned it. "A hideous monstrosity," she had called it.

Abby saw a similar chair in his sitting room. It accompanied a stiff-looking tan couch and a pair of homely end tables.

"I like it," she told him honestly, following him into the small kitchen. It didn't have much flair, but something about the space felt safe and easy.

"It's plenty big enough for me, and I got a great deal on it. No fees since I worked as my own agent."

"How's business?"

Abby's dad had been a real estate agent since before she came into the world. He loved his job, though Becky needled him constantly about selling mansions instead of welfare housing.

"Oh it's super. Look at this." He led her to a small office, tucked into the corner of the kitchen, with a desktop that folded down from the wall. A laptop sat on the surface along with a stack of her dad's brochures. He touched the mouse and his screen came to life.

"Newest software on the market. It's called Rate my Realtor. It's a social media platform for buyers, sellers, agents, you name it. I've got 4.7 stars!"

"Wow, congratulations," Abby told him, watching over his shoulder as he clicked on his profile. An image of her father standing next to a "sold" sign appeared on the screen.

"So what happened with you and Mom?" she asked, glancing behind her to make sure the others had stayed in the sitting room. She didn't mind if they heard, but knew her father would be reluctant to open up with strangers nearby.

He sighed and closed the laptop.

"After Sydney's funeral she just became impossible. You know I love your mother, Abby, and I have no intention of speaking ill of her now, but I couldn't live with her anymore. It's that simple. The moods, the rages. Sometimes I would come home from work and she'd attack me. Not just with words either, like she used to. She'd be throwing dishes at me before I even made it through the door."

"I'm so sorry, Dad."

He shrugged and held up his palms.

"She never handled change very well. I think you moving away and Sydney's death just became too much. But I have faith in her, you know? I think she'll work through this stuff and then maybe…" he trailed off.

Abby knew what he wanted to imply, but also sensed that he did not truly believe it. Neither did she for that matter. Once you escaped from someone like Becky, you were unlikely to ever go back.

"It's okay," Abby told him. "It's okay to do what's right for you."

He smiled at her and nodded, but he stared at the floor for several more seconds. When he looked up, Abby saw the sorrow in his eyes.

"She's had a hard life, you know. I never knew all of what went on, but I think something horrible happened to your mom when she was a little girl. I think she never got over it."

Abby frowned.

"She never said anything like that to me. What do you think happened to her?"

"I don't know. I tried to ask her a few times, but you know your mom, if she doesn't want to talk about it, she's not going to."

"What about this Cody character? Why on earth did she let him move in?"

Jim grimaced and a flash of anger passed over his normally placid features.

"He's an opportunist, a total user. He worked delivering packages for Anni's Custom Goods, you know that furniture shop on the west side of town?"

"Yeah, I remember it."

"Well he came by four or five times to drop off more of your mother's purchases, which has gotten out of control, by the way. Why Sydney left your mom all that money is beyond me."

"I don't think she intended for it to go that way."

"No, of course, you're right. What a tragedy. But I don't believe Rod killed her. Your mom was never fond of him, but I once saw him run into the street to pick up a turtle that was going to get run over. Not the kind of guy to murder anyone, let alone his wife, but then what do I know?"

"I don't think he did it either," Abby assured him. "Tell me more about Cody."

"Oh yes, Cody," he said the name like it left a bad taste in his mouth. "He started bringing your mom coffee with the deliveries and then cigarettes. He would stay and chat with her. After a couple of weeks, he quit his job and moved in. I hadn't been living there for a while so I didn't know right away. I stopped by every few days to check on her. One day he answered the door."

"It's not romantic?"

"No, no, at least I don't think so. Your mother would never…"

Though he didn't finish the thought, and Abby knew he felt as unsure about what Becky would do as she did.

"I tried to kick him out," Jim admitted, sheepishly. "I threw a bunch of his stuff out on the front lawn, called him a freeloader. Becky called the police. Can you believe that? They told me that I had to leave and he could stay."

Jim ran a hand anxiously over his freshly shaved chin.

Abby's heart ached for the complete bewilderment etched on his face.

She moved forward and wrapped her arms around him. He hugged her back, stiffly at first. Hers had never been an affectionate family. They stood that way for several seconds and Abby felt her dad finally relax against her.

"I'm sorry, Abby," he said into her hair. "I'm sorry that I let it go on for so many years. Your mother needed help."

Abby felt tears slide down her cheeks. She fought the sobs that seemed always to be hovering lately.

"I'm sorry too, Dad."

"Can I help?" Sebastian asked, walking into the kitchen. "Oh."

He started to turn away, but Jim stopped him.

"Sure you can," Jim exclaimed. He moved back toward Sebastian and opened a cupboard. "Got bowls right here if you want to get those out. Abby, biscuits are in the oven."

****

"I feel lost, Elda," Helena confided.

They stood in the scallop-shaped greenhouse that bordered the second lagoon. The glass windows were fogged from the warmth. Helena perched on a high stool and carefully trimmed a bonsai tree, searching for a calm that always seemed just over the next cut, breath or moment.

"It will take time, Helena," Elda soothed. She brought Helena a cup of tea from the thermos Bridget had prepared that morning. It contained a special blend of oils and herbs to aid in Helena's physical and emotional healing.

Helena took the cup and sipped it, looking toward the sky and wishing the sun would break through the clouds.

"I want to help. I want to dig into the curse. I want to track down Dafne. I have a thousand desires, but they are all locked in some chamber within me, and I appear to have lost the key."

"Your body knows better than your mind, Helena. Sometimes the only way to slow us down is to literally slow us down." Elda nodded toward Helena's cane.

"I don't want to be left out, though. I heard you and Faustine in the library. He went to see the Lourdes. Why didn't anyone tell me?"

"Because he didn't want to alarm anyone, dear. We're not hiding from you. We'll discuss our findings soon. Julian will reach out to Oliver and Abby and find out if they have any new information. It can't happen overnight. Not uncovering this curse, and not your recovery."

"Even Bridget is so involved. She's made a thousand of those powders that Julian created. She has two cupboards of anti-venom. I've never seen her so determined."

Elda chuckled, "I know, it's a terrible motivator, but it has brought us all screaming awake from our sleep."

"Why did Oliver and Lydie go back to Abby's?"

"Because I asked him to."

Helena frowned.

"I asked him to keep an eye on Abby. I'm concerned that this curse is working behind the scenes. More so, I'm afraid that the fire in the cave marked some transition and we're unaware. Abby drank the blood from that bottle, Helena. No one has talked about it, but Sebastian found it clutched in her hand and empty. That blood is part of the Vepar's ritual. How did she come upon it in the woods, in that blizzard?" Elda shuddered. "Something led her to it and she drank it and I'm positive that she has no memory of doing so."

"You think we walked into a trap?"

Elda looked far away and when her gaze returned, she appeared frightened.

"I think that Tobias, Alva, and most importantly Kanti got exactly what they wanted."

CHAPTER 10

"A VW Bus?" Abby laughed when Oliver and Sebastian drove up to the house.

They had returned from Lansing several days earlier to prepare for their road trip. Sebastian and Oliver had gone into Trager that morning to rent a vehicle for their road trip to New Orleans.

"Interesting rental choice."

"I bought it," Oliver said with a shrug, his eyes twinkling. "I need to be more portable."

"Ooh, a hippie van," Lydie squealed, catapulting from the porch into a giant snowbank that nearly swallowed her whole. She stood and shook her hair from side to side, flinging snow from her blonde tresses.

They all laughed. Abby realized that Lydie did need a vacation. In fact, they all needed an opportunity to get out of Michigan.

Once officially on the road, Abby settled comfortably into the crook of Sebastian's arm and dozed off. She felt a little tug in her heart as they pulled away from their new house, but also looked forward to the time with friends. It felt like a pre-witch experience, road tripping. Oliver drove the first shift with Lydie as copilot. They picked up Victor and Kendra in Chicago.

****

Victor offered up an iPod and Lydie found a playlist of Aerosmith and turned it on.

"Shouldn't you have picked the Jonas Brothers or something, Lyds?" Oliver teased.

"They're too naive," she said simply. "I prefer people who have done bad stuff. They understand more about the world."

Oliver grimaced, but didn't respond. In truth, he didn't want to know how deep Lydie's sadness ran. He had not told Elda about the road trip, despite his promise to communicate everything that was happening. He knew she would resist the idea and he didn't want the flack.

****

Helena returned to the library and settled into a chair by the fire. She shivered and layered an afghan over her lap. Despite the warmth in the room, she still felt a chill. The chill didn't often go away since the attack. She spent most of her time in heavy sweaters and layers of skirts. Sometimes when she grew really cold, the scars burned cold too.

She lifted a stack of journal pages that she had brought in from the Vault. There were hundreds of them, and the discovery process would be slow even with Victor's scanning contraption. Helena felt sure that the heart of their woes lay in those boxes.

The journal she read had been kept by a man named Christopher. Tiny cursive writing filled the pages. Helena closed her eyes for a moment and asked for clarity in the words and then returned to the pages. She skimmed through the first fifty pages, reading about witch sightings. Christopher himself had never seen a witch, but had been compiling stories from all over the state. People who claimed a woman cured their terminal illness with a tiny, sweet-smelling poultice, or a man who insisted his foe had vanished during a duel rather than fire his gun. Helena grew tired and blinked to stay awake. Only when her eyes drifted across the name Kanti did she suddenly snap back to focus.

Date 17 October 1856

I recorded this story by an Ojibwe elder:

He took her in broad daylight, the Algonquian man told me. Swept her into the woods like a shadow. Her mother woke, feeling the aching in her womb at the absence of her most magical child. The tribe searched the woods for days, weeks, months. They traveled to other tribes, they sent word along the trade lines, but not a speck of her remained, not a sighting or a detail. Only a single witness existed, Mukki, youngest son of Nootau. He told the mother and father of a giant covered in fur that snatched Kanti from the fireside. The boy was so terrified by the hulking beast, he'd burrowed back into his skins and fallen deeply asleep. Only later would he wake to the camp's hysteria and tell the others. By then it was too late.

What do we know about this Kanti? Was she a witch or merely a special tribal woman? She has appeared in the journals of others and I cannot help, but feel that she is important. When we find a piece of her history it is like discovering a small treasure, but having nowhere to sell the piece, it is valuable only to us, the collectors of history. We can only document it. But who was Kanti, and why is she woven into the history of the witches of the north?

The journal ended just five pages later. A few more stories and two short reflections by the author. Had the author died? Simply begun writing in another book? Helena set the journal aside, making a mental note to show the excerpt to Elda.

****

"It's huge," Lydie whispered, peering out the window at the towering Victorian Gothic house they had rented for the week. Lydie and Abby had spent most of their drive through the neighborhoods of New Orleans gushing over the sprawling mansions.

"It's beautiful," Abby added, surveying the bushes bursting with deep violet roses. They watched it through a black, wrought-iron fence with tiny spires poking toward the spider-like cypress trees.

"And spooky," Oliver said.

Sebastian pulled into the driveway and parked the van.

The house rose two stories with white Corinthian columns flanking the grand entrance.

While the group unloaded their bags, Abby went to the little black box over the door and typed in the house code. A metallic click sounded and she opened the heavy front door. Inside, the house smelled of lilacs. She slipped off her boots and padded over shining wood floors in her socked feet. She took a few steps and then slid. The floors, freshly polished, weren't quite as slick as an ice rink, but close enough. She trotted and then slid again.

She came to a stop in front of a set of French glass doors that opened into a cavernous bedroom. An enormous medieval bed stood beneath a copper chandelier, shaped like a many-pointed star. Colored light shone through the stained-glass window behind the bed and made rainbow patterns on the white comforter.

"Shotgun this room," Abby said when Victor walked in behind her.

"Wow, this is epic," he agreed, running his hand along the whorls and ridges of the bed frame. "It looks like a witch's bed."

They both laughed, but it did.

"What looks like a witch's bed?" Kendra asked. "Oh," she sighed. "It's gorgeous."

"And spooky," Oliver added over Abby's shoulder.

She elbowed him and laughed.

"It's not spooky, just…"

"Special," Sebastian finished. He moved in behind Abby and breathed into her hair. She pressed back against him.

"Whoa, look at that bed," Lydie squealed sliding into the room on her own socked feet.

They all laughed. Oliver scooped Lydie up and ran out. Abby heard his heavy footfalls on the stairs.

"Whee," Lydie called.

"Better catch them or Oliver's going to claim the second best bedroom," Victor joked, steering Kendra out of the room.

Sebastian moved to the window and looked at the stained glass.

"The Virgin Mary," he said, tracing the vague outline of a woman's shape in the reds and blues of the glass.

Abby followed the line that his fingers drew, and slowly the shape emerged.

"I didn't see it before," she said.

"Neither did I,' he admitted. "But then as I stared at it, she started to emerge. A good sign, I think. My mother always loved the Virgin Mary. She wore a little silver amulet with an inscription of Mary around her neck."

"Was your mother religious?" Abby asked, surprised.

Sebastian smiled and Abby saw the look of happy memories in his eyes.

"No, raised Catholic though, so she had a handful of superstitions. Her mother gave her the charm and she would have given it to Claire, but…"

"She was wearing it when she died?"

"I assume so. The truth is I don't know. I never saw it again after her death. I searched our house, but by then we were moving and everything was in boxes. I ripped the place apart, but no necklace."

Abby lifted Sebastian's hand to her lips and kissed it softly.

"I wish I could have known them-your parents and your sister too, Claire. I think in all of this, that is my only regret, that I met you after they were already gone."

Sebastian tucked a wayward curl behind her ear and kissed her.

"I wish that too."

****

Elda stood in front of the huge mirror and waited for the familiar sheen to slide down the reflective surface. They had bewitched it again, with the help of the Sorciére witches, into a two-way glass; however, it only transformed for two hours every first Friday. She saw the shift as the glass undulated before her.

As she began to walk through, Elda closed her eyes to avoid the dizziness that sometimes befell her. She stepped into the Coven of Sorciére's castle, into a small sitting room rarely used by the Sorciére witches. Galla had felt it prudent that the mirror remain secret from the coven, other than those witches directly involved in the happenings at Ula.

Elda steadied her hand against a tall chair back and then sat down, leaning her head back and closing her eyes. The transition through time and space had begun to take a toll on her, and she noticed more and more a feeling of vertigo when she made the journey.

The room was cold and dark except for a single lamp. The shade, hung with gold fringed tassels, trembled with Elda's movement into the room. She watched the shadows that the light cast on the floor and she remembered how enthralling she had found shadows as a young girl. She drove her parents mad with the elaborate monsters she envisioned in those dark shapes. In those days, candles illuminated everything and shadows were much more dynamic and, in her mind, sinister.

"You've arrived," Galla observed as she slipped through the doorway, holding a mug of tea. "I prepared a tonic for you. Faustine mentioned that you've been feeling a bit ill during the passage?"

Elda took the cup and sipped the sweet gingery tea.

"Yes, each time a bit more, it seems. Apparently I'm not sixteen anymore."

Galla chuckled and nodded her agreement. "Tell me about it."

"So have there been any findings?" Elda asked. She wanted to sit and relax and chat with Galla about trivial things, but her instincts told her that Galla had something to share.

"Yes, but not here. Let us go to my private chamber."

Elda did not ask more. There was only one reason Galla would prefer to speak in her private room: a need for secrecy.

Galla took a series of hallways and Elda soon lost track of their movements.

"Through here," Galla said at last, stopping at a heavy door adorned with a brass cat's face. Galla took a slender skeleton key from her pocket and clicked open the lock.

"You lock your door?" Elda asked, surprised.

"A coven decision," Galla told her. "After the attack on Ula, we've been reinforcing on all fronts. In truth, I think the news about Indra is what did it. If one of our own is capable of deceiving us, then we must protect ourselves from the enemy within as well as without."

Galla spoke with reluctant decisiveness. Only when they closed the door behind them, did she continue.

"I am less than thrilled about the changes," she told Elda. "But there is a sense of mutiny in the air. I am trying to put on a unified front even if my heart isn't in it."

Elda surveyed Galla's space. It was an apartment more than a room. Chunky old-world furniture was arranged in a sitting area next to a window that revealed an orange and pink sky as the sun began its descent. A kitchenette held tea things and sparkling wine goblets. One corner of the room overflowed with plants and a towering glass cylinder turned slowly, herbs poking from hydroponic pods. Another space revealed a claw-footed desk. The surface was perfectly clear except for a circle of crystals arranged around a single white candle. Beneath the desk, stacks of books rose from the floor.

"More tea?" Galla moved to the kitchenette and took an additional mug from the cupboard.

"Coffee?" Elda asked, the disorientation from her travel through the mirror still lingering. The tea had helped, but something strong and dark seemed in order.

"Of course." Galla smiled and waved her hands over their mugs. She set a sugar bowl and pitcher of cream on the little round table.

"Why is there upset in your coven, Galla? Because you're helping us?" Elda asked, settling into a chair and adding a drop of cream to her cup.

"It is the whispers mostly. Word has spread about your human Sebastian and how he disappeared from our All Hallow's Ball. There are rumors of a meeting."

"A meeting?"

"Oh, it's the same old stories. The Ancients will come together and pass judgment. They will seek to restore the old ways."

Elda cocked an eyebrow at Galla, who smiled an apology.

"There are witches who still believe in The Ancients? This is not the fifteenth century. Even if we did have such a group, they surely wouldn't cast judgment on their own." Elda spoke, but a shiver ran down her spine.

The Ancients were a bit like a fundamentalist version of God to early witches. It was they who created the rules to harm none and they who served punishment to witches that disobeyed. However, Elda had never known a living witch who saw or spoke with an Ancient. They existed in much the same way that God existed for humans, an all-seeing eye who tallied one's sins and eventually balanced the scales.

"I know," Galla agreed, waving her hand in dismissal. "I've seen too much of the world to discount any story as total fiction, but I do not believe The Ancients, if they exist, are lurking in the shadows waiting to punish us for our misdeeds. Furthermore, there was no malice in the actions of Ula. You merely tried to help a new witch feel welcome by allowing her human lover to be a part of her life. It seems to me that our role as witches should be more about inclusivity than superiority."

"I agree completely. Alienating ourselves is exactly why the Vepar's attack was so shocking. We were unprepared. We lived like hermits in our castle on the cliff and assumed that we could go on doing so forever. I wonder why we never asked if we should continue that way."

Galla drank her coffee, appearing thoughtful.

"Looking back is always easier. We see the whole picture instead of fragments. Are we meant to stumble blindly along in this life? I don't know, but perhaps, yes. We get the glory of these bodies and this decadent earth, but we have to view the world through a pinhole. Everything comes in sips when we want to open wide and swallow the whole thing."

Elda nodded, remembering. She had abstained so often. She loved

Faustine, but she had spent decades in a chaste, distant love with him. She rarely indulged. Even her magic was carefully moderated. Perhaps her reluctance to tap into her wild self arose from her pre-witch life. As a girl in Croatia, more than two hundred years before, she lived in poverty and destitution. Luxuries simply did not exist. It was not a matter of abstaining, but surviving. Long after she discovered her powers and moved to Ula, she continued to wake at night hearing her baby brother's hungry cries. He died at only ten months old. Their mother's milk had dried and the food that she could provide was not nutritious enough to sustain him. For decades, Elda devoted her work as a witch entirely to feeding the poor. She planted magic gardens, she filled empty pantries with food to last through famines, and she nursed the malnourished to a thriving health that they had never known. Somewhere through the years, her need to save others to make up for her brother's death had dwindled.

"Sometimes I feel very old," Elda sighed, inspecting a strand of her long silvery hair.

Galla smiled and shook her head.

"You are still a spring chicken, my dear," Galla reassured her. "It is I who am old."

Elda gave her a wry smile. "Well, older than me, anyway."

They laughed and then Galla set her coffee down, looking serious.

"Your Abby is with child," Galla revealed, watching Elda carefully. "I feel confident that your coven is not aware?"

Elda widened her eyes in surprise.

"Just now? We saw her only last week. Surely I would have…"

"She's hiding it," Galla interrupted.

"How do you know?"

"I still have her hair," she confessed. "I didn't take it intentionally. Thomas must have slipped it into my coat that day in the car when we found Abby injured. I discovered it when I returned here and tucked it into a drawer."

"Why didn't you throw it away?" Elda asked.

"I don't know. It just felt right to keep it, with everything that's happened. Hair is a direct link. It's a better conduit than material items. I hated to discard it only to discover a need."

Elda understood, but also found Galla opening that portal disturbing. Mostly because it hurt to think that Abby had withheld such important news from the Coven of Ula.

"Maybe she just wanted to wait until she felt sure. Many women miscarry and after Abby's injuries…"

"Perhaps," Galla agreed. "But there's another presence around Abby. I'm sure it's the spirit Kanti. I can feel her through Abby. I think that I can feel her through Abby's child."

Elda frowned.

"How could that be?"

"I don't know, Elda. This whole situation has confounded me on more levels than I care to admit, but we need to keep a close eye on her."

CHAPTER 11

Dafne tried to stand, but her left leg had been injured. Pain shot through her body and sent her crumpling back onto the bed. She groaned and bit down on a wad of blood-hardened blanket to keep from crying out. Dafne had felt pain. Sometimes her whole life felt like a series of monumental pains separated by years of listless monotony. Watching her friends die in the Ebony Woods fire, giving birth to the child she never knew, assisting Ula in its steady demise, remembering Tobias before he became a monster, and then knowing him after. At times, she thought all of the pain would take her swiftly in her sleep. When the nightmares became too much to bear, death would surely save her, but no, she lived on. Decades passed, but life never got sweeter; a little less bitter maybe, but then came the prophecy and with her growing awareness of the curse, a new pain consumed her life. She lived in terror for the witches of Ula. She owed them the shred of life she did claim and wanted only to protect them.

But what had all of her scheming brought her? A broken body, held captive in some dungeon that felt as dark as the center of the earth. She never heard a sound. Not a whisper. It nearly drove her mad. Sometimes she talked to herself out loud, sang even, but water did not come enough to allow for frequent speaking. The water only appeared after she had slept and she knew that they drugged it with their venom, but she had to drink. Drink or die.

Without light, she had no concept of night or day or how long she had been held prisoner. It might have been days or months. Where did they take Indra? Did she live? Or had they killed her and consumed her powerful blood?

Had the curse come to fruition and Sebastian risen as the next Vepar in Alva's clan? Perhaps her ignorance about what occurred, beyond her four walls, bothered her more than anything else. In the cell, she had no control. When she tried to call upon the fire of the earth, it did not heed her call. She wanted to believe they'd merely locked her in some chamber that blocked access to her element, but then she considered The Pool of Truth and wondered if the gods had stripped away her powers for good.

****

"Weird," Lydie murmured as they walked through an alley in the French Quarter, past a shop filled with tiny macabre heads hanging from strings.

"The shrunken heads of New Orleans," Oliver sang eerily.

"Hilarious," Abby quipped.

Even in daytime, the New Orleans streets throbbed with the sounds of jazz music. Intoxicating smells wafted from every store and restaurant.

Abby pointed out a two-story cafe called Silver Moons.

"Let's eat there, I see a sign for jambalaya."

"Do you think of anything other than food?" Oliver joked.

"Yes," Abby retorted, blushing and hoping that Oliver wouldn't notice. She might have been able to hide her pregnancy, but the symptoms not so much. Between hunger and fatigue and weird bursts of not-intentional magic, she felt pretty sure that her witch counterparts were starting to notice that something was up.

"I'm hungry too," Lydie said, in her defense. "And you ate half a bag of trail mix on the way here," she reminded Oliver. "No wonder you're not hungry."

"An acute observation, Lyds; food it is." He laughed. "You two get a table. I'm going to drop into this bookstore and have a look around."

Oliver wandered into a small, used bookshop that looked rather uninviting. Black ragged curtains covered the windows and a porcelain cat, who appeared somewhat hostile, guarded the door.

Though they all agreed that Lydie needed the road trip, they also decided not to involve her in seeking out the L'Obscurite. Oliver had explained to Lydie who they sought and why, but then made it clear that she got to skip the witch interrogation. Abby thought she might insist on going along, but then Oliver promised to take her to the zoo and she gave in.

Victor, Kendra and Sebastian volunteered to search for the L'Obscurite while Oliver and Abby took Lydie sightseeing. Though Abby would have preferred to explore New Orleans with Sebastian, Victor insisted he go with them. He thought a human addition to their group might make the L'Obscurite less suspicious.

Abby picked a table on the balcony and she and Lydie ordered sweet tea.

Their waiter, a short gentleman dressed in black slacks and a black turtleneck, told them enthusiastically about the specials. When he learned that they were visiting, he launched into a verbal tour of New Orleans, recommending a dozen or more restaurants and shops that they had to see before the left.

"Thank you, Abby," Lydie said seriously, after their waiter left.

"For what, Lydie?" Abby asked, mystified. All she had done was pass

Lydie a piece of bread.

"For bringing me here and for letting Oliver and me stay with you. I know it's probably not as fun with a kid along."

"That is absolutely not true," Abby assured her, squeezing Lydie's hand across the table.

Lydie, not entirely comfortable with any displays of affection, pulled it quickly away.

"We love having you. Honestly after you and Oliver stayed at Ula, Sebastian and I both felt a little lost. Our house is so big. It felt empty without you."

Lydie offered a shy smile and tore her napkin into bits. When she finished that, she started staring at the ice cubes in her glass, causing them to melt.

"See those candles over there?" Abby asked, giving Lydie a conspiratorial smile and tilting her head toward several tall candelabras along the balcony edge. "Think you could light them?"

Lydie looked at the candles and grinned.

"Easy as pie," she said, looking determined.

Abby knew they shouldn't play with magic, in public no less, but after months of being serious, she wanted to have a little fun.

Lydie gazed at the candles. Her fingers twitched on the table. One by one the candles lit. Another restaurant guest noticed as well. He looked at the floor as if searching for an electrical cord. A waiter stopped and loaded a tray with several empty glasses. When he stood, not realizing the candelabras had been lit, he stepped too close to the flame and his bowler hat caught on fire. Oblivious, the man continued cleaning. Abby stood quickly and flicked a surge of energy toward the half-empty pitcher of water on the table before him. The water spewed out and soaked the waiter and the couple at the next table, who both yelped in surprise. As if on cue, a cascade of red peony flowers showered the waiter and the couple from the sky. All three of them stared around in total astonishment, looking at one another with a mingling of awe and suspicion.

"Where did the flowers come from?" Lydie asked, giggling.

"I didn't want to miss all the fun," Oliver said from over her shoulder, startling Lydie and Abby both.

The waiter, finally noticing that his hat was smoking, held it to his face and gave it a distrustful sniff. Abby, Oliver and Lydie burst out laughing.

****

"This is the place," Victor agreed, looking at his smart phone.

Madame Lucinda's Wild Wares occupied a crumbling stucco house painted in vibrant greens and orange. The hand-drawn sign included skulls to dot the I's and little pitchforks pointing toward the open doorway. The smell of incense and cigarette smoke wafted into the already fragrant street.

Sebastian looked back the way they had come. He scanned the faces of people walking the sidewalks, but saw no one watching them. Still he couldn't shake the feeling of eyes. The hair on the nape of his neck prickled and he looked up into dark windows.

"Now or never," Kendra muttered, slipping her hands into the pockets of her jeans. Sebastian knew that she kept concealment stones in her pockets, as did Victor. They hoped to remain incognito while they got a feel for the place.

Kendra walked in first. Her long blonde hair hung in a thick braid down her back. She wore jeans and a plain red t-shirt. To Sebastian, she looked like any other human. Victor stood out a bit more. It was his eyes. They were dark, nearly black, and his dark hooded sweatshirt, paired with dark jeans, only added to his mysterious image. He wore his hair, also dark and long, tied at the base of his neck.

They had all tried for the casual look. Sebastian didn't own anything else so that simplified things. He also wore jeans and a well-worn Van Halen t-shirt that had belonged to his father. He had kept most of his dad's clothes, even the stuff he hated like pleated jeans and polo shirts. Not that his dad had often worn those things. Many of the clothes sat in a storage unit in Ohio. One day he would go back and clean it out, though the thought of it made his stomach knot.

Inside the shop, skeletons dangled. Colorful beads hung around their necks and funky hats were perched atop their gleaming skulls. Shelves, jammed with glass bottles, hand-sewn dolls and an assortment of magic supplies from tarot cards to leather-bound journals, lined the walls. Behind the glass counter, filled with elaborate looking jewelry and huge geodes, a tall, dark-skinned woman read from a book titled The Wild Woman's Guide to Potions and Poultices. The woman wore tiny dark sunglasses, despite the dim lighting, and had rows of braided hair woven with little orange beads. She did not look up from her book when they entered.

Kendra glanced at her and then wandered to a shelf of candles, picking each one up and holding them to her nose. Sebastian looked at a tattered book about shifter spells and mildly flipped through the pages, keeping an eye on Victor from the corner of his eye.

"Hi there," Victor said to the woman at the counter. "I'm looking for a friend of mine who may have stopped through here. She's been missing for a month now and we're pretty sure she came this way."

The woman set her book down and watched Victor with a bored expression.

He held out the photo of Dafne that Oliver had supplied them.

The woman took it and squinted at the image.

"Never seen her," she said, but even Sebastian could see the lie in her face. He knew that Victor and Kendra saw it as well. Subtle, well-practiced at deception, but still a flick of her eyes toward a dark beaded curtain and a tightening of her jaw.

"Is there anyone else here, who might have?" Victor asked, gesturing toward the curtain.

"Nope, just me," the woman lied again.

Sebastian walked over and smiled.

"We really don't mean to bother you," he said. "But this person is important to us and we need to find her. It's life and death here." Sebastian chose his tone carefully. The thinly veiled threat was not obvious, but it was there. He placed his hands on the counter.

Kendra shot him a questioning look and then joined the two of them in front of the woman.

Victor bored into her with dark eyes, imploring her to open up.

She frowned and glanced openly at the curtain now. She was human, but she had begun to sense that they were not.

"I told you, I've never seen her," she said again, and this time her voice shook.

As if the person behind the curtain sensed her distress, a man swept in from the back room. He wore a long navy robe with buttons running high up his neck. His white blond hair, cropped close to his head, was streaked with silver and black. Intense blue eyes, catlike, stopped on the three of them.

"How can I help you?" he asked, not bothering to conceal his hostility.

"When was she here?" Sebastian barked, jabbing his finger at the picture.

He knew that both Victor and Kendra were taken aback by his forwardness, but something urged him on.

The man barely glanced at the picture.

"Never seen her," he said.

"Mitchell? It is Mitchell, right?" Sebastian could not say how he knew this man's name, only that it appeared in his mind like a block of black text on a white screen.

The man recoiled and his eyes turned to slits.

Sebastian leaned forward and seized the man's wrist.

"My name is Sabre," the witch said, through clenched teeth. He tried to jerk his arm away, but Sebastian held tight, daring him to react.

"Your chosen name, sure, but I'm talking about the name your parents gave you. You know, the people who brought you into the world?" Sebastian continued, unperturbed by the witch's growing anger.

Sebastian knew things about this witch. He could feel the energy snaking off him, crawling over Sebastian, inspecting. An air element, he thought.

The woman behind the counter stood and disappeared into the curtain.

"We're not looking for trouble," Victor chimed in, though his voice too held a note of warning. "But we've come a long way for this information and one way or another, we're going to get it."

Mitchell, Sabre, glanced between them and smiled an angry-looking grin. One of his front teeth was pierced with a small blue diamond.

"You're way out of your league if you think you're bringing trouble to my store."

Two more people emerged from the curtain. A man and a woman. The man was short, stocky and reminded Sebastian of a feisty jungle cat. The woman, also short, but slender and silver-haired, looked like a much older, much wiser witch. She cast her light eyes upon them, and the title of a book that Sebastian's father had kept in his study popped into his mind "Something wicked this way comes."

Sebastian dropped Sabre's arm and the older witch nudged Sabre aside.

"I do apologize for my associate's reluctance to assist you," she said in a soft, breathy voice. Her greenish eyes regarded them with false kindness. "Please, join us in a more comfortable space."

She beckoned toward the curtain beyond them.

Kendra looked alarmed, but Sebastian nodded. They followed the three witches into the back room. The woman with braids returned to her seat.

They walked along a dark hallway. The silver-haired witch pushed open a doorway that led into a small alcove with a spiral staircase. They followed the witches up the stairs and through another door that opened into a cavernous space.

The room, or bar, was dimly lit with red string lights that hung like garlands from the bare beams of the ceiling overhead. A long polished bar, carved from the enormous trunk of a twisted oak tree, stretched along one wall. Behind the bar, dark bottles lined the glass shelves, lit from behind by a bluish glow. Couches and plush footstools surrounded knee-high glass tables. Several other people, all witches, Sebastian thought, occupied seats around the room. Some of them looked up when the silver-haired witch entered, but their gazes did not linger.

"Have a seat," she suggested, beckoning toward an empty table. "Sabre, some drinks?"

Sabre nodded and walked away without argument.

"My name is Ethel and this is Maze." She gestured to her companion. "And you are looking for the dark-haired witch from the north? The fire witch?"

"Yes, Dafne," Sebastian responded.

Ethel narrowed her eyes and regarded him slowly. His skin prickled as her stare traveled from his face and down over his body.

"Interesting," she concluded, but did not say more.

"You're the L'Obscurite then?" Victor asked, curiosity getting the best of him.

Ethel laughed, but Maze continued to watch them, unblinking. His face was a mask of neutrality. He made Sebastian nervous.

"We go by many names, dear child. Such young witches you are. Babies really."

Victor stiffened, but did not retort.

"Exactly," Kendra agreed. "And we need all of the help we can get. You must understand that? This is our friend and she has disappeared."

Ethel turned her eyes, now a milky blue, on Kendra. Sebastian realized that the woman's eyes were beginning to look like Kendra's.

"Your friend? The witch that I met had no friends. She had passion yes, purpose maybe, but no friends. You have some other reason for being here. Why don't you enlighten us and then perhaps I can help you."

Kendra noticed the witch's eyes and looked at Victor, startled.

Ethel shifted her gaze to Victor and her eyes began to darken, blue giving way to brown, now almost black.

Victor stared back at her.

"Neat little trick you have there," he sneered.

Ethel only smiled and continued to watch him with his own eyes.

"I didn't know Dafne," he admitted, with a shrug. "But she was part of a coven that I do know and they are my friends. I am here to help them."

"She was part of a coven? Has she been removed then?" Ethel asked.

"I couldn't tell you," Victor replied, looking impatient. "What does it matter to you anyway?"

Ethel folded her hands on the table and regarded him.

"How am I to know what does and does not matter if I only have pieces of the truth?"

Sabre returned with a tray of cocktail glasses, each filled to the rim with amber liquid.

"Apricot brandy. A specialty of mine," Ethel told them.

Sebastian looked at his glass. The liquid turned in a lazy circle around and around. He watched as the golden swirls moved hypnotically. The spinning grew faster, creating a cone in the center of the glass that seemed to extend beyond the glass, beyond the floor of the bar, somewhere… He brought the glass closer to his face.

CHAPTER 12

"The humans are too weak." Dafne heard the words through the veil of unconsciousness. She swam somewhere between waking and sleeping. Days passed in such a state and then she might get a few hours of complete awareness. As complete as oblivion would allow. She had no concept of night or day, of hour or month. Somewhere in the time before this moment, she had attempted to count the days. Whenever she found a lucid spell, she would scratch her fingernail into the dank wall of her prison. Then one day as she brushed her hand along the wall, searching for her markings, she found nothing. Scraped away? Had she been moved? No way to know.

But those words, "the humans are too weak," lingered in the fog of her mind. She clung to them and like a lifeline, she crawled up those words, hand over hand, until her eyes started to open. Her eyelids, as heavy and dry as sandbags, lifted until she could see the space before her through the tiniest of slits. Light. The first light she had seen in ages and shadows moving across the room.

Her eyes, too heavy to hold open, closed. She focused instead on sound.

"The other witch is dying, nearly dead I think. The witches are wasted on her trials." The same voice again, familiar. Dafne fell and fell into the vacuum of her memories. Endless sinking, but she kept a hand clasped around the rope of those words, the sound of that voice. Somewhere in the eternity of her life, she found its source. Dark and tall and beautiful and he had loved her, but then he'd hated her and she'd hated him more. Tobias.

The thought of his name sent a spasm of pain and grief through her body, and she jerked in her bed. It didn't feel like a bed though. It felt like a hard metal table. It felt like a morgue.

"Is she waking up?" Another voice now, and this one also familiar. Alva. Dafne found the name quickly this time. They went together after all. Tobias and Alva. Two parts of the same evil.

"They're creepy and they're kooky, mysterious and spooky. They're all together ooky, The Vepar Family." The song, modified, ran through her head and she snorted laughter.

Again, she focused on her eyes and the lids lifted. She saw the shadows, the Vepars, closer now.

Tobias walked to her bedside and looked down into her face. His black eyes, rimmed with red where white should have been, roved along her body. He smiled and revealed his glistening white teeth, sharper than she remembered.

"Just a taste," he told her and lifted her wrist to his mouth. He punctured the skin and she saw that tiny red wounds dotted her entire hand and trickled down her wrist. He had been biting her. That was how he kept her unconscious. The venom in his teeth. She tried to jerk her hand away, but found no strength to pull and then no strength to keep her eyes open. They closed and she began to fall again.

****

"I'm going to take a walk," Abby told Lydie as she slipped out the door.

Oliver napped on the couch and Lydie sat at the dining room table reading a book. They still had not heard from the others, but decided that might be hopeful. Perhaps Kendra, Victor and Sebastian had managed to find out something after all.

She trailed her fingers along the wrought-iron fence and pushed out of the gate and onto the sidewalk. Romantic, sprawling mansions towered amongst the subtropical landscape. She marveled at their size, their beauty, but most of all their presence. Each house seemed an entity all its own. Some of them hulked and glowered while others seemed to smile as she passed.

She turned the corner and continued down another street and another until she came to an older neighborhood with houses in disrepair and abandon. She stopped at a massive structure. In the same style of the house they rented, with giant beams extending between the roof and ground, the house seemed to sink into the black soil around it. Looking at the house, Abby felt something akin to terror. It started at her hands, clasped on the iron rail, and crawled up her arms like tiny spiders. She took her hands away and shuddered, staring at the black windows, and almost expecting a figure in white to rush forward from the darkness.

"Haunted, that one." The voice startled her and Abby stumbled back, tripping on a split in the sidewalk and landing hard on her butt.

She stared up at a tall, slim man wearing a moth-eaten suit and a top hat. His gaunt face surrounded two bottomless black eyes that watched her with interest. He did not offer to help her up.

"It looks abandoned," Abby added, struggling back to her feet and wincing at her tender backside.

"Oh no," the man disagreed. "No one ever leaves that place."

They both stood and watched the house. The man turned to her suddenly and leaned close to her face.

"Have the sight, do ya?"

She recoiled at his hot, sour breath.

"I can see her, you know?" he accused. "The brown-skinned woman in fur."

"Kanti?" Abby asked, suddenly unnerved by the strange man.

He nodded and shifted his gaze over her shoulder.

"Spectral, dark witch," he spat, continuing to watch over her shoulder.

Abby turned, expecting to see Kanti's spirit hovering in the street, but only the desolate neighborhood returned her gaze.

"Can't outrun the dead ones," he whispered, shifting from foot to foot as if agitated. He dropped his voice even lower so that Abby had to lean close to hear him. "Leona French, she knows what to do."

He stood abruptly, turned and shuffled back down the sidewalk. Abby watched him until he turned the corner.

She gazed back at the house for another minute and then turned away, hoping that she would not run into the strange man a second time.

****

Sebastian blinked. In his hands he held a pile of roses in the early stages of soft decay. Their sweetness overpowered him and he shoved them away. They toppled off his lap into a heap on the concrete. He looked around. He sat on an iron bench in a deserted graveyard. Both Victor and Kendra sat on the grass, leaning against a large concrete tomb heavy with moss. In their laps lay mounds of spoiled roses.

He felt dizzy, and when he stood a wave of nausea forced him back to his seat.

Victor stirred and then yelped in surprise. Sebastian watched him fling the roses away, disgusted. His movement startled Kendra, also lost in a strange reverie. She turned slowly to look at them both.

"Where are we?" she asked and then in slow motion tilted her head to look at the flowers. She lifted one to her face and wrinkled her nose. "Ugh, they smell rotten."

"Does anyone know how we got here?" Sebastian asked. He tried to stand a second time, holding on to the bench for support.

Victor frowned as if searching his memory.

"We were in the bar. I didn't even take a drink..."

"Neither did I," Sebastian said, "but I looked at it."

"It was moving, the brandy, like a whirlpool," Kendra said.

"Yeah, I saw that too."

"Me too," Victor agreed. "But how? I mean how could that have led to this?" He motioned toward the cemetery.

Tall concrete tombs stood in rows along the sparse grass. They could not see an entrance or exit, only endless tombstones.

"Ethel Myers," Kendra read, pointing at the tomb that she and Victor had been leaning on.

"Same Ethel?" Victor asked, still disoriented. He heaved to standing. "1856 to 1906."

"Do witches fake their deaths?" Sebastian asked.

"Some do, sure. I mean once you live past a hundred people start to ask questions," Kendra responded, also studying the gravestone. "But usually they change their names."

"And move," Victor added with a hoarse laugh.

"Let's get out of here," Sebastian exclaimed. "This place is giving me the creeps."

"I second that," Victor agreed, helping Kendra to her feet.

They walked slowly, not unlike a funeral procession. It took several false starts before they found a path that led them out of the graveyard. Victor talked, all the while trying to determine how the L'Obscurite had hypnotized them.

"And why a cemetery and roses? Is it a warning?" he demanded, searching Kendra and Sebastian's blank faces.

"I'm curious too, I swear," Kendra told him, patting his arm. "But right now I want to get that cab over there and go get a glass of water. I feel like I've been eating dirt."

****

"Dafne went to the Lourdes during her pregnancy. She sought her help," Faustine told Elda.

Elda paused at the cauldron before her. Tendrils of steam drifted from the basin, and she closed her eyes and slipped momentarily into the sweet scent. A spell for Abby's child. She had confided the pregnancy to Helena and Faustine, but asked they keep it to themselves.

"Why would she do that?"

"Somehow she knew. She knew that the Lourdes had been the previous victim and went to her for guidance. The Lourdes told her to kill the child."

"No." Elda gasped.

"She abandoned her own child, Elda. I don't know why I hadn't thought of it before, but now it all makes sense. She left her baby to die in the woods, beneath the red willow, before it was red, before it was deadly."

Elda added a handful of hibiscus flowers and stepped away from the potion before her tears could fall and taint the mixture.

Elda wiped her cheeks and shook her head.

"Sometimes I want to escape from this, Faustine. The truth is so hard to bear. Have I grown weak? If we cannot sit with the horrors of the world, who can?"

Faustine took Elda in his arms and rested his chin on her head.

"It should hurt, my dear. It should feel unfathomable. That is where we find our strength to bring about change."

"So who saved her child then?"

"That I do not know, and perhaps it is not relevant, although I would be curious. It is clear that this spirit, Kanti, needs the continuation of the blood-line. Could she have influenced someone to save the child two hundred years ago? I have preferred to believe she's only recently come into her power, but this information confounds me."

Elda sighed and waved her hand above the potion, which vanished. Her grief had ruined it. She had watched the oils move from intricate spirals to thick clumps. She would have to make it another time, when happiness felt more accessible.

****

"I just don't want you to go," Sebastian insisted for the second time.

Abby and Sebastian sat on a wooden porch swing in the backyard. White twinkle lights hung from the cypress trees, weaving through boughs of moss. Abby could see bits of stars through the opening in the trees, but the moon was covered by low drifting clouds.

"I know you're looking out for me," Abby said. "And I appreciate it. You know that I do, but I'm in this. Maybe I'm the only one who can speak to this witch Ethel. Have you thought of that? This world is mysterious. Some of these witches wait for a sign or an energy or an aura. Maybe I'm the one who has it."

Sebastian slid off the swing and got down on his knees, taking Abby's hands and looking into her face.

"They were playing with us, Abby. They had no intention of giving us any information. They didn't care who we were or why. I'm telling you that they're dangerous. I haven't felt right since we woke up from our trance, or whatever they did to us. I'm not sure they didn't plant something in our heads."

"Kendra and Oliver performed every revealing spell they could think of and nothing showed up."

"I don't care if Elda and Faustine had performed every spell they know. These are not ordinary witches. They're dealing with a different kind of magic and they don't play by the rules." He squeezed her hands, exasperated, and she saw the fear in his eyes, for her.

As she gazed at him, she suddenly understood the concern etched in the lines of his face. His parents and Claire, his entire family, had been ripped away from him far too soon. His grief still lived in his every cell, every thought, word and deed.

Abby pulled his hands to her face and kissed them. She tugged him back up and then nestled into him when he sat on the bench.

"I love you and, even though I want to have my way, I'm going to choose the path of least resistance right now. I will not go to the L'Obscurite. However"-she held up a hand when he started to kiss her-"If no one gets any information before it is time to leave, then I am going to try. We are not going home without finding out exactly what they told Dafne."

Sebastian cocked his head and nodded.

"I can live with that. If it does happen, then we'll all go together, and we'll lure them into the light of day where they can't play us like puppets."

From the house, Abby heard the scratchy croon of Etta Jones.

"There were birds in the sky, but I never saw them winging, no I never saw them at all, till there was you," Abby sang along, one hand on her belly and the other tight in Sebastian's own warmer, larger hand.

Sebastian's stomach growled and he sighed.

"You're hungry," she said.

"No, not yet. I want to remember this moment. Keep singing." He kissed her temple.

She continued to sing, not knowing all the words and making them up as she went along.

****

Galla stepped through the mirror into the library at Ula. Her short white hair hung limp around her gaunt face. Julian held out his arm and she placed her weight heavily against him. She settled into a chair and looked at the witches of Ula. Faustine, Elda, Bridget and Helena sat around the room.

"Indra is dead," she told them. She lifted a delicate silver locket as if it offered proof. "I've been handling it every day. Before the All Hallow's Ball, I never saw her take it off, so I knew it was my best chance for an impression of her. When I picked it up this morning, a horrible grief overtook me. She is dead."

"Oh," Helena moaned and put her hand to her mouth.

"I'm so sorry," Elda murmured, going to Galla and sitting close to her. She wrapped her in a hug and Galla laid her head on Elda's shoulder.

Faustine walked to the window and stared out at the lake.

"Dafne? Did you hold Dafne's ring?" Faustine asked, his back to the group.

Galla nodded. "I did, and nothing has changed. No images, but no…"

"Darkness," Bridget finished.

"Yes. I am sure that she still lives, but for how long, I do not know." Faustine pressed his palms together, frustrated.

"Where have they taken her? Where? We've scoured the woods. Every Vepar lair that we've ever heard of has been searched. Tobias has fled. All of his old lair's are abandoned. What does it mean?"

Elda stood and went to him. She held his hands and looked into his face.

"The cave of elders. They were of great service to us last time; we must go again."

****

Elda and Faustine returned from their astral travel to an expectant Helena. She sat in the dungeon, perched on the edge of the raised stone slab. Elda opened her eyes first and then Faustine.

"No elders," Elda told her, disappointed. "No fire in the cave. Just cold night air."

"Surprising," Faustine added. "I can count on one hand the number of times in my life I've gone to that cave and found it empty."

"I've only been to the caves once," Helena admitted. "Right after I discovered I was a witch, for the initiation. They took me into their arms. I've never felt so loved. It was like I was being hugged by my mother, my grandparents, my siblings, everyone who ever cared for me all at once."

"Yes, I remember it too," Elda agreed. "It was the one moment of light and ease during those turbulent years. After I met the elders, I knew that I would be okay."

"So why are they gone when we need them?" Helena asked, concerned. "Are they punishing us, Faustine? For all that transpired at Ula?"

Faustine's face darkened, but he said nothing.

CHAPTER 13

"I have an appointment," Abby told the girl at the counter.

She had found Leona French in an online directory. A psychic, medium and tarot reader, the woman operated out of a second-story tearoom on Canal Street. Sebastian had agreed to check out shops while Abby went in for a reading.

The girl led Abby to a back room and then closed the door firmly behind her.

"Sit with me," the old woman said, patting the couch beside her. "Can't see ya with these old eyes, but my hands know better anyhow."

Abby glanced around the room, taking in the antique furniture, cluttered together, and the shelves jumbled with bones, feathers, stones and books.

The woman sat hunched on her sofa, a spread of tarot cards fanned on the table before her. Thinning black hair showed patches of her scalp, spotted with age. She wore a dark robe, the hood resting on her shoulders.

Abby looked into the woman's face and saw blue eyes veiled by a white film.

Leona took Abby's hands in her own and stiffened. She traced her soft, worn fingers along Abby's palm, over each finger, gently probing the joints and knuckles. She released Abby's hands and moved to her face. She softly brushed Abby's eyes and lips and then continued to her skull, cradling her head and pressing into the bones along Abby's jaw and spine.

Satisfied, she leaned back into the couch and folded her hands in her lap.

"A water witch," she concluded.

"How can you tell?" Abby asked, studying her hands for some clue.

"I can feel it moving through ya. Cool and slow and deep. I can hear it in your voice. Nothing to it, honey. When you lose your eyes, that's when you really learn to see."

"That's amazing."

"It just is," Leona told her. "Now tell me about your ghost."

Abby glanced at the cards on the table. She saw a moon suspended above two dogs and several cards with swords.

"Are you a witch?" Abby asked.

Leona cocked her head.

"Is it fear that's got ya tongue tied? This ghost is haunting you good, ain't she? I'm a witch and a non-witch. I'm a little bit of the whole world and I'm nothin' at all."

"Her name is Kanti."

Leona frowned and nodded. She reached for the table and shuffled through the cards. She turned over a card. Abby read "Justice" upside down.

"How do you read the cards?"

Leona only smiled and lifted the card close. She held it in her hand for a long time.

"Vengeful, this ghost of yours. Gonna get what's rightfully hers."

"Can you feel her? Kanti?"

Leona nodded and her whole body moved with the gesture.

"She's here and then she's gone. Comes and goes real quick and dark. Has other business in the world, I think, but she's after you real good. She's old. How did you find this ghost, child? Diggin' a grave where you shouldn't'a been?"

"No. She's connected to a blood curse. I was hoping you might be able to tell me more."

Leona chuckled.

"You young ones are always so hopeful. Lookin' outside yourself for the truth that lives right here." She tapped two fingers on Abby's chest.

"A man directed me to you. He said that you would know what to do."

Leona sighed and hung her head.

"Father Ralph. He's been dancin' with skeletons long as I'm knowin' him. Still thinks I've got the holy grail, but darlin', look around you. Is this a palace of gold?"

Abby stared at the floor and fought the sudden desire to cry. She wanted to be rid of the curse and Kanti. She wanted to welcome her child into a happy world where evil did not exist.

"Gotta be protectin' this one here," Leona said, placing her hand on Abby's stomach.

Abby shrunk away from her.

"It's this one your ghostie is after."

****

"You know what's been bugging me?" Julian said suddenly, breaking the dinner silence. "How did Alva get to France? He obviously didn't board an airplane to bring Dafne, Indra and the human woman home. So how did he get them back to Michigan?"

"Do we know that he brought them back to Michigan?" Bridget asked, reaching across the table for a cornbread muffin.

"That's been bothering me as well," Faustine agreed. "And yes, I think they were all brought back. We know that Sebastian saw Isabelle in the Vepar's lair."

"Is it possible that they had access to a magic mirror? That they somehow entered Sorciére through the coven's mirror?" Julian wondered aloud.

Elda shook her head.

"How could they? Only covens have access to those mirrors, and they are bewitched for only that night."

Faustine stared into his stew, frowning.

"What are you thinking?" Elda asked him.

"Indra. From the beginning she has been the outlier. Why was she involved? She betrayed her coven, and for what? Because Dafne believed that Sebastian and Abby were next in line for the curse. Look at the risk she took, the peril she put her coven in for a witch she had a casual friendship with."

"They were close, Dafne and Indra," Bridget objected. "Wouldn't you help your friend?"

"No," Julian said bluntly. "Not at the risk of losing my coven and damaging my relationship with the magical world. Indra didn't just offer Dafne advice, she conspired. She helped her manipulate the energy in the Pool of Truth, she broke magical laws."

"And now she is dead," Elda sighed. "I don't get the impression that she gained from her choices."

****

"We have a plan," Victor announced.

They had spent the day doing tourist things. They took Lydie to the zoo, visited a music museum and stuffed themselves on seafood and pecan pie. After an exhausting day of sightseeing, they had returned to their vacation house to nap and talk about how to approach the L'Obscurite a second time.

The witches huddled around a wide leather ottoman. A round silver tray sat in its center, on which were arranged several glass bottles. Two of the bottles held a muddy red liquid and the third a greenish-hued paste.

"I hope it involves dinner," Sebastian told them, eyeing the bottles dubiously. He and Abby had taken a long nap and despite the day of eating, he talked of food the instant they woke up.

"No worries, my man," Oliver assured him. "Pizza is on the way."

Satisfied with pizza, though Sebastian always preferred home cooking, he moved closer to the group.

Abby took a seat on the floor between Lydie and Victor.

"A plan for the L'Obscurite?" she asked.

"Yep," Victor stated, pointing to a notebook revealing stick figures and little thought bubbles.

"Looks professional," she joked.

"Hey," Oliver quipped, "I'll have you know that Lydie gave those stick figures an A+."

Lydie smiled, but subtly shook her head toward Abby.

"These witches are dangerous, right?" Sebastian broke in, scowling at the page. "It feels like you guys are making a joke out of this."

He glanced toward Abby and she scooted closer to him, rubbing his back. She felt his heart beating rapidly through his back ribs. She had not told him what Leona French had said earlier that day. She knew that he was nervous enough without any additional stress.

"Don't worry," Kendra told him, gesturing to the paper. "This is just a brainstorm. We have no intentions of approaching these witches again without a serious plan."

"We're just having a little fun," Oliver added. "Ever heard of it? Fun?"

Sebastian narrowed his eyes at Oliver, but before he could retort, Abby jumped in.

"Okay, tell us the plan."

Victor picked up one of the bottles.

"This is a truth serum. We can't risk approaching Ethel, she's clearly the mastermind, but Sabre is a newer witch and should be way easier to crack. Abby will wander into the store like any old tourist and lure him out for a coffee or a drink."

"No," Sebastian blurted. "No way. Abby is not bait."

"She's not bait, Sebastian. She's a witch, a powerful witch and..." Oliver cut in.

"No."

"Sebastian," Victor began, looking to Abby for help, "we need Abby. Kendra can't seduce him because he's already met her. It's Abby or Lydie, and I'm guessing he's not the type to go for twelve-year-old girls."

"Honey," Abby said gently, hugging Sebastian closer. "I'll be fine. I've never felt stronger than I do right now. And I'm doing the easy part."

"The easy part? Going into that store and trying to lure him out under the nose of what? Twenty other powerful dark witches who are sitting upstairs having a drink?"

Abby bit her lip and looked to Kendra. She needed another woman's voice.

"Look at the big picture here, Sebastian," Kendra started. "We're here, we need this information. If you have another plan, then we're all ears, but as it stands..."

"I'll go," he said simply. "I'll go and talk him into meeting me."

"You're not a witch," Victor interrupted.

"Exactly," Sebastian agreed. "That's exactly why it will work. That guy was an arrogant bastard. He'll jump at the chance to get me alone to work some spell on me that he can run back and share with his friends. They get off on it. You saw what they did to us."

The other witches looked thoughtful. Only Oliver seemed to want to argue.

"He may have a point," Victor agreed. "And you really pissed him off when you called him Mitchell. He'd probably like a go at you."

"I'm not buying it," Oliver protested. "If you called him out, isn't he going to wonder how you knew his name?"

"How did you know his name?" Abby asked, realizing she had not heard that part of the story.

"I don't know," Sebastian shrugged. "It just popped into my head."

Oliver frowned, but Victor and Kendra had clearly come to a conclusion.

"It's settled," Victor said. "Sebastian draws him out. It's ideal. We'll still use the potion to cloak Sebastian so that the other witches can't pick up his thoughts while he's in the store, but now we can spare Abby's virtue."

"Oh thank you." Abby laughed. "I truly was concerned." She rolled her eyes.

"Pizza," Lydie shouted when the doorbell rang. She jumped up and ran to the front door.

Lydie's scream pierced their conversation. Kendra dropped the bottle of truth serum and it smashed on the wood floor. Oliver was already gone, racing from the room in a blur. Sebastian lifted Abby up by her arms and shoved him behind her as Victor ran for the front door.

CHAPTER 14

"Oh gosh! I'm so sorry! I didn't mean to scare you," a woman yelped from the front of the house.

Abby and Sebastian walked to the front door where the others stood staring at a dark-skinned woman with beautiful black braids. She hovered on the front stoop with a red rubber mask clenched in her fists.

"It's just a mask," she told Lydie, holding it out as proof. "I brought it just in case I saw one of the others."

"You thought a red devil mask was less conspicuous than your own face?" Victor asked suspiciously.

"In New Orleans? Pretty much. I'm Audra, by the way."

"Audra who knows nothing," Sebastian said over Abby's shoulder. "She worked in the store," he told her in explanation.

"I'm not stupid," she snapped. "Do you have any clue what Ethel would have done to me if I talked to you?"

"So why are you here now?" Kendra demanded, crowding into the entryway with Oliver, Victor and Lydie.

Audra glanced behind her and shifted uncomfortably.

"Can I come in? I feel exposed out here."

"No, you can't come in," Kendra began, but Lydie interrupted her.

"Let her in. She's scared. I can feel it. She came alone."

Oliver glanced toward Lydie in surprise, and the woman gave Lydie a grateful look.

The other witches stepped back and Audra walked into the house. Her eyes darted around the room as if already planning her means of escape.

"I came because I did meet your friend," Audra informed them, moving away from the windows to stand along a wall where she could not be seen. "Dafne."

"Why don't we move to the dining room," Victor suggested. "We can sit. The windows face the backyard," he reassured her.

After they found their seats, Audra reached into her pocket and pulled out several sheets of paper, torn from a book.

"Dafne wanted a book while she was here. I don't know the name of it.

Only that it involved spirits that find a way to survive after their bodies are gone."

Oliver frowned and looked toward Lydie. She watched Audra with wide eyes.

"Why would she want to know that?" Victor asked, addressing his question to Oliver.

"Your guess is as good as mine."

"Did she get the book?" Abby asked.

"Most of it," the girl said, pushing the papers across the table. "There were other things she wanted to know as well. I missed some of it because Ethel took her out of the store. I overheard something about an invisible pond."

"The Pool of Truth," Oliver corrected her, looking at Sebastian.

Dafne had somehow manipulated the Pool of Truth to reveal Sebastian as dead when he was in fact very much alive.

"Your witches helped her with that?" Abby asked, enraged. "Why don't they just call themselves Vepars?"

Audra flinched at the word.

"They're not my witches," she exclaimed. "That store has been in my family for generations. I didn't make any agreement with those witches, but my great-grandmother did and I'm bound by her oath. It's as simple as that. I don't support their methods. My great-grandmother didn't either, but by the time she realized what they were, it was too late."

"So they told Dafne how to bewitch the Pool," Victor cut in. "What else?"

"Like I said, I missed a lot of it, but she came back a few days later and she mentioned a curse. She seemed to believe that she was under some kind of curse and that a spirit had created it. She wanted to figure out where the spirit was getting its power and how it continued to live after its body had died."

"Kanti," Abby breathed and Victor's face darkened.

"Ethel gave her a book?" Oliver asked.

"But she tore out these pages first." Audra pointed toward the torn pages.

Oliver pulled them from the table and read them quickly.

"They're about possession."

"Possession?' Lydie asked, looking scared. "Like when a spirit takes over someone else's body?"

Audra nodded.

"Why would she tear those out?" Kendra asked.

"I don't know," Audra told them.

"So that Dafne wouldn't know what she was up against," Sebastian broke in. "So that she wouldn't be afraid of getting too close."

Oliver grimaced and continued to study the pages.

"Are we talking about this spirit possessing Dafne?" he asked, though he clearly did not expect an answer.

"Why are you giving us this information?" Kendra looked at Audra.

"Because someone should know what they are," Audra replied. "I tried to tell Dafne, to warn her away from them. Everything comes at a cost with them. A terrible cost."

****

Like dreams, but not dreams. Dafne saw snippets of life. She felt a burst of cold water rushing over her bare thighs and slippery pebbles beneath her feet. So cold that it shocked her. She danced on the edge of a cliff in the moonlight, hands outstretched with a brilliant ball of flame roiling at the tips of her fingers. She lay beneath Tobias as he devoured her with his sharp teeth and tongue and black hungry eyes, but when he called her name, he called her Kanti.

When she woke between these visions, her body throbbed and tingled. She felt bruises and aching muscles. Her head felt raw, as if someone had pulled her hair. She smelled the sooty remains of her own power, exercised without her knowing.

"What is happening?" she asked the room and silence, that endless agonizing silence, greeted her.

****

Kendra arrived back at the house just as Oliver finished creating the circle. They had moved all the furniture against the walls, and he had drawn a large circle in chalk on the floor. Lydie and Abby moved through the house collecting candles. Lydie directed her fingers at one of the candles and they all lit at once.

"It's a special magic," Kendra said, glancing through the window where the setting sun glowed purple on the horizon. "Something we've wanted to try, but we never had the water element." She inclined her head toward Abby.

"Dream Magic," Oliver said. "Julian once told me about it."

"Is it a good idea to be performing new magic on these witches?" Sebastian asked.

"It's not new," Oliver continued. "Just new for us."

"Which is my point."

"She did it," Victor announced, striding into the room. He held a brush thick with long silver hair.

"I hope they don't hurt Audra," Lydie said, staring at the brush. "She shouldn't have taken the whole brush. The lady might notice it's missing."

"Audra said there wasn't time to steal hairs, so she grabbed the brush and brought it to me in the alleyway," Victor explained. "I'd say the lack of time applies to us as well, so let's get moving."

Kendra took the brush and pulled out a handful of the hairs. She took a small doll from a paper bag. The doll had button eyes and large black stitching around its arms and legs. Abby felt a stir of uneasiness looking at the thing. She knew very little about voodoo dolls, but this one gave her the heebie-jeebies.

"Have any of you used one of those before?" she asked, nodding toward the doll as Kendra quickly sewed the hair onto its head.

"I have," Oliver admitted. "Sort of. Julian taught me. We used a doll to heal a woman who'd been attacked by a Vepar."

"It worked?" Sebastian asked, looking skeptical.

"Julian made the doll right there in the woods. He ripped off part of the woman's shirt, stuffed it with leaves and sewed it with fish line. He took some of the woman's hair and added it to the doll. Then he performed the ritual to animate it with her spirit. I wasn't much help, as you can imagine. I mostly just watched with my mouth hanging open catching flies. Then he took a bottle of anti-venom and soaked the doll. The woman was unconscious in the woods and had nearly bled out. He was concerned that giving her the potion directly might poison her, and we didn't exactly have a lot of options."

"And?" Abby asked, incredulous.

"It worked, or seemed to. The woman came to about twenty minutes later. She needed a blood transfusion so we took her to the hospital and dropped her off. Julian muddled her memory a bit, but he checked on her later and found no traces of the venom."

"Traces?" Sebastian asked.

"For most humans, the venom of the Vepar kills them outright," Oliver admitted. "The ones who aren't killed usually wander around until their bodies go completely toxic, and that kills them."

Sebastian frowned.

Abby knew that he thought about his own experience with Vepars. He had been bitten more than once and not suffered those horrific outcomes.

"You're strong," Abby told him.

"Some people have a certain immunity," Oliver added. "Possibly because your sister was a witch."

"Well she obviously wasn't immune," Sebastian snapped.

"I didn't say she was," Oliver challenged.

Abby put her hand on Sebastian's arm. She could feel his pulse thumping against her fingers. He looked at her for a moment as if enraged that she had stopped him, and then his eyes softened.

"If you guys are done, maybe we could begin?" Kendra asked.

The tension in the room buzzed like a live wire. They were attempting unexplored magic and dabbling with a witch who'd likely make vengeance a priority if she discovered what they were up to.

Kendra finished the doll.

Oliver set up a ladder and climbed to a chandelier suspended in the center of the room. He tied a string around the waist of the doll and then fastened the other end to the fixture. The doll dangled above the circle. They placed a chair in the center of the circle and Kendra sat down. They had only one broom. Abby walked through the space sweeping the floor and whispering the incantations Elda had taught her to purify a space.

"Why can't you just set the doll on the floor?" Sebastian asked, watching the grim little doll sway back and forth.

"We're entering the land of dreaming," Victor said. "It's all about air and fluidity. If the doll were on the floor, we might wake Ethel up, bring her back to the physical world."

****

Lydie arranged herbs in a mesh pouch. Each of the witches would wear one during the ritual. Some of the herbs would be the same: peppermint for help in dream travel, frankincense as an offering to their element and fennel seed for protection from psychic attack. Additional herbs magnified their individual elements. Lydie would add cinnamon to her own pouch, aloe leaves for Abby, for Oliver bark from the cypress trees and a handful of dirt, and for Victor and Kendra anise. Oliver and Lydie had found most of the herbs and stones at a new age bookstore in town. The health food store Mama's Miso sold the rest of the herbs in bulk. Kendra's pouch would contain extra herbs and stones because she would be their primary conduit during the ritual.

They arranged themselves in the four directions according to their element. As an earth element, Oliver took his position at the north of the circle, Abby at the west, Lydie to the south and Victor to the east. Kendra sat in a wooden chair in the center of the space. The chair was positioned directly beneath the doll.

"Ready," Victor said and Sebastian flicked off the lights, leaving the room awash in candlelight.

The four witches on the perimeter of the circle gazed at one another a final time, and then they each closed their eyes.

Oliver began:

"I call to the Watchtower of the West, energies of the water, goddess of dreaming. Guide and protect us as we navigate your fluid scape. Protect us with your strength and your grace."

Abby joined him as he repeated the call a second time. She felt a heartbeat in her belly, but did not know if it belonged to her or the baby. As Abby's voice rang out, she sensed the ball of blue energy at the base of her spine igniting and growing stronger.

"I call to the Watchtower of the South, energies of fire, sun god Ra. Guide and protect us as we navigate the land of dreaming. Shield us with your fierce energy."

Lydie joined him during the second invocation.

"I call to the Watchtower of the East, energies of the air, god of the mind. Guide and protect us as we move into the realms of memory. Protect us with your wit and cunning."

Victor repeated the call.

"I call to the Watchtower of the North, the energies of earth, of my own true nature, goddess of Gaia. Guide and protect us as we move away from your solid bearings. Protect us with your steady hand."

As Oliver invoked the elements, the candle flames danced and flickered. Outside the wind grew fiercer. Leaves and branches scraped the windows.

As the witches felt their energy heighten, they directed the flow toward Kendra. She held a sharp silver blade in her hand. Carefully, she stood on the chair and drew the blade across an emptiness in the air above the doll. Though she appeared to cut nothing at all, she created a doorway into the world of dreaming. She sat and closed her eyes. Her body hummed with the funneling power and her chair knocked rhythmically on the wood floor.

****

In her astral body, Kendra left the circle. She directed her energy up, beyond the earth and the sky and the universe. She pressed harder and higher until she burst through the barriers of consciousness into the land of dreaming. The blackness terrified her, but soon it gave way to a thousand images flashing in every direction. Colors and streaks of light and ghostly drawn faces wove and cascaded around her. A cacophony of sounds penetrated her mind—music, laughter and crying. She lifted a hand, stared at her own shimmering body, and tried to remember. She had a purpose, a mission, but found only a million glittering worlds, and she longed to fall into each one. A slithering darkness moved past her. She felt her astral body begin to melt toward the shadow.

In her mind, Victor appeared. Not in the astral plane, but in her thoughts. He held up an image of the doll and she remembered: Ethel.

She focused on the doorway above the doll, turning through space until she noticed a sliver of red light. She moved toward it, ignoring the dreams that swirled around her. She reached out and allowed her hand to pass through the opening. Immediately the dream pulled her into its scape.

Kendra stood in an old shack. Rain beat against the tin roof and dripped onto sodden rugs and a dirt floor. Candles stood on a stack of planks in the center of the room. Half-empty plates of thin stew surrounded the candles. A young woman, her back to Kendra, stood at a washpot near the door. Two snoring women slumbered in sagging cots against a wall.

Kendra did not recognize Ethel, but knew her to be the angular girl washing dishes. She might have been fifteen. Malnourishment gave her the appearance of a boy. Her black hair hung down her back in tangles. Sharp shoulders and ribs stood out in her gray cotton dress.

Ethel glanced at the women sleeping and then began to whisper under her breath. Outside, the rain grew louder and the wind began to howl. The shack shook and groaned. One of the women woke, scared, and turned to Ethel. Ethel stared back at her and then a streak of white lightning, followed by a deafening clap of thunder, struck the shanty. Kendra smelled smoke and flinched as the front wall burst into flames.

She started to cry out, but the shack, the women and the fire dissolved. She looked around, confused, at a long stretch of stony beach. The gray half-light of dawn revealed a choppy, cold-looking lake or ocean. Ocean, Kendra thought. She tasted salt in the air.

Ethel, older now, stood waist deep in the water. She drew her hands up and the water followed in streams and tornadoes and cyclones. In a burst, she flew straight out of the water and spun with her arms outstretched to either side.

She's dreaming, Kendra reminded herself. Of course she can fly.

Kendra joined her. She drifted up and began to spin around and around. Ethel did not seem startled, only continued her twirling and then dove, hard, into the dark waters below. She emerged and flew up again. Kendra followed her. She dove into the water and then rose into the sky. It was strange manipulating her astral body in such a way. She always knew that she could defy natural laws in the astral space, but rarely did so. Finally, Ethel tired of her game and returned to the shore.

Her black hair was now cropped short above her shoulders. No longer the sickly teen girl, she appeared as a healthy, glowing witch. Her green eyes, like two shards of beach glass, regarded Kendra with interest.

In dreams, the tangible world with all its stories ceased to exist. Ethel might know Kendra and she might not. Kendra hoped for the latter.

"Tell me about Dafne," she said.

"Dafne?" Ethel asked, but something sparked in her eyes. Recognition and memory.

If Ethel had not remembered Kendra, she did now.

"Clever witches," she said, staring out at the sea. "Clever and stupid to approach me this way."

"No, I don't think so. I think this was the only way."

Ethel smiled meanly.

"Don't assume I'll make it easy."

She vanished and Kendra reached out, grabbing at nothing.

Another scene materialized. Ethel could shift her dreamscape, but Kendra had already entered it. Wherever Ethel disappeared to, Kendra emerged as well.

Kendra looked at a towering medieval castle. Angry black turrets stretched toward a sweltering red sky. Black roses grew in massive heaps along the road that wound toward the castle gate. Kendra saw Ethel standing on the stone steps. She turned and ran toward the castle entrance and Kendra raced after her. She had to reach her before she crossed through the door—something horrible awaited them on the other side. So close, she reached out and clutched for Ethel's black cloak, but the door swung out and Kendra stumbled back, terrified. Ethel disappeared into the black interior. Kendra heard screams and laughter and howls of pain.

"This is a dream," she reminded herself, but suddenly felt less sure. She paused and allowed her mind to connect with the other witches who sat around her body in New Orleans. She felt Victor, Lydie, Oliver and Abby. They could not see what she saw, but they surely felt her panic.

Kendra drew her attention back into the dream and to the doorway.

"She cannot hurt me," she whispered and strode into the darkness.

****

A huge stone foyer greeted her. Far away she could see a hearth as tall as a house. A massive fire blazed and she moved toward the flames. She searched for Ethel, but the flames seemed to stretch and fill every space. She could no longer see anything, except the flames. Inside the blaze, another scene materialized. Kendra moved closer, watching as a dark street slid into view. A beautiful house surrounded by a heavy black iron fence. Now she could see a window with white curtains billowing. Beyond the flickering candlelight, she saw her friends sitting in a circle, their eyes closed, their lips moving. In the center, Kendra saw herself. Above her hung the doll.

****

Sebastian paced around the witches. He stared at Abby's face, searching for any sign of distress. If something happened, he would rip her out of the circle. None of the witches moved, only Kendra shifted and moaned. Sometimes her fingers twitched and her eyes blinked open, but he knew that she did not see.

Outside the wind continued to rise. Leaves and branches pelted the roof and windows. The sound grew in intensity until it thundered through the entire house. The candles started to flicker and then all at once blew out.

CHAPTER 15

"Run!" Kendra screamed in her dream, and the scream traveled through dimensions until it exploded into the witches' minds. Abby felt the scream burst within her. Her eyes snapped open, but darkness met her searching gaze. She fumbled out of her chair and tripped over a soft form in the darkness. A person. Dead? She knelt down, trying to steady her breath, and felt the shape beneath her. Her hand trailed over long hair—Kendra. Pressing a hand on the woman's chest, she felt the rise and fall of her breath. She was alive.

"Abby?" Sebastian whispered, and she nearly cried out in relief.

"I'm here," she said and held out her hands, standing and moving toward his voice. When she finally felt his strong hands grasp hers, she pressed her face hard into his chest.

"Guys?" Lydie's voice now.

"We're here," Abby whispered. She moved away from Sebastian, but kept one of his hands clutched in her own.

"What happened to the light?" Oliver asked.

"Sshhhh," Lydie croaked.

They all listened. The wind continued to howl beyond the house, but they heard another sound too, a crackling.

"What is that?" Victor chimed in. His voice was high and alert.

"It's fire," Lydie shrieked. "I feel it everywhere."

The light from the fire began to pour into the room then as it grew in the trees surrounding the house. Through the windows, they saw the trees burning.

"I can't stop it," Lydie yelled, her fingers stretched toward the flames.

Abby moved toward the window at the front of the house. A woman stood in the street. Her silver hair flew wild around her head and a mad-looking grin stretched across her lips. She fixed her gaze on Abby and in the firelight, Abby saw her light eyes turn darker, black.

Abby felt a terrible pain shoot through her head. She stumbled and fell against the wall. Sebastian ran to her. He looked toward the window and saw the witch outside.

"It's Ethel," he yelled.

Abby braced her hands on the windowsill to keep from throwing up. She watched the witch lift her hands toward the sky. The fire from the tree snaked into her hands and up her arms. She conjured the fire into a massive roiling ball and turned back to the house. Abby knew the witch would throw the ball of flames at the house. She would burn them all alive.

And then a shape darted up behind the woman. Slim and dark with a long woven braid. Kanti.

Suddenly the fire dissolved in Ethel's hands. Her face screwed up in pain and she dropped to her knees on the pavement.

"She's fallen," Abby croaked, gesturing wildly at the window.

"Go get her," Kendra cried weakly from the floor.

Oliver, Victor and Sebastian ran into the street, but Ethel had already disappeared.

****

"Makes me feel like the techies are the real wizards," Helena told Julian as they watched the pile of papers queue up at the scanner and then zoom to one of the boxes on the floor.

"Agreed. I keep trying to read the files as they show up on the screen, but they disappear before I make it through ten words. I may be going blind at this point."

"Time to tackle that box then? According to Victor, the important stuff would get sorted into that one." She pointed to the box labeled "Important."

"Kind of obvious, huh? It's almost like he thought we're old geezers or something." Julian laughed.

Helena laughed too.

"Since that attack, I do feel like an old geezer."

"Maybe I could work on you?" Julian asked. "I spent a lot of years in study after I left Ula. A good portion of that time I devoted to energy healing. I might be able to help."

"I'd take a miracle cure from an infomercial if I thought I might feel better. Yes, please."

"It's settled then. How about we devote an hour to reading and then we'll spend some time in the healing room ."

Julian carried a stack of papers from the box to a table by the fireplace. They found seats and divided the paperwork between them.

"Mostly journal pages," Helena complained. "Not exactly easy reading."

Julian pressed his face close to a page.

"No they're not. I get the feeling penmanship wasn't a priority for a few of these folks. The Sydney journal pages are quite legible though." He held up a page with Sydney's initials, SBA, monogrammed across the top.

"I would have liked to have met her," Helena said. "Abby described her as larger than life."

"You know, I can feel that? It jumps off the page. Pretty strong energy if I can still feel it through these notes."

"Have you spoken with Oliver much?" Helena asked, wondering if Oliver had confided the details of Sydney's death.

Julian had trained Oliver when he first arrived at Ula. Helena traced Oliver's bloodline, but Julian became his mentor. Oliver took it hard when Julian left the coven. She knew that he took it a bit personally too.

"Very little. I get the feeling he's still sore with me."

Helena nodded.

"It was hard on all of us when you left, Julian."

He looked up, surprised.

"I was under the impression that most of the coven preferred that I leave."

"Not Oliver and not me. It hurt to see you go. It hurt even more when we didn't hear from you."

Julian's eyes softened and he looked at Helena with regret.

"I missed you too, Helena. I hated to leave, but I couldn't stay. I was haunted. Even now it's hard."

Helena looked at her hands. They trembled as they often did since the attack on Ula. She shoved them into the folds of her colorful patchwork skirt.

She gazed at him steadily, stared into his nearly transparent blue eyes and wished that she could read his mind. She had loved him when he'd left. She wondered if she loved him still.

"I am truly sorry, Helena, from the bottom of my heart. If I could have stayed, if I could have made it work, I would have."

"But you did stay, Julian. After Miranda—" She paused, her voice caught on the name. "After Miranda passed, you stayed for decades. And then suddenly you left."

"Murdered," Julian corrected her. "Miranda did not pass," he closed his eyes as he said the word, "peacefully in her sleep. She woke to chaos and violence. He killed her without a thought, without a purpose."

Julian's eyes had grown distant with the memory. Helena could sense the dormant rage just beneath the surface of his pain.

She nodded stiffly and returned to the journals. Her eyes grew tired after only a few pages. She closed them and leaned her head back in her chair.

"This is interesting," Julian said suddenly.

He held up an old journal entry. The paper looked yellow and stained.

"It's a map," he said.

Helena stood and went to his chair, balancing on the armrest.

The map, clearly drawn by a novice, showed a shoreline and scribbled trees. The blank space beyond the shore was labeled Lake Michigan. Within the trees a small x and the word "body" were crudely marked.

"Well that's useful. It could be anywhere," Helena said.

"No, look." Julian pointed at a single, tiny word in the upper right corner of the page. "Trager."

****

As Sebastian maneuvered the van down the long paved driveway that led to their home, Abby sighed and rested her head against the seat. The drive had taken them twenty hours. No one wanted to rent a hotel. All of the witches and Sebastian preferred to put as much distance between them and the L'Obscurite as possible.

"I'm beat," Oliver groaned, pulling open the back door and stepping out. He dropped into several squats and stretched his arms overhead.

"Me too," Lydie mumbled.

"Bed sounds good," Kendra agreed, rubbing her temples and blinking a few times. Since her journey into Ethel's dreams, she had complained of a constant headache.

Sebastian offered to make breakfast, but the witches opted for bed.

In their bedroom, Sebastian pulled the comforter over Abby and lit a fire.

"Come lie with me," she said when he finished.

He looked alert, despite the long drive, but nodded and climbed into bed. She pushed her back into him and he wrapped his arms and legs around her, breathing her in.

"You're experiencing powers, aren't you?" she asked. She had felt them during the ritual in New Orleans. Though he was not in the circle, his presence hovered around them like a shield.

"I think so," he admitted. "I haven't turned into a wolf at the full moon yet, so that's rather disappointing."

She laughed and wiggled her butt against him.

"Earth, I think. That's only a guess though. You just feel so solid lately. Sometimes I notice that around Oliver. Like he has roots growing out of his feet."

Sebastian stiffened slightly.

"He likes you," Sebastian said.

"We're friends."

"He likes you as more than a friend. I know that you know, so let's not act, okay? There's enough confusion in this life without the pretense."

"Okay," she sighed. "Yes, I'm sure that's true, but those aren't my feelings. He's not a threat to you, not ever. I love you, Sebastian. I love you in a way that I didn't even know existed. A thousand lifetimes kind of love."

He pulled her tighter and began to kiss the back of her neck. She felt her body grow warmer.

"I love you too," he murmured into the bare flesh of her back. "And I want you."

He stripped her clothes off slowly. She lay beneath him and watched as he took his own shirt off. She traced the muscles of his chest down to the v shape that tapered into his pants. He pulled his pants down and kicked them onto the floor.

He made love to her slowly. They stared into each other's eyes. Abby longed to draw him into her completely, to somehow make a single person from their two bodies. Afterward, he wound his body around her and they slept.

****

"I thought we could stay here for a couple more days and then Lydie and I will make the trip back to Ula to fill them in on New Orleans," Oliver told Abby the following morning.

Kendra and Victor had woken early to return to Chicago.

"Of course. Are you okay with waiting?"

"Yeah. Lydie's worn out. I think she wants to read books and play with your cat and pretend she's not a witch for a little while."

Abby laughed.

"I think I'll join her."

"You and me both," he said. "But I figure two days max and then we need to leave. I want to get this information to Faustine, especially the book pages. If he could track down that book, maybe..."

"Maybe we'd have another five hundred pages of stuff to sift through," Abby sighed. "Seriously, how are we ever going to get through the journals and the information from the Asemaa?"

"Victor set up a pretty stellar system in the Vault and everyone at Ula is reading. We have a lot of eyes on that stuff."

"A lot less eyes while we were road tripping south."

"Still, we needed to go," Oliver said. "I think this is important."

"It's scary is what it is. Possession? I don't even want to go to sleep at night."

"You have plenty of protective spells around this place, Abby. No spirits are coming in unless you invite them."

Abby nodded, but she thought back to the presence in the nursery two weeks before. She had only mentioned the experience to Victor, preferring not to alarm the others.

"We made an enemy out of that witch Ethel and didn't even get any useful information," Abby continued.

"I get the feeling she has a lot of enemies. I doubt we're at the top of the list, and we did get useful information. Kanti wanted us to live. She stopped Ethel from burning the house down."

"Yeah, but why?"

Oliver shrugged.

"I'm afraid that's where my vast knowledge comes to an end, but still, it's good to know, right?"

Abby bit her lip.

"I wish I knew."

"So, not to change the subject, and I don't want to step on toes, but is everything okay with Sebastian?"

Abby looked away, struggling to meet Oliver's questioning gaze.

"Yeah, of course," she lied. "He's just edgy. Who wouldn't be, right?"

"You can talk to me, Abby; you know that, don't you? About anything?"

She thought of the secrets that she currently harbored. The baby growing inside of her. Sebastian's burgeoning anger coupled with a darkness that came over him. As a human she might not have noticed it, but as a witch, she sensed energy in a wholly different way. When he lapsed into his moods, the light and energy seemed to drain from the space around him.

"I do know, Oliver, and I appreciate it, truly. I think everyone is going to be a little off until..."

"Yeah exactly, until. From where I'm sitting, I don't see an end in sight. And this possession stuff that Ethel kept back, she did that for a reason."

The kitchen door swung open and Abby's black-and-white kitty Baboon strutted in with Lydie on his heels.

"I just gave him a good brush and rubdown ," she told them. "And now I want to bake cookies."

Oliver laughed and hopped off his stool. He squatted down to pet the cat, who purred and rubbed against him.

"Be careful, too much petting and he'll bite you," Lydie warned.

As if on cue, the cat turned his head and snapped at Oliver's outstretched fingers.

"Ouch, little fur devil."

"That's my angel you're insulting," Abby joked. "What kind of cookies do you want to make, Lydie? I can definitely get on board with cookies."

"Me too," Oliver said, pushing Baboon onto the floor and rubbing his belly. The cat playfully batted Oliver away.

"My mom used to make snowdrop cookies. I've been thinking about those lately," Lydie admitted, wistfully.

"Seems appropriate." Oliver tilted his head toward the window where snow had begun to fall.

"Any clue what the recipe is?" Abby asked.

"We're witches," Oliver said.
"We'll improvise," Lydie finished.

****

Oliver, Helena, Elda and Julian stood in the castle's oratory. Oliver and Lydie had returned to Ula that morning after two days of cookies, movies and pretending that they were not witches.

Sun shone through the stained-glass windows and cast rainbows of light on the scarred wooden desk they hunched over.

"I don't recognize the writing," Elda admitted, studying the torn pages that Oliver had brought from New Orleans.

"Nor do I," Julian agreed. "Although something in the tone is familiar."

"It's the content that is disturbing to me," Helena added, pulling over a chair and sinking into it. Weakness continued to plague her, and standing for more than a few minutes at a time fatigued her. "It speaks of spirit possession."

"Through bloodlines," Elda finished.

Oliver pointed to a passage.

"The writer says that possession is short-lived. Hours at most. So what would be the purpose?"

"To have a body," Julian said simply. "It's one thing to manipulate through the mind, through dreaming and visions. It's quite another to pick up a knife and stab somebody with it."

"You think she wants to kill someone?" Helena asked, trembling. She grasped the edge of the desk to steady her quaking hands.

"I think she's had several hundred years to build this rage. I don't believe that she even found the strength to communicate until recently. Look at the history. We find traces of the curse, but no evidence of her as an actual participatory entity until the last twenty years. Victor started receiving visions of her. Abby is having dreams. She's clearly working with the Vepars, but before that? Nothing."

"So what happened? Who opened the gate for her to come through?"

"That's the million-dollar question, I think," Julian replied.

"And she appeared in New Orleans and stopped this witch Ethel?" Elda asked, frowning.

Oliver knew Elda had been angry when he admitted that he and Lydie and the other witches had gone to New Orleans, but she was biting her tongue.

"Yes. Abby saw her. She described her as phantom-like, so she doesn't have a body yet."

"But Dafne is still missing," Helena murmured.

CHAPTER 16

"It's so good to see you." Gwen moved forward and gave Abby a fierce hug. "And to meet you officially, Sebastian."

Gwen hugged Sebastian and then gestured them toward a cozy booth in the back of the restaurant.

They passed a case of croissants and Abby's stomach growled. They had eaten breakfast, but Abby noticed that breakfast barely satisfied her these days.

"Which one do you want?" Sebastian asked, grabbing her hand.

"The almond are amazing, and the chocolate," Gwen told them, winking at Abby.

"One of each," Sebastian declared and returned to the counter to order.

Abby slid into the booth next to Gwen.

"I appreciate you coming all this way," Gwen told her.

Abby and Sebastian had driven to Detroit to meet Gwen, who had been an integral part of the Asemaa and the first person to enlighten Abby about the curse. Gwen and her daughter Ebony had fled to Detroit after several members of the Asemaa vanished. Though Gwen offered to come to them, Abby thought it best if she remain outside of Trager until they had a better grasp of the Vepar's intentions. Oliver had told Abby about seeing Stephen in the Vepar's lair, which meant that Gwen was right about the danger their group was in. She had not told Gwen about Stephen's death and dreaded the prospect.

"We were happy to come," Abby assured her. "And we're actually taking a little trip to Ohio, Sebastian's hometown, so this was on our way."

"Oh good, it gives me hope to see you together. Sydney would have been over the moon."

"How's Ebony?" Abby asked, wanting to avoid a conversation about Sydney. Her pregnancy created too many turbulent emotions, and great sadness might result in the bathroom flooding or a sprinkler system going off.

"She's happy. I've done my best to keep her in the dark—she is only four, after all. Four going on twenty." Gwen shook her head and smiled. "She's home with me so we have a lot of fun."

"How about your other friends? The ones who originally took Ebony?"

"They're okay. Everyone is okay, as far as I know. I reconnected with Lorna. Though I haven't seen her, just a few quick phone calls. She's in Canada, but Stephen, still nothing from him."

Sebastien returned with their croissants and a tray of coffees. He slid next to Abby.

"I have news about Stephen," Abby told her, taking Gwen's hand.

Gwen studied her face and then her eyes began to fill with tears.

"He's dead?"

Abby nodded.

"I'm so sorry, Gwen. I dreaded this moment. Oliver," she dropped her voice, "another of the Ula witches, recognized his body in a Vepar's lair."

Gwen inhaled sharply and clenched her eyes shut.

"A lair?" She said it out loud as if that might make it more true. "But why? Because of the Asemaa?"

"I don't know, but probably, yes. We've been going through the information and, frankly, it's overwhelming. One thing we know is that the Vepars are strongly connected with the curse, and we're pretty sure they know more than us."

"Maybe not," Sebastian interrupted. "They seem to have a direct connection to the creator of the curse, but I get the feeling they're in the dark. I think she's playing them."

"She?" Gwen asked.

"Kanti," Abby told her. "We believe that she created the curse, although even that, we're not sure of."

Gwen pressed her palms into her eyes and shook her head.

"I don't know if I should hear this." She looked up, afraid. "What if they come after my child? Is this information going to sign our death sentences?"

Sebastian glanced at Abby.

"I don't think so, Gwen, but I get it. If you don't want to know, you don't have to."

"If they believe you have information, I don't think claiming ignorance will save you," Sebastian added.

Abby shot him a warning look.

"It's true," he told her unapologetically. "These aren't people to be reasoned with; they're not even people. I don't know how much you're aware of, Gwen, but if you have even a sense of what Vepars are, then you know better than to think they'll leave you alone if they believe you're valuable to them."

Gwen shot a distressed look at the door as if a Vepar might stroll in at any moment.

"I never would have joined the Asemaa had I known. I love Sydney, but I want out of this. I can't put Ebony in danger."

"They followed me to France. They took the woman I was staying with and killed her too. You can run from them, but like I said—" Sebastian continued.

Abby put a hand on Sebastian's arm to stop him from saying more.

"I would be scared too, I am scared, but Sebastian is right. Still, they didn't attack you in Trager, and it may be that they're not as invested in the Asemaa as we think. Maybe Stephen went to them."

"You think he confronted a Vepar?" Gwen asked, incredulous. "He was impulsive, but not stupid."

"You never know, Gwen. They look like you and me. One of the detectives working Devin's case was a Vepar."

"What?"

"Yes," Abby confirmed. "Alva was his name. He's a major player in their world and yet he's involved in the investigation of a witch they'd killed. It's strange."

"But why? Why do they even bother?"

"We think it has to do with Trager specifically," Sebastian chimed in.

Abby looked at him questioningly.

"I was talking with Oliver about it," he told her. "Oliver couldn't think of another time he'd seen a Vepar place himself within an investigation, but Trager seems to break all the rules."

"What about Claire?"

"He was there," Sebastian admitted. "But on the sidelines. A bystander watching the chaos unfold."

"Do you think you could find out what Stephen discovered in Texas?" Abby asked.

Gwen had told Abby that just before he disappeared, Stephen told her he intended to meet someone in Texas who had information about the curse.

"I doubt it," Gwen sighed. "But Lorna might know. Like I said before, she was a lot more involved than me. She took the whole thing really seriously."

"She fled to Canada?" Sebastian asked.

"Yeah, she has friends there. I think she's been moving from place to place."

"Is she being followed?"

"She doesn't think so, but she's suspicious by nature."

"Can you call her?" Abby asked.

"No, she'll call me. She uses disposable phones and then throws them away."

"Do you know when she'll call?"

"Probably in a few days."

"Can you set up a meeting?"

"Yeah, I think she'd like that. She asks me if I've had contact with you every time she calls."

"Does she say that she has information?"

Gwen shrugged and wrapped her hands around her cup of coffee.

"Not really. She tries to keep the calls neutral. I think she's afraid, but she doesn't admit it."

"Set it up then," Abby told her. "We need to talk to her."

****

Abby scooted across the seat and leaned her head on Sebastian's shoulder. He took a hand from the wheel and squeezed her leg. His knuckles were pale and clenched. As they got closer to his hometown, he seemed to grow more nervous. She saw it in the set of his jaw and his incessant need to thrum or tap on something. When he stopped doing that, he scratched absently at the dark stubble on his chin. He changed the radio station to alternative music and then classic rock. Frustrated with the radio, he asked Abby to hook up his new iPod. He scrolled through ten songs before finally landing on Bob Marley.

"Are you up for this?" she asked, not for the first time.

He glanced at her. His blue eyes glittered. She hoped their baby inherited his eyes.

"Yes," he assured her. "I want to take you. It's time."

He got off the freeway and they drove through the meandering countryside. In January, it was hardly a sight to behold. Only a dusting of snow coated the frozen Ohio ground. The gray sky and barren trees made Abby shiver and snuggle closer to Sebastian.

They passed a small concrete sign perched on the roadside. It welcomed them to Grimville, Ohio.

"So you grew up here?" Abby asked, scanning the buildings as they passed through the little town. "It's pretty charming."

Shop windows still held Christmas displays with fake snow and strings of garland. Red and white striped light poles lined the sidewalk.

"Yep, had my first kiss in that movie theater."

Abby looked at the marquee, unlit in the day.

"They're showing a football game?"

Sebastian laughed.

"It's a unique place. They show sports games, political discussions and obviously movies."

"What movie were you watching during your first kiss?"

"Donnie Darko," he admitted.

"Kind of creepy for a first kiss," Abby teased.

He laughed.

"Yep. Lilly Hanes thought so too, so creepy that she kissed me rather than look at the screen."

"Oh my, sounds very romantic."

"Tell me about your first kiss."

Abby blushed, remembering.

"Jay Stine in my friend Kim's bathroom on her fourteenth birthday. It was a dare."

"A dare? Now that's really romantic!"

She laughed and returned her gaze to the window.

"Interesting shops," she noted. They drove past The Apothecary, Merlin's Metaphysical Wares and a bookstore called The Ember Goddess.

"Part of the reason my mom agreed to live here," Sebastian told her, smiling. "I was born in Detroit. My dad brokered mortgages and my mom was a social worker. After I came along, they stayed a couple more years. They wanted me to have a real life, not the rose-colored glasses of middle-class suburbia, but then a kid got shot down the street. So they packed up and moved to Grimville, Ohio."

"Detroit? I didn't know that."

"I barely remember. I was two when we moved here. All of my memories are here."

"Why Grimville?"

"My mom hated the name, but my dad found a great deal on a really unique house. It had an artist's studio. My mom loved to paint. If they moved here, she could work as an artist. They could live on his income. They wanted another baby so it made sense."

"How do you know all this?" Abby had little insider information on her parents' lives before she came along.

He looked at her curiously.

"Really? Didn't your parents ever tell you how they met? All the details of life before Abby?"

She shook her head.

"You met my mom—not exactly forthcoming."

"My parents loved to talk about their memories. My mom had stacks of scrapbooks. They took road trips, they backpacked around Europe, they lived a lifetime before Claire and I showed up. Honestly, I loved the stories. Instead of tucking me in with tales of the three bears, I heard about my dad proposing on the subway, in New York City, in a car so packed that when he tried to get on one knee, he ended up sitting on some old guy's lap."

"That's amazing," Abby laughed, "and terrible. Couldn't he wait until they got off?"

"That's what my mom always said, but my dad insisted that he just knew it had to be that moment and if he let it pass they were destined for tragedy. Seems ironic now."

Abby's smile fell and she reached her arms awkwardly around Sebastian for a hug.

"I'm sorry you lost them."

"Me too. I wish you could have met them."

They drove in silence and then Sebastian turned down a wooded driveway. They came upon a large brick house. A glass-walled building sat off to the right.

"Does anyone live here?"

"No. A friend of mine from high school is a real estate agent, and I asked him to let me know if it ever came back on the market. About a year after Claire died, the people who bought it moved to Florida. So here it sits."

They got out of the car and walked to the door. Turquoise pots holding browned flowers squatted on the front stoop. Sebastian punched a code into the lockbox and a key dropped out.

"My friend gave me the code. I told him that I was thinking about buying it again."

"Are you?" she asked, surprised.

He shook his head.

"There's nothing left for me here. My life is with you now." He wrapped his arms around her and she pressed closer to the warmth of his breath.

She felt him gathering courage to step across the threshold.

They walked into a bright foyer. Blond wood floors and white walls greeted them.

"It's different. My mom hated white walls. Too boring. The entryway used to be orange—creamsicle, she called it."

They moved through the house. Sebastian pointed out rooms and their previous colors. He showed her the jagged scratches on the bathroom wall where his dad marked his and Claire's growing height. He took her to his old room, empty of furniture and also painted white. Abby tried to imagine the New York skyline his mother had painted on the wall and the hammock that he had strung from the corners of the ceiling.

"One of my friends called our house the Twilight Zone. It was pretty eccentric."

"Why did you sell it?"

Sebastian stepped into the master bedroom and sighed, as though disappointed that no evidence of his parents remained.

"Because they were gone. We didn't need the money. They both had life insurance, but living here, we couldn't seem to move on. I really felt it with Claire. She'd walk in the door after school, all bubbly and excited, and the minute she stepped foot in the house, she lost something. It was like she deflated. Sometimes I would wake up at night and she would be wandering around touching the walls and the furniture. My mom created this place. You can't see it now, but before, she was everywhere."

Abby walked to the window that looked out over the backyard. She saw evidence of a garden. She pressed her hand on the window frame and felt the energy left behind. Love stolen at its peak.

They ended their tour in Claire's room.

"My mom called the paint color Lemon and my dad said it was Unmellow Yellow."

Abby laughed.

"You're inspiring me to paint when we get home."

"Claire added her own touches. She painted flowers on that wall over there. She loved comic books and pasted pictures of the X-Men all over her ceiling. Her room was like something out of Willa Wonka's Chocolate Factory meets Alice in Wonderland."

They left Sebastian's childhood home and drove to a little cemetery on the edge of town. A frozen stream cut through the hillside. He parked in front of three gravestones.

"They didn't leave instructions," he told her, as if apologizing. "My grandmother on my mom's side made the arrangements. Looking back, I wish I hadn't let her. My parents wouldn't want this." He gestured to the blocky stone structures. Jared Hull, Julia Hull and Claire Hull—all in a sad little row. No flowers adorned the frozen ground in front of their gravestones.

"Where is your grandmother?"

"Florida. We were never close. My mom's parents were pretty distant. They moved south when I was young and our contact included Christmas and birthday cards. I loved my dad's mom. She was friends with your Grandma Arlene, but she died when I was ten."

"My grandparents died when I was young too."

"Death seems to be the only thing we know for sure," Sebastian murmured. He opened the car door and stepped out.

He walked to the headstones and squatted in front of Claire's grave, pressing his hands against the stone face. Abby walked behind him, but gave him space. After several minutes he stood up.

"One more stop on this depressing tour," he told her.

"Hey." She put her hands on his shoulders. "I want to be here. There's nothing depressing about seeing where you come from."

He sighed and nodded.

"Maybe it's just depressing for me."

They drove to a storage unit. Abby waited in the car while Sebastian ran in and grabbed a plastic tote.

"What did you get?" Abby asked, when he returned.

"Mostly photo albums."

"And women's clothes?" Abby could see a red dress speckled with little yellow moons.

"I used it to wrap some frames so that the glass didn't break."

It was a logical explanation, but Abby studied Sebastian as he drove away. His tone implied another motive for taking the clothing. She didn't have a clue what that could be and didn't want to press the subject. When it came to Claire, Sebastian was touchy.

CHAPTER 17

"Anything related to the map?" Faustine asked. He used the mouse to click the file marked Important. He pulled up each document.

"Finally a way to read that doesn't cause an instant migraine," Helena said, scanning the enlarged script.

"Nothing in the box," Julian said. "But it's still scanning."

Faustine opened the map on the screen.

"That looks like Abby and Sebastian's property," Oliver said suddenly, walking closer. "I recognize the shape of the shoreline."

"I admit that was my first thought when Julian showed us the map," Faustine confessed.

"So a body was buried on their property?" Helena asked to no one in particular.

"It seems so," Faustine said. "Though perhaps we're looking at a planned dump site for a body."

"And it's possible that it was an animal's body," Julian cut in. "How do we know this isn't a hunter's map?"

"Why did it get sorted into the Important file?" Elda asked. "It doesn't have any of the keywords that Victor specified."

"That is strange," Julian agreed. "How do we contact him?"

"We have cell phones, but they never work here at Ula. I gave him a shell. We may be able to reach him through that."

"I'll try," Helena said. She left the library to retrieve a shell.

"I should go there," Oliver said. "Right now."

"Abby and Sebastian are gone, love," Helena told him kindly. "Remember they took a trip to Sebastian's hometown."

Oliver frowned, but didn't say more.

"He used magic," Julian continued. "So his intention must have been made known and the program is sorting according to that intention, beyond simply the words he specified."

"Which is even more valuable to us," Elda concluded. "Did you and Helena find anything else notable?"

"We hadn't made much progress when I found the map."

"It pertains," Faustine remarked. "There's no other explanation. This map is related to the curse and if it depicts Abby and Sebastian's house, then they found that location for a reason."

"Perhaps they were led there."

"Exactly."

****

Lydie sat in the floating garden. Despite the blistery cold of the day, the garden remained warm year-round . The temperature ranged between seventy-two and seventy-five degrees. Centuries ago, the witches of Ula had created the flower sanctuary, shielding it from the elements. The only caveat was walking to the garden from the castle. Fighting through drifts of snow that she couldn't melt fast enough with bursts of fire left her sodden and chilled when she finally reached the garden.

Though it was invisible to the eye, an energy dome surrounded the flowers and trees, blocking the garden from wind, rain and, of course, evil. As new witches arrived at Ula, they added their own special magic to the space. After Lydie's parents died, she planted a lemon tree in the garden. Fortunately, everything grew in the magic garden. Michigan was generally not an ideal place for lemon trees, but Lydie's mother had grown them at home as well. As a water element, Lydie's father had a special talent for coaxing the roots deeper and helping them to draw the nutrients they needed from the soil. Her mother, a fire element like Lydie, enchanted the air around the trees to ensure they always had sunlight.

She pulled out her battered copy of The Thornbirds and folded her coat beneath her head. She had read the book before, several times in fact, and loved Meggie. She saw herself in Meggie, though her own family had died and she had no great love. Someday, though. Someday she wanted what Abby and Sebastian had. She wanted a love and a life separate from the coven, far away from the evil that pursued witches.

****

Sebastian woke in the shed. The darkness and cold startled him and he looked around desperately before he got his bearings. He stood and braced his hands on the workbench. Feeling along the wall, he found the light switch and flicked it on. The desk was scattered with pictures of Claire. When had he retrieved them from the tote he brought home?

He had tucked the tote into a downstairs closet, unopened. Abby insisted that she wanted to go through them with him so that they she could learn more about his sister.

He picked up a photo of Claire. She sat cross-legged in front of the scanty Charlie Brown Christmas tree they had chosen for their first Christmas after their parents' deaths. She wore a green sweatshirt, with a picture of a grinning reindeer, and black sweatpants. Sebastian knew that he wore a matching sweatshirt behind the camera lens. He bought them as a joke to cheer Claire up. She begrudgingly wore hers on Christmas morning. He remembered the catatonic way she opened her presents and ate the banana French toast that he cooked. He remembered thinking that he might not be able to handle it. He too grieved the loss of their parents, and he couldn't believe that Claire was his responsibility. He was terrified that he would fail her.

"And I did," he told the room.

He glanced at the other pictures, but did not sift through them.

"You could bring her back," he said out loud and then looked up, startled. His own reflection stared back at him in the shed window. Why had he said that? Of course, he couldn't bring her back.

A memory stirred in his mind. He stared at the scattering of pictures and willed it to come back.

Someone had told him that Claire could come back. That magic could return her to life.

"She's been in the ground more than two years. There's nothing left to bring back."

He spoke, but the memory continued to plague him. Elements and particles and cells. With enough power the body could just rematerialize. It wasn't easy, but it could be done. Who had told him that? One of the witches of Ula? Julian? No. It wasn't their kind of magic. There was a lot of magic in the world. Some called it dark, but those were just words. Once upon a time, the earth was flat and people were segregated by color. To a Catholic the pagans were heathens. To the pagans, the Catholics were out of touch with the natural world. Good magic versus bad magic. Who made the call? Who decided that one was right and the other wrong?

Even as the thoughts swirled in his mind, he struggled to separate his own ideas from those that seemed to belong to another. Had someone messed with his head? Several times now, he had woken in the shed with no memory of getting there. He needed to know what was happening, but dared not tell Abby.

He shuffled the pictures together and tucked them in a drawer in the workbench. He didn't want Abby worried that his obsession with Claire had returned. With the pregnancy and all of the other drama in their lives, she didn't need to worry about him as well.

****

Abby heard knocking, but it sounded far away. She lay curled on the living room floor, in a heap of blankets that she had been folding fresh from the dryer. Suddenly tired, she had crawled into the center and fallen asleep.

"Sebastian?" she called meekly, hoping he might answer the door. She remembered that he had left to buy steaks for dinner. He must not have come home yet.

She fumbled out of the blankets and walked, drowsy, to the door. Elda and Helena stood on the stoop. They both wore heavy wool cloaks.

"Hello, lovely girl," Helena said, pulling Abby into a hug.

"Oh hi, wow, I didn't know you were coming," Abby stammered. "Come in."

She moved into the house and Helena and Elda followed. They took off their snow boots and cloaks and hung them on the coat rack before following Abby into the kitchen.

"Can I make you some tea or coffee?" Abby asked, rubbing the sleep from her eyes.

"No, no, you sit," Helena murmured, guiding Abby to a chair.

"Julian joined us as well. At Faustine's urging, he is going to work with Sebastian today."

Elda glanced around the room as if looking for Sebastian.

"He went into town for steaks," Abby told her. "He's a foodie. Everything has to be fresh. I swear he goes to the grocery store every day."

"He's finding his groove," Helena said, smiling. "That's wonderful for you both."

Elda watched Abby with interest.

"You know, don't you?" Abby asked, seeing the knowledge in Elda's face.

She nodded.

"We didn't want to invade your privacy, Abby," Elda assured her. "Galla sensed your pregnancy and she confided to me."

Abby looked down, suddenly embarrassed.

"I hadn't intended to hide it," she confessed. "But when I realized..."

"Have some tea, honey." Helena placed a mug of hot cinnamon tea in front of Abby and then prepared two more for Elda and herself.

"We're not upset," Elda continued. "It has been a big year for you. Probably the most transformative of your life."

"I'll say," she agreed.

"And a baby, oh, it's so exciting," Helena gushed. "But we understand why you wanted to keep it to yourself."

"Do you?" Abby asked. "Because I'm not sure that I do."

"What do you mean?" Elda asked, concerned.

"I guess I just feel off, and it's not only the hormones. I feel like the baby wanted me to keep her a secret. Does that sound insane?"

The older witches exchanged troubled looks.

"Is it possible that it's not the baby communicating that to you?"

"You think it's Kanti?"

"I think that Kanti is very invested in getting into your head. I don't know why, but it seems strange that just as you became pregnant, she shared the birth of her own child with you."

"A child that she cursed," Abby said gravely.

"Maybe," Helena said, and they both turned to her in surprise. "What if she didn't intentionally curse the baby? What if her pain and anger acted without her?"

"I will challenge you on that with this. If she didn't intend to create the curse, why does she appear to be perpetuating it? Imagine the energy it would take to inadvertently do such a thing. And then the energy to maintain it. The energy to make contact with and manipulate the Vepars," Elda continued.

"The energy to make contact with and manipulate us," Abby murmured.

"I guess that is difficult to argue with," Helena admitted.

"We have another reason for dropping in on you today, Abby."

Abby waited, her body tense. Had Oliver mentioned that Sebastian had been acting strangely?

"Julian found a map at Ula," she continued.

Abby relaxed, letting the breath she had been holding rush out.

Elda cocked her head to the side.

"You know about it?"

"No, just had some nausea coming on. It passed," she lied and immediately felt guilt at the deception. "What kind of map?"

"A map that appears to mark a burial site. When Oliver returned to Ula, he recognized the shape of the peninsula. He thinks it may be here on your property."

"A graveyard?" Abby wrinkled her nose.

"No, not a graveyard. A single burial."

"And you found this in the Kanti Files?"

"Exactly," Helena affirmed. "In the Important box. Julian noticed it right away. It was marked Trager so we knew it had to be in this area."

"And Oliver confirmed that it's here?"

"Not confirmed, but felt pretty sure. Julian is on a walk right now. He's hoping to ascertain whether the map depicts your property or not. Can I ask you, Abby, what compelled you to buy this home?"

Abby stood and set her empty mug in the sink, suddenly needing to feel busy. She refilled the teakettle and shuffled through the cupboards for the sipping chocolate that Sebastian had brought home on his last adventure to the market.

"European sipping chocolate?" she asked, holding up the container.

Elda waited patiently and Helena nodded, lifting up her cup.

"I dreamed about it," she confessed.

The water boiled quickly and the teakettle began to shriek. Abby jumped, startled.

"We had been looking at houses for a few days. We stayed at that big hotel on the bay, The Cherry Resort. It has glass breezeways that connect two sides of the hotel. One night, I woke up and I walked into the hall and down to one of the breezeways. When I looked out, I saw this enormous old house surrounded by woods. It looked like a real-life dollhouse and I swear my dream took me right up to the sitting room window. Inside the house, this giant fire blazed in the brick fireplace and the room was filled with people. You were all there, plus Lydie and Oliver, Sebastian and me, even my parents. I don't know that I'd ever felt so safe and loved and just...home. And then I woke up."

Helena breathed and looked toward the window and the sweeping view of the snowy shore.

"It is beautiful."

"How did you find it after your dream?"

"I didn't have to," Abby went on. "Sebastian had already set up three viewings for us that day. This house was our first stop."

"It didn't concern you at all? That you dreamed of the house and then you found it?"

"No. The Kanti dreams are different, Elda. I'm in her life, they're more like memories and half the time, I'm not even sleeping when I have them. This dream felt guided by me, my energy, my spirit."

"But you feel her here? Kanti?"

Abby bit her lip, wishing she could deny the question.

"Yes, but maybe she is focusing her energy more on making contact. I don't see why it should have anything to do with our property."

"Because if her body is buried in those woods," Elda murmured, "her connection is a lot stronger."

****

"The greatest barrier to your elemental energy is right here." Julian tapped two fingers on the side of his head. "Therefore, you must practice quieting the mind. Ancient practitioners of yoga called this yogash chitta vritti nirodhah—or the mastery of the mind's activity so that you can rest in your true nature. Buddha referred to this as taming the monkey mind. In any discipline that involves detachment from the ego and the material world, you will discover the same guidance—you must quiet the mind."

Sebastian nodded and shifted from foot to foot. They stood deep in the trees on his and Abby's property. They had hiked more than a mile in, until

Julian stopped suddenly and said it felt like a good place to start.

"You'll sit in the snow in silence. Let's start with a half hour."

"Are you serious?" Sebastian asked, incredulous. If meditation was the training, why couldn't he sit by the fireplace where he wouldn't freeze his balls off?

"I know it seems counterintuitive. I bring you into the cold, clearly rain is on the way. You are uncomfortable, probably irritated, but all of those distractions are the truth of your brain in any given moment. It is much easier to meditate in comfort, but it only teaches you to still your thoughts in moments of peace and tranquility. I want you to still your thoughts when everything in you is talking—when your body is crying out for attention, when your mind is questioning the validity of my guidance. That is a rich space of learning."

Sebastian opened his mouth and then closed it. He wanted to argue. Part of his nature tended toward stubbornness, and it had been many years since anyone told him what to do. He almost couldn't help but question the old witch's tactics.

Julian watched him carefully, but gave away no evidence of his thoughts. Was he expecting Sebastian to argue?

"Okay," Sebastian said, finally.

He looked around for a suitable place to sit and finding none, plopped onto the snow. He folded his legs awkwardly. He had not worn snow pants, believing the physical exertion would have him sweating in no time, but now he regretted the decision.

Julian wandered away from him.

He closed his eyes and tried to focus. A hundred thoughts darted around his brain.

"It's like a pinball machine in here," he muttered and then cracked an eye open to see if Julian had heard him. The man was nowhere in sight.

He shut his eyes again. He focused on his breath, counting to five on the inhale and eight on the exhale. Abby had taught him that one and it often helped him to fall asleep at night. As he counted the seconds of his breath, his legs and butt shifted from cold to tingling and then finally numb.

When a thought arose, he envisioned encasing it in a bubble and watching it float away. That tip he'd learned from Claire, and she had learned it from Adora. Claire had wanted to help him with his temper. One night she sat him down, legs crossed on a pillow, and walked him through a guided meditation. Each time he had an angry thought—that particular day Sebastian had been livid over a neighbor who kept taking his parking space in the apartment complex—he should imagine the thought moving inside a bubble and then floating into the sky.

As he remembered the evening, he lost track of his empty mind and started to think of Claire. Thoughts of Claire ignited his most recent memory of waking in the shed with ideas of her resurrection. It was utter madness and yet something sparked in him at the thought of her. He imagined Claire holding his and Abby's newborn baby. He envisioned her sitting on the porch in the summer, sipping ginger ale , her favorite, and talking with Abby about life as a witch. Abby would have a friend and he would have his sister back.

He realized that his whole body had grown tense with his contemplations and he had taken hold of something in his hands. When he opened his eyes he saw a crow, its dark wings slick, crushed in his grasp. Its head hung to the side and its black eye stared at nothing. He gasped and flung the bird away from him.

He looked up to find Julian watching him through the trees.

CHAPTER 18

Abby stooped to pick up a tiny onesie, freckled with pink and yellow elephants. She ran her hands over the soft fabric and felt a rush of warmth spread through her body. She added it to her basket.

It felt good to shop for baby clothes. The experience felt so fabulously normal. Unfortunately, her thoughts veered into a very non-normal space-specifically to conversations from the day before. Elda seemed convinced that something sinister had led Abby and Sebastian to their house. She disagreed. When she asked Sebastian about it, he barely said two words before complaining of a headache and slipping off to bed. She wondered if his work with Julian had exhausted him.

A hand clamped down on her shoulder and she swung around, basket in front of her, ready to defend herself.

"Whoa." Victor took a step away and held his hands up. He grabbed a white blanket from a shelf and waved it in the air. "I surrender."

"Good grief, are you trying to send me into early labor?"

He laughed and cast his eyes down.

"I would imagine that's not a risk just yet."

She smiled and shook her head, exasperated.

"Still, I prefer not to start a rainstorm in the Stork Stop."

"It is quite a place, this Stork Stop. I saw a bib back there that said I shizzled in my dizzle."

Abby groaned.

"I think I'll skip that one, but how cute is this?"

She held up the onesie.

Victor furrowed his brow and pretended to examine it carefully.

"I'm not sure how realistic yellow elephants are."

"It's for a baby. The goal is cute, not realistic."

"You say that now, but have you seen the pink bunny pajamas in A Christmas Story? That kid was ruined for life."

"I appreciate the clothing tips, but what are you doing here? It's an awfully long drive from Chicago to help me pick out baby clothes."

A black look passed over Victor's features.

"Buy this stuff and then we'll talk. I don't want to ruin your baby bliss."

Outside the store, Victor steered Abby to his car.

"There's a little coffee shop down the way. It looked pretty empty on my way here. Let's go there."

"Milk and Honey," Abby told him. "Coffee and ice cream. My kind of place."

Victor chuckled.

"Always have food on the brain, don't you?"

"Yes," she admitted. "But Milk and Honey is extra special because they have organic ice cream, so it's a guilt-free indulgence."

"You're gonna need it," he mumbled.

She gave him a questioning look, but he ignored her.

At the coffee shop, Abby ordered a decaf coffee and espresso ice cream with caramel and brownie. Victor asked for three shots of espresso.

They chose a table near the window, though they had little risk of being overhead. Other than the young woman scooping ice cream, the place was deserted.

Victor pulled a notebook from his backpack. He laid it on the table and flipped to a series of drawings.

Abby gasped and nearly dropped her ice cream.

She looked at a familiar jut of tree-lined peninsula along the Lake Michigan shoreline. Standing at the water's edge, the sliver of moon shining overhead, stood Sebastian and Dafne. Dafne looked different. Thin, as if she'd been starved, but with wild magnetic eyes. Sebastian's eyes appeared wide and vacant. Dafne held an object in her hand. As Abby leaned closer, she recognized the jeweled dragon from the Vepar's ritual. The dragon that held a pulsing blade and a life of its own.

"This is our peninsula," Abby whispered. "Sebastian said he wanted to hang a swing from that maple tree."

"I thought it was," Victor agreed. "But I wasn't positive."

"Is this real?"

"I think so. It came to me in the night about four days ago. I woke up, feverish, and just started drawing. I didn't even look at it until yesterday and then when I realized what I was seeing, I came right away."

"Her eyes are different." Abby pointed at the dark magnetic eyes staring from Dafne's face.

"They're Kanti's eyes."

****

"I don't think you and Sebastian should be alone right now."

They had returned to Abby's car parked by the baby store. She stared at the snowflakes crystallizing on the side-view mirror. Beautiful and intricate, Mother Nature knew her stuff.

"I love Sebastian. I have faith in him. He's not dark. Nothing could turn him into one of them, nothing."

"I'm sure Dafne believed the same thing about Tobias."

Abby glared at him, stung.

"Sebastian could never be Tobias. You don't know him, Victor."

She started to get out of the car, but Victor grabbed her arm.

"Don't do that. Don't use anger at me to ignore what's happening. I know you're freaked out. I am too. But this," he tapped his notebook, "is real. If you play dumb, then you're doomed. We're all doomed."

Abby bit her lip and fought a sudden urge to reach across the car and slap Victor. She took several deep breaths. She stared at the little white bag with pink tissue paper sticking from the top. The cashier at Stork Stop had even added a tiny plastic rattle to tie the bag closed. She thought of her baby girl and wanted to cry.

Settling back into the car seat, she reluctantly nodded.

"I know. I don't want to know, but I do."

"So what else has been going on?"

"Sometimes he disappears at night. Not often," she added quickly, wanting to soften the revelation. "Maybe once a week, twice at most. I'll wake up and he's not there. One night he came running into the room like something had spooked him. I was too groggy to question it, but I asked him about it the next morning."

"And?"

"And he said he went for a walk outside because he couldn't sleep. He thought he heard a noise in the house and ran back to check on me."

"Did you believe him?"

"I wanted to." She sighed. "But no, I didn't believe him."

****

Abby returned to her car and pulled away from the curb. She needed to drive home. She needed to confront Sebastian, but her head had begun to ache. The throbbing traveled to her eyes and she shut them against the white glare of the sun on the snow. She drove onto the shoulder of the road and leaned her head back.

The headache had come on suddenly and with it came a rush of nausea. Flinging open the car door, she barely got her head out before she threw up. Aching, her vision blurred, she pulled the door closed and reclined her seat. She had made it far enough into the country that few cars drove by. She could already feel her astral body trying to disengage. She closed her eyes and gave in to the pull.

She stood in the cave. Her last two visits had called her to the Pool of Truth to reveal unknown death. She wanted to return to her physical body, but her astral body moved of its own volition. She drifted down the sloping tunnel, the slimy walls surrounding her with dense familiarity. She was not pulled to the Pool of Truth. Instead, she floated into the path that branched to the right. A yawning cavern opened before her and she saw the small shimmering puddle of blue water that had beckoned her previously. Remembering that splendid journey into the water, she knelt down and cupped the water in her hand. In a rush, it took her. She surged through the cave in the water, as the water, and burst into the night sky. She rained into the lake as a million particles of water and then reformed as a single entity. She bolted through the water, watching the fish and the seaweed, but searching for the cyclone that she knew to be there.

It appeared suddenly, swirling above a bed of rocks, thick with algae. She moved toward the tempest as an image gradually appeared.

She saw a sleeping Dafne in a dungeon room cast in darkness. She lay curled in the fetal position with her black hair fanning out on the dirty mattress beneath her. Her already skinny body looked further emaciated. Bones showed through the skin of her face and chest.

The door to the dungeon swung open and a hulking Tobias moved into the room. He glowered at the sleeping form and then leaned over her. Pushing the hair away from her neck, he leaned down and bit her. Abby saw the red of Dafne's blood on his white chin. He wiped it away and then stared at his fingers. He licked them clean and stood.

Alva entered the room behind him. He held a syringe filled with a clear, luminous liquid.

"She's growing weaker," Tobias told him. "Look at her back. There's barely an ounce of flesh left on her."

Alva handed him the syringe.

"Inject her. Kanti travels tonight."

The image blurred and disappeared. Drawn back through time and space, Abby awoke in her car. The sunny day had grown overcast.

Abby thought about her vision. She felt a hollow aching for Dafne. Her anger at the witch who had betrayed her and Sebastian still burned, but less as she realized the fate that had befallen her.

CHAPTER 19

"You must really miss me if you're pulling out the seashells," Oliver joked.

His voice blasted out of the shell and Abby held it away from her ear, temporarily forgetting that it didn't work like a telephone.

"Well I would have liked to use a cell phone, but Ula might as well be on Jupiter when it comes to cell service."

"Yep, we prefer tin cans and string in these parts."

"It's probably more effective than cell phones out there, but I have a reason for reaching out."

"Other than a desperate need to hear my sultry man voice?"

Sebastian glowered at her from the couch, but Abby only laughed. She had wanted to ask Sebastian about Victor's dreams, but the vision of Dafne had felt too important to not share with Ula immediately.

"No, I have Sebastian for the sultry man voice. He's here with me, by the way."

Silence from the shell and then Oliver laughed.

"Hey man, how's the snow blowing going?"

Sebastian started to respond, but Abby interrupted.

"He can tell you all about his power tools when you come back. I had a vision of Dafne today."

"It's not a power tool," Sebastian argued.

"A vision? As in a dream or something real?"

"It was real, I astrally traveled. It's happened to me before. I could see her in a dungeon. I saw Alva and Tobias too."

"Wait, let me snag Helena, she's walking by."

In the background, Abby heard Oliver yell for Helena.

"Okay we're both listening."

"I saw Dafne sleeping in a dungeon. She looked ill, skinny, bruised, but alive."

"Oh thank the Goddess," Helena breathed.

"Tobias bit her. I think he's using venom to keep her unconscious. Tobias told Alva that Dafne was getting weaker and then they injected her with something."

"Injected?" Oliver broke in. "That's not a tactic I've seen a Vepar use before."

"Any idea what they injected her with?" Helena asked.

"No, something clear and sort of, well, magic looking, for lack of a better word. It was shiny, like liquid light."

"Like mercury?"

"No, more like light cast off a pearl or an opal."

"The stuff from the lair, that they were extracting from everyone," Sebastian jumped in, excited. "I couldn't think of how to describe it, but that's it, Abby. It was like looking at an opal in the sun, but as if the opal were melting."

"You're right," Oliver agreed. "I didn't spend much time examining it, but I had a similar thought."

"So they're injecting her with the essence they removed from everyone in the lair?" Helena asked. "How come?"

"I don't know," Abby answered, honestly. "But they said something else. Tobias told Alva that Dafne was getting weak. He seemed to be implying that they shouldn't inject her, but Alva told him to do it anyway. He said Kanti travels tonight."

****

Elda tapped her fork against her glass until the din around the table died.

"A porpoise!" Oliver finished with a guffaw, and Julian burst into laughter beside him.

They continued to laugh until Elda stood and cleared her throat loudly.

"Oh sorry." Oliver held up his hands in apology.

"I want to take a moment and thank you all for being here this evening. When we're all together like this, I have real hope for the future of Ula."

"Here, here," Bridget declared, holding up her glass.

Abby smiled and nodded her agreement. The Coven of Ula felt especially magical that evening. They had come together to celebrate Imbolc, the middle of winter and the shift toward spring. They had also gathered to create a plan for the map that Julian had found. Abby felt much less excited about the prospect of that conversation.

"It is especially auspicious that we celebrate Imbolc because we are honoring the cycles of birth and death. As winter and darkness die, the spring and sun are reborn. Birth is a powerful ally in the rebuilding of a coven, and though we have agreed to spend this night in merrymaking rather than discussion about all that has transpired, there is one announcement that must be made."

Elda paused and looked to Abby.

Abby felt her face flush. Beside her Sebastian clasped her hand and squeezed. She stood awkwardly and he stood with her. She had never been a fan of public speaking and though she knew and loved the witches around her, she felt a little nervous as she prepared to talk.

"Well, I guess I should just come right out and say it," she told the group, locking eyes with Elda, who gave her a smile of encouragement. "Sebastian and I are having a baby."

Lydie's mouth dropped open and Oliver's eyes widened in surprise. The other witches looked less surprised, and Abby knew that Elda had likely confided the secret before their dinner.

Helena stood and walked around the table, sweeping Abby and Sebastian into a hug.

Bridget joined them.

"Oh, it's so exciting," Helena beamed.

"We'll spoil that baby rotten," Bridget added. "It's a sign. Of course, it is. There are no better happy tidings than a baby."

"Congratulations," Faustine announced.

"Yes, congratulations," Julian agreed.

"Wow, does that mean I get to babysit?" Lydie chirped. She had moved into Helena's empty seat to eat her unfinished banana cake.

"Absolutely," Sebastian told her. "She's going to need someone to show her the ropes."

"She?" Oliver asked. He smiled, but Abby could see a look of hurt in his eyes. "Are you far enough along to know that it's a girl?"

"Not technically, no," Abby confessed. "At least not by medical standards, but I still know."

She broke from the group hug and walked closer to Lydie and Oliver.

"I'm sorry that I didn't tell you guys sooner. I just felt like I should wait."

"Yeah, of course," Oliver agreed, taking a long drink from his glass of wine. "Suddenly your cravings for peanut butter and pickle toast make sense."

Abby laughed.

"And noodles with hot fudge. Gross!" Lydie added.

"Hey, that was a secret," Abby grimaced, covering her face with her hands.

"Really?" Sebastian asked, grinning. "You have your very own chef and you're resorting to college stoner food?"

"I couldn't help myself," Abby admitted. "I'm just happy that no one saw me eating sardines on apple slices."

"Eeeew!" Lydie moaned, finishing Helena's dessert and moving to Bridget's chair.

"You know, Lydie, Bridget has more cake in the kitchen," Elda told her.

"Why waste these?" she asked.

"Good point," Julian agreed, reaching across the table to swipe Faustine's remaining cake.

"So, you're engaged, with a baby on the way," Oliver said. "Going for the Happily Ever After experience?"

Abby smiled and nodded as Sebastian grabbed her from behind and whirled her to face him. He kissed her and then pulled her against him. She savored his smell and the soft texture of his T-shirt. She didn't want to turn back and face Oliver. He was hurt, as she knew that he would be. Not because she was pregnant, but because she had been keeping secrets.

"So when do we get to have the baby shower?" Helena asked. "Bridget is already planning the menu."

****

"How are you feeling?" Abby asked Helena, joining her in the breakfast room.

Helena sat at a small table with a violet blanket draped over her shoulders. She wore gold satin slippers and a long silver robe, but still looked cold.

"Better every day, I think," she told Abby, taking a sip of her tea. Steam rose from the dark liquid and Abby smelled a pungent garlic aroma.

"Doesn't smell like chamomile."

Helena laughed.

"Bridget has me on some superpowered concoction. Almost made me gag when I first started drinking it, but it's growing on me."

"I thought we could use some of my blood today."

"Your blood?" Helena looked at her quizzically.

"Elda mentioned it before. She believes it could be healing. I want to help."

Helena stared into her tea and Abby thought she might cry.

"I'm not sure of the process, obviously," Abby explained. "But I'll do whatever it takes. Maybe you and Bridget could find some way to develop it into an elixir for other ailments too."

Helena nodded and some of the light returned to her eyes. She looked hopeful.

"Only if you're sure, Abby. Lately, I feel like I need a miracle, and the old me saw miracles every day. This new version, well sometimes, I see storm clouds even on sunny days."

"Of course, you do. We all do. I can only avoid depression and anxiety if I turn my brain off. The moment I have an hour of free time, my mind goes..."

"Apeshit," Helena finished and they both burst out laughing.

"What's all the ruckus about?" Oliver called from the doorway. "And where's the food? I figured Bridget would have left breakfast out until noon at least."

"Bridget said any late sleepers have to fend for themselves today. She's hot on the trail of a new anti-viral potion. She's spending the day in the greenhouse."

"Yeesh," Oliver complained. "Guess I'll have to survive on leftovers. No Sebastian either? I've gotten rather used to his protein pancakes."

"He's at the lagoon," Abby told him. "Cold cereal for you, my friend."

Oliver sauntered off to the kitchen and Abby turned back to Helena.

"Did Dafne ever mention Kanti?"

Helena's face darkened, but she only shook her head.

"Never. We didn't have a clue, Abby. Not that she was pregnant, that she'd been with Tobias, that her friends had died. We definitely didn't know about Kanti. A part of me believes that she didn't know about her either, but maybe I'm wrong."

"Why would I be the only one having these dreams? I feel like she's reaching out to me."

"We've talked about it, a lot, in fact. Faustine believes that she's grown stronger. He thinks that each time the curse has struck, Kanti has captured the energy in some way. Now she finally has enough power to manipulate energy. She can appear in spirit form, she can send you her memories."

"But why?"

"I wish that I had an answer. We have a dozen theories and I believe we're getting closer to the truth, but we're still very much in the dark. Let me ask you this. Why do you think she's contacting you?"

Abby paused.

"She wants something. I know that. She wants something from me, but she can't come right out and say it. Maybe because she's not strong enough or maybe because she wants it to remain a secret until the last possible moment."

Helena sat up straighter, nodding her head.

"You're the direct link to her. You have to remember that. Trust your feelings and intuitions. You have more information than any of us, but be wary. She is giving you access to the cruelty that was inflicted upon her. She wants your empathy. Why?"

****

Abby sat on the bed in the healing room. Bridget and Elda bustled around the space, preparing the tools to extract Abby's blood. Helena sat on the edge of the huge stone tub that occupied a large corner of the room. Lotus-shaped candles floated on the surface. The glass dome overhead revealed the purple sky of the half-light as the day waned.

Bridget placed two glass pitchers on a rolling cart and wheeled them to Abby's side. Next to the pitchers, an array of bandages, herbs and unfortunately needles sat in a row.

"You won't feel a thing," Bridget promised.

She rubbed a smooth stone over Abby's skin. Abby felt a light tingling sensation when Bridget lifted the stone away. She swabbed Abby's arm and tapped gently on a blue vein. Attaching a needle to a long clear tube, she deftly slid the point into Abby's arm.

Abby stared at her skin, surprised. She really hadn't felt anything.

"Was that the effect of the stone?" Abby asked. "It numbed me?"

"The stone and a bit of placebo effect," Bridget confessed, smiling. "You believed me when I said that you wouldn't feel it, so you didn't feel it."

Elda moved to the tray and helped direct the flow of blood into one of the pitchers. After several minutes, she quickly shifted the tube into the second pitcher.

"Will you do a transfusion?" Abby asked, looking toward Helena, who had swung her legs into the tub.

"Yes," Elda responded. "A transfusion with the blood from one pitcher, and the other we will study and attempt to create a tincture from."

"We'll have to separate and isolate the different components," Bridget explained.

"You know how to do that?"

"We've been around a long time," Elda replied. "It's hard for me to even imagine everything we've learned."

"Abby, we've also been talking about your mother," Helena mentioned.

Abby had told Helena and Elda about the event with her mother over Christmas. She had been reluctant to confide the experience, but at Oliver's urging had done so in the hopes that they might offer their insights.

"It's not safe to bring her to Ula, unfortunately," Elda said.

"But we can take the healing to her," Helena chimed in. "Faustine has a very special crystal that I am able to utilize with my sight. Hopefully I can discern what sort of energy or experience is plaguing your mother, and then it's only a matter of performing the proper magic to rid her of it."

"That sounds great. I'm just not sure how to present it to her so that she willingly participates."

Abby didn't mention her other concern. After a lifetime of observing her mother's mood swings, she didn't feel confident that even magic could help her.

"Don't you give it another thought," Helena told her. "We're working that part out."

After they collected the blood, Elda encouraged Abby to soak in the healing waters of the bathtub. They would wait until morning to do Helena's transfusion.

Abby stripped out of her clothes and stepped into the steaming water. Oils floated on the surface and reflected the glow from the flickering candles. She settled onto a stone bench and closed her eyes as the water lapped against her chest and the base of her neck. She would only stay for a few minutes, having read that hot water submersions were contraindicated for pregnancy. She pressed a hand on her belly and imagined the tiny person already forming within her.

"The size of a poppy seed," she said out loud, thinking about the book she had been reading about baby development in utero. As she marveled at the awesomeness of the physical body, an image of Kanti rose in her mind. She saw Kanti holding her own baby in the snowy cabin, a baby that she hated.

"She won't hurt you," Abby spoke to her unborn child. "I promise."

CHAPTER 20

Abby stood on the stone slab, shivering. She pulled her cloak tighter and tucked her face beneath the hood to protect her chapped lips.

Elda and Faustine stood on either side of her. They both swayed and murmured. Elda had created a cone of water that rose out of the lagoon. Faustine had conjured a cone of sand that emerged from the beach. The two witches brought their energies together. The cyclone of sand and water swirled faster, and then with a thunderous clap it exploded into the slab beneath Abby's feet. She felt the jolt as the energy traveled through the rock and into her body. It burst through her fingertips and the top of her head. She stumbled and Faustine caught her around the waist before she plummeted off the slab.

She pressed her hand to her belly and looked wildly at Elda, afraid that the energetic blast had hurt the baby.

"Don't worry, honey," Elda told her quickly, helping her into the wooden chair that sat on the slab. "It will shield the baby. It didn't hurt her."

Elda lifted the hood on Abby's cloak so that it covered her red-rimmed ears.

"I can sense you sensing her," Elda confided. "And I sense her a bit too, though she's just a tiny little light right now. Though that energy is getting bigger every day."

"Do you think she will be a witch?" Abby asked, feeling for the child and smiling when the flutter responded.

"Unlike the sex of the baby, it's much harder to tell if she will be a witch. Do you want her to be?"

Abby considered.

"I don't know. There's a part of me that believes the human world is safer, but I know that's naive. How do I hide my true identity if she's not a witch? How do I protect her if I don't hide it?"

"Those are some of the hardest questions we face in the witches' life. And the reason that many witches do not have children. They are not a burden, no—if anything, it is our gift that can sometimes feel burdensome—but they change our reality. They make us vulnerable in a way that we never imagined possible."

"Did you have children, Elda?" Abby asked, noticing a tremor in the older witch's voice.

She looked at Abby and shook her head.

"I wanted to and it broke my heart to turn away from that part of myself, but Ula needed me and I needed her. If I would have chosen the mother's life, I could not have stayed here on the island. It doesn't support a child and a family."

"Why not? I feel like Helena and Bridget would love a baby to look after."

"Now it is time to activate your light body," Faustine said briskly, closing the conversation.

Elda looked at him. Abby thought she saw hurt behind Elda's gray eyes, but the older witch hid the expression.

"My light body?" Abby asked, shifting back and forth on her feet. The initial magic had warmed her up, but now she felt the cold again through her cloak.

"I'm sorry you're cold, honey," Elda told her. "We can't do any additional magic that might interfere, but I promise, I'll warm you up before we return to the castle."

"Oh, it's okay, Elda," Abby reassured her. "It's strangely energizing. I've been so tired lately, it's nice to want to hop up and down."

"Your light body transcends the physical world. It is woven into the collective light of the universe," Faustine explained.

"I like to call it harnessing the power of the stars," Elda added romantically.

"Close your eyes, Abby," Faustine directed. "Focus on the chakras, beginning with the space just above the crown of your head. As you guide your vision down the center of your body, feel the wheels of energy begin to spin."

Eyes closed, Abby directed her attention toward her subtle energy body. When she first learned of her powers, the subtle body had felt like a concept that she might never grasp, let alone truly experience. Now she found the space easily. As she kept her attention there, she sensed the vortices of energy, like orbs of light, pulsing through her body.

Elda's soft cool hands took hold of her forearms. She felt Faustine's bony, and surprisingly strong, hands settle on her shoulders.

"Allow an opening at the crown of your head. Feel the beaming white light, the whole of the universe, traveling through those waves, coursing into your body," Faustine spoke with vigor.

"Now beneath your feet an opening," Elda continued. "As if the world is breaking apart to let you in. Another beam of light, golden, sparkling. It moves into your feet."

"Connect the beams of light," Faustine and Elda spoke together.

Abby felt her body growing warmer. She began to vibrate, but Faustine and Elda held her firmly in place. The beams of light grew brighter, larger, until she couldn't feel her body at all. She felt as if she had swallowed the sun. A billion rays of light burst from every cell in her body. She lost connection to Faustine, Elda, the stone beneath her feet, the sense of skin or hair or limbs.

Energy, vibrant and hot and heavenly, coursed in every direction. She might have been a glowing waterfall cascading down a mountain ravine or a geyser spitting into the sky. Time dissolved. She knew only the sweet oblivion of oneness with all that existed.

When it ended, Abby felt the earth drive up to meet her. She fell forward into Elda's strong embrace. The cold moved into her like an avalanche and sucked the breath from her body.

An uncontrollable sob rose up from the depths of her belly. The sorrow at the loss of the light, at the return to her aloneness, overwhelmed her. She pressed her face into Elda's shoulder and cried. Behind her, Faustine continued to grasp her shoulders. He squeezed firmly and she heard him whisper an incantation. Elda too murmured, and soon the weight of grief softened and then slid away.

Abby lifted her head up, raw now as the cold bit her wet cheeks.

"Pretty amazing, huh?" Elda asked, smiling.

****

"It's truly unbelievable," Helena announced, striding into the oratory with a spin. Her red and yellow dress fanned out in a cascade of fabric as she twirled. "I feel like a new witch."

Elda laughed and clapped, standing and hugging her old friend.

"Thank the Goddess," she said, holding Helena at arm's length. "You look like a new witch."

Helena laughed and spun again before settling into a chair.

"The question now is how to utilize Abby's blood to the greatest benefit."

"We have to be back in the hospitals," Helena urged.

Elda shook her head and frowned.

"I don't think so. They've become overrun by power and money. I'm not sure that anyone is getting healed anymore. We would be met with suspicion and perhaps outright persecution. Victor mentioned a free clinic that they created in Chicago."

"Oh yes, please, I am so ready to be back in the world."

Elda smiled, but as so often lately, her eyes looked troubled.

"We performed the shielding spell on Abby and the child," Elda changed the subject.

"Oh how lovely. Did she enjoy her light body?"

"Immensely."

Elda returned to the pages before her.

"From New Orleans?" Helena asked.

Elda nodded.

"Yes. I keep thinking if I read them enough times, the author and book title will miraculously appear."

****

Sebastian scanned the titles in the library. The books shined as if each had been dusted and polished. Titles in gold and black cursive shone in the candlelight.

He took out a title called The Life Beyond, flipped through it quickly and returned it to the shelf. He tried two more, but didn't find what he searched for. Finally, he picked a thin, tattered book, nearly swallowed by the ornate volumes surrounding it, and sat down.

Fifty-two pages of tiny cursive writing. Sebastian's eyes ached before he finished the introduction.

"And I told her that I would bring her back. I would find a way and I did. A decade of searching, experimenting. The dead will rise again," he read.

The door to the library creaked open and Sebastian stuffed the book into the back of his jeans.

Oliver stepped into the room, not seeing him at first. He moved toward the fireplace and then stopped, noticing Sebastian.

"Insomnia following you as well tonight?" Oliver asked, plopping into a sunken chair.

"Yeah." Sebastian tried to conceal the tremor in his voice. He felt criminal, as if he'd nearly been caught looking at pornography instead of a book in Ula's own library.

"Tried Helena's tinctures, some yin yoga, I even read half a book on the uses for compost, but here I am. Walking the halls like a cat."

Sebastian faked a yawn and stood from his chair.

"Probably better give sleep another shot," he mumbled, making his way to the door.

As he stepped into the hallway, the book fell from the back of his pants. It hit the wood floor with a thud and he saw Oliver's eyes wander to the cover. Sebastian stooped and grabbed it, pressing it against his chest.

"Goodnight," he added.

As the door to the library swung closed, Sebastian saw Oliver watching him uncertainly.

****

The next day, Abby stepped out of the castle. She pulled her dark cloak tighter around her body. The wind whipped and howled. A storm was coming. She moved down the steps slowly, carefully avoiding patches of ice. From the window, she had glimpsed Sebastian near the lagoon. She searched for him along the water's edge, but saw no one.

As she took the path that wound through the cherry trees, shrunken in winter, she spotted him. He stood on a faraway bluff with Julian. Even her keen senses could not decipher their words, but Julian's hands flew as he spoke and he looked angry. Abby watched for several minutes until Julian grabbed Sebastian's arm and pulled him out of sight.

She returned to the castle, wandering the rooms until she found Oliver in the dining room. He sat at a small table reading a paperback and eating a bowl of something that smelled like curry.

"Hey Abby pants," he called and held up his book. "Ever read Eckhart Tolle? He's my man!"

She smiled and shook her head no, pulling out the chair next to him.

"I have a question for you."

"Shoot," he said.

"What's Julian like?"

"Julian?" Oliver studied her face. "Can I preface your question with a question? How come you're asking?"

She sighed and picked up his book, glancing at the words without really seeing them.

"I get a funny feeling maybe, and I'm curious. Tell me about him."

Seemingly satisfied with her ambiguous answer, Oliver leaned back in his chair.

"He's awesome. He's a witch who does what it takes. Faustine once told me Julian lives by his own set of rules. He believes in the witches' oath and he follows the laws of the universe impeccably, but he also has his own reasons for what he does and he adheres to those as well."

"Do you trust him?"

"With my life. He's different, that's true enough, but I get him. He's good to the marrow of his bones, Abby. I don't know what he was like before his wife died. Helena mentioned a few times that her death changed him, which is no big surprise."

"But he was reckless as your teacher, wasn't he? When you first arrived at Ula?" Oliver had mentioned a couple of experiences with Julian that had given Abby pause, including forcing him to eat nutmeg until he hallucinated.

"Unconventional," Oliver corrected. "Not reckless in my mind, though Elda and Faustine might have viewed his methods that way. He pushed me, he challenged me. With Julian, I learned what I could do. That training proved invaluable. Do you know how many Vepars would have killed me by now if not for Julian?"

"Well probably only one," Abby teased.

He laughed.

"True enough, but the point is Julian understood that we weren't playing at life. If I wanted to hunt Vepars then I had to stare down death and live to tell the tale. Elda, Helena and even Faustine live in a different kind of reality. They don't face the enemy head-on, they cast spells, they collaborate and plot. I thought of Julian's tactics as military style. He prepares you for what lies ahead and he reminds you of what's at stake. So, tell me about your funny feeling."

Abby looked toward the window, unsure of how much to say. She imagined the dark look on Julian's face as he spoke to Sebastian.

"I get the feeling he and Sebastian have a relationship that I'm not aware of. I saw them arguing outside just now."

Oliver nodded, considering.

"Julian found him in France. Maybe he finally got a change to chew his ass for blowing them off in New York."

Abby hadn't considered that. Julian had probably been very angry when Sebastian disappeared from the hotel in New York. In the chaos of everything else that had happened, that detail had seemed inconsequential. She wanted to believe Oliver's theory, but something in Julian's expression revealed a deeper quarrel between him and Sebastian.

CHAPTER 21

A week later, Abby's mom checked into the spa.

Ezra guided her to a room and instructed her to get undressed and lie facedown on the massage table. Specially designed purification candles lit the room and a blend of oils, created by Helena, wafted from a diffuser. Even the music was magic. A creation of Dante's that incorporated beats meant to train the mind combined with the sounds of a magical flute that when played lulled the listener into a trancelike state.

"Ready for me?" Ezra asked, slipping into the room and closing the door.

Becky lay on the table in the candlelit room, a linen sheet covering her body. Facedown, Ezra saw only the back of Becky's head and the birdlike bones of her shoulders and back.

"Mmm-hmmm," Becky murmured.

The spa weekend had been Helena's idea. As a healer, she knew how much progress could be made in a weekend of healing touch and, more importantly, it offered them access to Becky's mind and body. Any other option would have created suspicion, but when Abby told her mother that she had booked her a weekend at the spa, Becky accepted.

Helena had not met Ezra, but Victor insisted she would be the perfect addition. Ezra, a nurse and a healer by nature, had also studied massage.

Ezra knew a space in Chicago they could rent for the weekend. They equipped the Spa Bed and Breakfast with massage rooms and an array of elixirs, both magic and not, for use in divining the source of Becky's continued unraveling.

Ezra rubbed a blend of almond oil and lavender on her hands. The oil sat in a stone basin filled with raw amethyst. The gem assisted in sleep and also clearing negative energy.

Resting her palms on Becky's back, she felt the woman stiffen beneath her touch.

"Try to focus on your breath. Take a big inhale through your nose, hold it, and release through your mouth to a count of six. Great, and one more time."

As Becky's breath grew deeper, Ezra felt her muscles begin to release.

Gradually her body softened. Ezra massaged her back, pressing into the knots of muscle. She felt a chaos of energy swirling through the woman. Sorrow and fear flowed from her in bursts that tingled through Ezra's hands and arms. Despite the protective barriers Ezra had placed around herself before the massage, touching Abby's mother still drained her. When an hour had passed, she placed her hands on the back of Becky's head.

"Helena will join you now for the cranial sacral massage," Ezra told her, leaving the room. Becky did not stir.

Helena sat on a chair in the hallway. She had pulled her long auburn hair into a bun and she wore a simple white shirt with black pants.

"How'd it go?" she whispered, cocking her head toward the door.

Ezra yawned and gently massaged her shoulder. She would need a massage now too.

"She's got a lot pent up in that little body," Ezra explained. "A lot of fear that has wound itself tight."

"Any visions?" Helena asked.

"No, but I've never been prone to visions. I did feel her energy though, and it's stuck all over the place," Ezra explained.

"Okay, thanks, Ezra." Helena touched Ezra's hands, allowing a bit of her energy to flow into the other witch.

Ezra sighed and smiled.

"Thank you."

Helena went into the room. Becky breathed long and slow, fast asleep.

"I'm going to touch your head now, Becky," Helena explained, but Becky did not respond.

Helena pressed her hands into Becky's scalp. She massaged along the back of her skull and down her neck. As her hands moved and pressed, she closed her eyes and focused on transitioning Becky into deeper states of relaxation.

Helena, an air element, could manipulate the mind. The visions, the secrets, had begun for her in childhood. After moving into the Coven of Ula, she worked for many years with Faustine on developing her psychic abilities; however, they often went unused. Helena struggled with guilt when she invaded a person's mind without their consent.

To aid in her psychic work with Becky, Faustine had given Helena the Crystal Pendant of Sight. The crystal helped magnify the energetic connection between the two minds. More importantly, it could store thoughts and memories retrieved during mind exchanges.

She slung the delicate silver chain around her head and situated the crystal over her third eye. If she could conjure enough energy, the crystal would channel Becky's memories and Helena would be able to examine them.

As she massaged, Helena caught glimpses of Becky's inner state. Colors, mostly dark reds and blacks, wove through Helena's mind. Helena began a low chant, heard only as a vibration; it called out to Becky to release the darkness within her.

Becky moaned and sighed. Suddenly, she sat up, her spine stiffening. She clutched at the air and screamed. Helena stopped the murmuring and rested her hands on Becky's shoulders. As quickly as the episode began, it ended. Becky collapsed onto the bed, her eyes closed.

Helena touched the crystal on her forehead and directed her gaze through the prism of light. A flash of Becky's past grew larger in her mind's eye. She saw through Becky's eyes. A ghastly face loomed out of the darkness. Empty black eyes sunken in a ruined gray face. The woman held Becky's shoulders with cruel, gnarled hands. She spoke in rapid bursts that Helena could not understand, but one word she heard for certain—curse.

Helena pulled the pendant away from her head. She closed her eyes against the face, like a corpse, looming in Becky's memory.

The Lourdes of Warning.

***

The cold couldn't reach her. In the orb of her body, the heat rose and Abby started to sweat.

Helena called the ritual "Harnessing the energy of the dark moon."

Ezra had chosen the space, an open field tucked miles outside of the city. The black sky held a billion tiny stars and in the far distance the lights of the city cast an opaque glow on the horizon.

After they'd cast protective barriers to block wanderers, Julian had erected the pyre. At first, Abby balked. They could not place her mother's body on a bonfire, for God's sakes, but the older witches prevailed. If not for Helena insisting that the magic was not only safe, but necessary considering Becky's condition, Abby would have refused. Helena had told Abby that a spirit memory tormented Becky and that she would fall into deeper decline until they rid of her of the toxic energy.

As the inferno grew brighter, Abby twirled and chanted. Her arms reached out to either side and soon she lost the feel of her body. The wind whipped and howled around her though she knew the night, beyond their field of energy, was still.

In the center of the snowy field, her mother lay on a bed of coals. The fire burned red and ominous. The heat snaked through the ground and rose into the witches' feet through their heavy boots and clothes.

Abby's mother did not make a sound. The elixir of tranquility would keep her unconscious for hours, so Julian promised. Abby, Julian, Sebastian, Oliver, Helena and Ezra acted out the magic. Carefully chosen by Faustine, who consulted his crystals and reassured them that their energies matched the task.

Abby's mother had not blinked an eye. Sebastian called it "being in the flow." When your plan, your path, unwound before you like a ball of silk rolling down the stairs, perfectly, without a snag.

Abby had poured the vial of liquid into her mother's wine after her massage. So easy, weirdly easy. Abby watched her mother lift the wine and shoot the amber drink in a single go. Becky's bloodshot eyes lingered on Abby's for only an instant longer, and then she slumped over the table and began to snore.

They had carried her to Oliver's van.

Ezra and Julian had already begun preparations in the field. They filled a pit with coals coated in an enchanted dust that purged the energy body. As the fire burned, the smoke would wind through Becky's body, into her lungs, through her skin and bones and blood. It would seek to release the darkness harbored there.

When they began the ritual, Abby's fear and doubt slowed them. She had moved reluctantly, filled with anxiety at the thought of her mother waking up. Finally, Julian had clapped his hands hard in her face.

"Snap out of it," he barked. "Of every witch here, your energy is the most connected to your mother. If you don't show up, then neither will she." He had gestured to Becky's prone form. He did not look angry, but vexed.

Abby's doubt arose from the fear that the darkness lived in her mother as fully as the woman herself. Not an insidious outsider, but an aspect of Becky's spiritual makeup that could not be purged with magic and ceremony.

As the chants grew louder, her body lighter and the fire burned hotter still, Abby's doubts slipped away. She closed her eyes and spun. She sang and laughed and cried. The longer she twirled through the field, the sky a spinning mass of sparkling black, the more she left the physical world and the story of her life behind. The lifetime of Abby—her thoughts, feelings and experiences—ceased to matter. They were merely roles that she played for a little while, but the vastness of divinity lived just beyond the veil. She had only to pull it back, step across that thin line and leave the dense form of Abby behind her.

"Dark moon, we call upon your dormant light," Julian sang into the clearing. "Pull the madness from her body, pull the darkness from her soul, release the woman Becky, give her back her purity, her liberation from pain."

Abby barely heard the words, but sang them anyway.

A shadow slithered from Becky's body. Abby slowed in the firelight and watched it approach her. When the wasted face of the Lourdes reared up, Abby's eyes bulged and she screamed. She fell back into the snow and her head struck the ground.

Sebastian rushed to her and scooped her into his arms.

She saw that he too glistened with sweat. His blue eyes shone from his sooty face.

"I'm okay," she whispered. "I thought I saw..." But as she looked around the clearing, she saw only darkness.

The others continued to sway and chant.

Only Julian had paused. He moved closer to Becky. He held his palms above her body and the fire rose toward his palms.

"No," Abby screamed and scrambled to her feet. She ran toward him. Her mother would burn alive.

"Stop," he commanded her, and the force of his energy drove her back. She gasped for breath as if he'd physically pushed her.

"She's nearly there," he bellowed. "If you enter her space, you will disrupt the connection."

"What connection?" Abby shrieked, sure that her mother was burning within the flames.

Julian gestured to the sky and as Abby's gaze trailed up from her mother's body, she saw thousands of tiny luminescent filaments entering her mother's body.

"I saw a shadow leave her," Julian exclaimed. "It is working."

Abby started to move closer to her mother. She had an overwhelming desire to reach her hand into the silvery threads, but as her fingers reached out, a sharp spasm cut through her stomach. She clutched her belly and doubled over.

On hands and knees, she watched the muddy ground swim and tilt beneath her.

She sensed Sebastian touching her, talking to her, but his voice sounded far away.

"There's something wrong," he called to the others and the alarm in his voice should have spurred her to action, but her hands and knees felt cemented in the mud. If she moved, she would get sick again.

"What hurts?" Ezra asked, squatting in front of Abby and holding a bitter-smelling satchel.

Abby jerked her head to the side and shook her head.

Ezra took the satchel away. She touched Abby's face.

"She's feverish," Ezra announced.

"Sebastian, take her back to the room, we're not finished here," Julian commanded.

Abby heard Sebastian stand.

"No, she needs medical help. Ezra, can you come with us?"

"No," Julian snapped. "We're nearly there. We need the collective energy to maintain it."

"Julian," Helena said, an acid tone in her voice. "Let them go, the spell is nearly complete."

Abby sensed Helena close to her, but she closed her eyes and tried to breathe.

"What's happening?" Oliver murmured as if he'd only just woken from the reverie of the spell.

"Can I pick you up, honey?" Sebastian asked, resting his hand on her back.

She watched spots of light dance at the backs of her eyes. Could he? She wanted to say yes and get far away from the muddy, smoky field, but the thought of shifting, even an inch, terrified her. She pushed her attention to the baby and tried to connect. She felt life, a stirring perhaps, but nothing to convince her that their baby girl was okay. What if she moved and the baby died?

Abby's arms shook as tears ran down her face.

Sebastian pressed his hand into her chest and eased her up. She cried harder as spasms snaked through her body. She reached a hand again toward the silvery light, but then Sebastian had lifted her into his arms and begun walking across the field. She could no longer see the altar that contained her mother. She watched the twinkling stars and tried to feel the child inside of her.

****

"Are you sure she's okay?" Sebastian asked again. He hovered over Ezra's shoulder as she removed the blood pressure cuff from Abby's arm.

Ezra squeezed his hand and smiled.

"She is, Sebastian. Blood pressure is down, fever is down. I think that level of spell casting, it pulls in such a huge amount of energy, and just caused a nasty attack of pregnancy sickness. It's normal, you know? I'm not a midwife, but I've worked with a lot of pregnant women. Abby's body gets fatigued easier, simple as that."

"Which is why she should be taking it easy," he muttered.

Ezra nodded.

"True enough, but consider things from her perspective. She's a brand-new witch with all these powers and energy in the midst of a major crisis. Even if she wanted to lie around all day, she probably couldn't."

"At what point should she start doing that?"

"I don't know. It's going to depend on her body. I would recommend this: get one of the witches of Ula on board as a midwife or ask them to connect you to a witch midwife. This is her first baby, both of yours, and you're going to have questions and need the support."

"That's a good idea," he confessed. "Funny that we hadn't even thought about it."

Sebastian moved to Abby's bed. He smoothed the tangled curls away from her face. She looked pale and drawn. Her cheekbones seemed more pronounced and her lips small and colorless in her face.

He knew if Ezra put the blood pressure cuff on him, it'd be through the roof. He could feel blood pounding in his ears and pumping through his veins. The death of his family, the murder of Claire in particular, should have made him stronger, more capable of dealing with illness, but it had the opposite effect. He grew anxious, scared and then finally angry. He wanted to make Abby better. He wanted to punch Julian in the face.

"Here." Ezra held out a handful of heart-shaped candy.

"What is it?" he asked, examining the tiny red and yellow candy.

"Tranquilizing treats, or Kendra calls them sugary sedatives. Many names, same impact."

Sebastian shook his head.

"I don't want to sleep."

"They won't make you sleep, just relax a bit. They're mostly herbs, a bit of honey and drop of magic. They can really soothe the senses. I promise you'll be fully present, just a little less..."

"Nuts?"

"I was going to say anxious."

"How's she doing?' Oliver asked, creeping into the room and edging the door closed.

He had returned an hour earlier with Julian and Helena. They had a special room set up for Becky on the first floor, and Helena would stay with her through the night to observe and ensure that nothing strange occurred.

Sebastian took the candy and threw them into his mouth. They tasted sweet and flowery.

"She's doing better," Sebastian told Oliver, though he said it more for himself. He touched her face, relieved to feel her skin cool to the touch. Her temperature had been down for a while, but he couldn't help checking every few minutes.

"You're like a long-tailed cat in a room full of rocking chairs," Oliver joked.

Sebastian glared at him, but bit back the retort on his lips. He could easily direct his anger at Oliver. The guy just rubbed him the wrong way. If he dug deep, he knew his feelings arose from envy. He felt envious that Oliver was a witch, of his easy friendship with Abby, of his carefree attitude with life.

"Don't you take anything seriously?" Sebastian asked, trying to temper his outrage.

Ezra looked back and forth between them, cocking an eyebrow.

"I see," she said finally.

"You see what?" Oliver asked, ignoring Sebastian's question and stare.

"Like two sides of the same coin, you guys are so alike that you magnetize apart."

"Hardly," Sebastian scoffed.

"Maybe if I were an angry, brooding goat," Oliver countered.

Ezra laughed and shook her head.

"It's true. I'm a witch, remember? I know these things."

****

"I don't feel the heaviness," Helena admitted, rubbing her hands along Becky's temples.

"It's gone, the shadow. I watched it slip out of her. I think Abby saw it too," Julian said triumphantly.

Helena narrowed her eyes at him.

"You were out of line out there, Julian. You do know that, right?"

Julian's face darkened.

"This isn't high school, Helena. You know that if we broke that spell, all of our efforts would have been wasted."

"You said yourself that the shadow had already left."

"And may have been lurking nearby, tethered to Becky's energy body. As long as that light was coming in, we needed to hold the space."

Helena sighed and looked away. There had been a time when she felt so close to Julian. Miranda had been her best friend. She had loved them both without condition, but after Miranda's death, Julian delved further into the extremes. He lost some critical piece of his humanity. Helena had secretly hoped that the years had restored it, but could see they had not.

Julian moved along Becky's body, letting his hands drift just above her.

"Nothing dense," he said finally.

"I'm going to make a cup of coffee and then you can head to bed," Helena told him.

****

"So, what now?" Abby asked Helena after they had returned to Abby and Sebastian's house in Trager. Abby's mother had checked out of the spa with a smile and taken a cab to the train station to return to Lansing. Becky was in the dark about the true intentions of the weekend and did not realize her daughter had been watching her from an upstairs window. Abby couldn't help but feel hopeful.

"Now we wait. I know that's the last thing you want to hear."

"Actually, I don't mind hearing that. I'm exhausted."

Helena took her hands and squeezed.

"You're living for two. One life is tiring, two, well...you're getting a glimpse of that experience."

"Speaking of the baby," Abby added. "Sebastian and I talked this morning about a midwife. Ezra thought you or Elda might know of a witch midwife?"

"You're looking at one," Helena beamed. "I haven't delivered a baby since Lydie, but I would love to care for you, Abby, if you'd have me."

"Wowm really?" Abby asked eagerly. "You delivered Lydie?"

"With my own two hands."

She held up her hands and looked at them.

"Thanks to you they're good as new and now we're practically family." Helena referred to the blood that Abby had given Helena to heal her.

"I'd love for you to be our midwife, Helena."

"And I would be honored, honey. When can we get started?"

"Started?"

"Sure, go over all the fun changes that are happening in your body, make sure you're eating and doing all the right stuff."

"Lamaze?"

Helena laughed.

"We will cover breathing, but at this point your meditation training will have taken care of a lot of that."

"Sebastian's going to be so excited," Abby told her.

He would be too. Sebastian loved Helena. She was by far his favorite witch at Ula, excluding Abby, of course.

Abby hugged Helena goodbye and walked into her house. It smelled like home, and she inhaled deeply as she moved through the rooms. It also felt freezing cold. She shivered and wrapped her arms across her chest. She walked to the heater and checked the thermostat. Fifty-six degrees. She turned it up and waited to hear the furnace kick on. Silence.

Gathering some newspaper from the recycling bin, she squatted in front of the fireplace and quickly made a fire. Adding two logs and lighting the kindling, the fire gradually came to life. She held her hands in front of the heat and rubbed them together.

A floorboard creaked overhead and she paused, listening. She heard it again.

Hating to abandon the warmth, she plucked a blanket from the couch and wrapped it around her shoulders. Oliver and Sebastian had gone to the woods to check out the area that they believed the map discovered in the Kanti Files depicted. As she walked up the stairs, Abby wondered if she shouldn't wait for them to return.

"Don't be silly," she said. "You're a witch after all."

Before she reached the door to the nursery, she sensed the energy inside. Abby touched the knob, ice-cold, and slowly turned the handle.

Gathering her energy, she shoved the door open and lunged into the room, ready to confront the evil waiting for her. For an instant, she saw her. Kanti.

CHAPTER 22

The spirit dissolved just as she turned her black eyes on Abby. Abby stood rooted in place, frozen by the pure hatred that had shone from the eyes of the ghost. The tiny white birds above the bassinet swayed as if agitated by the presence.

Downstairs she heard the door open and then slam closed.

"Abby?" Sebastian called.

She waited for another moment, finally allowing her breath to release. She fought the urge to race downstairs and tell Sebastian about the spirit. Abby didn't know why she preferred to keep the secret, but she feared revealing that Kanti had come into their home.

****

Tall and thin with wiry dark curls, the woman moved through the terminal like she owned the place.

"I think that's her," Abby whispered, elbowing Oliver and nodding her head.

Abby and Oliver had driven to Michigan's Upper Peninsula to meet Lorna after Gwen had called Abby to inform her that she'd finally talked to the woman and set up a meeting.

Sebastian had allowed Oliver to go in his place because he insisted that he needed to fix their furnace. Abby had almost argued with him, hating to leave him behind, but realized it would be an icy night if they didn't get it fixed. She also knew how important it was for Sebastian to take care of things around the house and she didn't want to strip him of that by insisting that he go.

"How do you know?" Oliver asked from the corner of his mouth. He wore a long tan trench coat and a bowler hat cocked to partially cover his face.

"You look ridiculous," she reminded him, yet again.

"I look like a P.I.," he corrected her, still talking out of the corner of his mouth. "Think Sherlock Holmes, Inspector Gadget, you get the drift."

He winked at her from the eye not covered by his hat and she sighed, exasperated.

The woman stopped by the fountain in the center of the terminal and scanned the faces around her. When her gaze moved over Abby, she paused.

Abby lifted her hand and smiled.

The woman's eyes shifted to Oliver and she frowned.

"She's going to freak out and run," Abby told him, reaching up to snatch the hat from his head.

Oliver laughed and tried to grab it back.

"Okay, you win, no hat," he told her, holding up his hands. "Let's go meet her."

He grabbed Abby's hand and began to pull her towards the woman who watched them suspiciously. She did not run.

"Lorna?" Abby asked, stopping in front of her and extending a hand.

"I recognize you from Sydney's pictures," Lorna said.

She shook her hand briskly.

"But who are you?" She looked at Oliver distrustfully.

"Oliver," he offered a hand and a huge smile. "Sorry for the outfit, Abby tried to tone it down, but I couldn't help myself."

"You think this is a joke?" she hissed.

"No, of course not," Abby insisted.

"No," Oliver added. "I'm really sorry. I didn't mean to offend you. We've been under a lot of pressure. I was just trying to lighten the mood."

Lorna studied him for another moment, her lips pursed in a thin line.

"There's a cafeteria upstairs. I'm assuming you have some way to muffle our conversation?" Her words held an accusatory tone.

Abby looked at Oliver questioning. She didn't know any magic to block their conversation.

"Yeah, not a problem at all," he assured them both.

They followed Lorna to an escalator. As they rose toward the second floor, the woman continued to scan the room. Occasionally her eyes narrowed on a person walking through a doorway or talking on the phone, but she didn't reveal her suspicions, if she had them.

She chose a small table tucked into a corner and sat with her back to the wall.

"Can I grab us a few coffees?" Oliver asked, gesturing toward the counter.

"If you want an ulcer." Lorna replied coldly.

"I'll take an ice tea, please," Abby told him, smiling.

"Nothing for you?" Oliver tried again. "A soda?"

She shook her head.

"I don't drink from public places. Who knows what someone might slip into my cup."

Oliver arched his eyebrows at Abby, but didn't say anymore.

As he moved toward the counter, Lorna relaxed, leaning back in her chair.

"Gwen said that you would bring Sebastian. I am familiar with him. This person," she flicked a hand toward Oliver, "is a stranger to me."

"I'm sorry about that," Abby said. "But you're a stranger to me as well and Sebastian couldn't make it. Oliver is my friend and he's a good…"

"Witch?"

Abby nodded.

"Are you in hiding?" Abby asked.

"Yes."

"Do you have any reason to believe that they're after you? The Vepars?"

Lorna's eyes darted around the room.

"The problem Abby is that I don't know what I'm looking for. I don't have the gifts you have. One of them could sell me a bus ticket and I'd be none the wiser."

"Well I hardly think…"

"Of course you think that's ridiculous. So do I, but the truth is that I am powerless against those creatures. Powerless!" Her voice began to rise and Abby looked desperately toward Oliver.

He paid the cashier and returned to the table.

"Now I see why we need to shield our voices," he joked, but Lorna gave him an acid look. "This will just take a minute."

He walked in a circle around their table, pretending to look for something that he'd dropped, but actually whispering an incantation under his breath.

He took the seat next to Abby.

"We're all good," he told them.

Abby sipped her tea and continued.

"I can see that you're scared Lorna and I get it. I'm not going to lie and pretend that it's unjustified. The truth is that we don't know what the Vepars are up to either."

"But they killed Stephen?"

"Yes," Abby admitted. "Oliver saw his body."

"You?" she narrowed her eyes on Oliver.

"Yeah. I recognized him from his pictures."

Lorna closed her eyes as if trying to regain her composure.

"They were my family. The Asemaa. Sydney, Gwen, Stephen, Karl and Meghan, and of course, Ebony. Now they're gone. Dead or scattered. Our lives have been stolen. We can never go back."

"I'm so sorry." Abby took her hand and Lorna started to pull away, but then stopped.

"Can we help?" Oliver asked. "Help you find a safe place? Cast protection spells around your home?"

Lorna sighed, defeated.

"I never thought I'd want out. I believed, like Sydney, that the Asemaa would be my life's work. Without them I am nothing, the work is nothing. I never realized how much the group meant to me."

"What about Gwen and Karl and Meghan? Can't you go to them?"

Lorna shook her head.

"It's not safe for us to be together. We're sitting ducks. Gwen and Ebony have separated from Karl and Meghan. Maybe someday…" She looked far away and Abby waited, allowing Lorna her reverie.

"We've been reading your material. It's kind of mind blowing, the volume alone."

"I'd say," Lorna agreed. "I remember a Saturday night years ago, sitting on Sydney's porch, drinking wine and reading one of those journals. I thought, 'who knew this is how I'd choose to spend my Saturday nights.' But I loved it, we all loved it. It made us special, which you can understand, of course."

Abby smiled sadly.

"Be careful what you wish for, huh?" Lorna asked.

"Exactly," Abby agreed.

"A lot of it's anecdotes, tales from the road for those tobacco traders. It takes a lot of reading to find the juicy stuff. We didn't know about the curse until a few years ago. That's when we started going back through and searching for links, but we all had lives. We never got around to organizing it."

"We're so grateful that you collected it to begin with."

Lorna offered a short, dry laugh.

"If I could do it all over again, I'd have taken those boxes out to the woods and set the whole lot on fire."

"Why is that?" Oliver asked.

"Isn't it obvious? They're dead. Sydney, Stephen, they're dead because they knew about the curse. If I were you, I'd get as far away from Trager City as possible."

Abby felt Oliver stiffen. She wondered if he thought about the night that Sydney had died, the night that he had killed her.

"Why do you think it's isolated to Trager City?"

Lorna threw up her hands in frustration.

"I don't know why. It's all there though. And yet we're drawn back to that place, knowing full well that something terrible is waiting, still we return."

Oliver looked at Abby and she sensed his anxiety about her and

Sebastian living in the lake house.

"Why was Stephen writing about a vampire cult in Trager? It almost seemed like he was luring the Vepars to him," Abby asked, changing the subject.

"Stephen had a strange sense of humor and, honestly, something of an underdog complex. I think he believed that they would seek him out and he could get close to them."

"Close to them? For what?"

"He had this notion that he could reveal their lair to Adora. It was a crazy scheme that he went back and forth on. A lot of days, he knew it was nuts and abandoned the plan."

"Was he in contact with Adora then?"

"Yes, they talked on the phone once every couple of months. I had hoped to hear from her after he disappeared, but we couldn't wait around. It wasn't safe. Are you in contact with her?"

Abby's face fell.

"She's dead, too?" Lorna shrieked, not bothering to lower her voice.

Startled, Abby looked around, but no one had heard her, apparently Oliver's concealment spell had worked.

"We think so," Oliver answered her. "But the Vepars didn't hunt her down. She went to their lair. I'll spare you the details, but we all went in knowing that we might not make it out alive."

Lorna put her face in her hands and shook her head.

"Do you know what Stephen found in Houston?" Abby asked, gently.

"Yes," Lorna admitted, her voice muffled by her hands. She looked up and her eyes appeared watery and close to tears. "He came to me a few days before he disappeared. Showed up on my doorstep in the middle of the night. He'd literally gotten off the plane from Houston and driven directly to my house. He met a man that knew about Kanti."

"Knew what?"

"He knew that she had existed, for starters. He was involved with a group of men that dug up her body more than fifty years ago."

"Dug up her body?" Oliver asked, surprised.

"Yes, at the time, the man believed they were digging up the grave of a wealthy tribeswoman. The men had been told that the woman was buried with gold and jewels. However, when they uncovered the bones, the only treasure was a copper amulet with strange inscriptions. The man who organized the dig, insisted that they bury the body at the base of a tree or she would haunt them for the rest of their lives. That night he disappeared with the amulet."

"The man who organized the group to dig her up?" Abby asked.

"Yes, according to Stephen's contact the man who set-up the dig was named Ira."

"Ira?" Oliver asked.

"Ira who later became Alva," Abby finished. "A Vepar."

"But why would he organize human men to dig up Kanti's body? Why not just have Vepars do it?" Oliver wondered.

"The man in Houston, his name was Jack, told Stephen that Ira acted very strange. He wouldn't touch the bones himself. He started off digging with the group, but then retreated into the woods. When Jack pointed out the amulet, Ira insisted that he hand it over, but first asked Jack to wrap it in a black cloth, like he didn't want to touch it."

"How did Stephen find this guy?" Oliver asked.

"Believe it or not in a chat room about Native American History. Stephen has been posting for a few years. Every month or so, he'd go in and write a request for information about a Native American girl named Kanti. He never had a hit until this August. Jack sent him an email and said that he would tell him a story, but Stephen had to fly to Houston and receive the information in person."

"What's the significance of the amulet?" Abby wondered out loud.

"Stephen believed that the amulet was the key to breaking the curse. Destroy the amulet - end the curse."

CHAPTER 23

Sebastian trudged through the snow watching for the gnarled tree that Abby had described months earlier. He barely distinguished the knotted gray tree from the drifts of snow as he lumbered along. Fortunately a raven, perched on a tenuous branch, caught his eye. He gazed at the misshapen trunk and found the symbol embedded in the wood.

He turned west and moved on, noticing that the trees looked different. Many were misshapen, either abnormally large or shrunken and withered. As the snow started to thin, he spotted the crimson weeping willow looming over the white landscape.

He gaped at the tree in dreadful fascination. He had never seen anything like it. He doubted that another existed in all the world. He touched the blade that Oliver had given him, sheathed beneath his jacket. In another pocket, a pouch held the berries of the belladonna plant.

He crouched beneath the willow and scooped a handful of the stinging red moss into the glass jar he had brought with him.

The root stairway that plunged into the earth left little room for his large feet. He pressed his hands into the dirt walls to keep his balance as he descended. The dank hovel smelled of rot. He saw the table piled with putrefied food. Despite the cold, maggots crawled along the rotted fruit and meat.

"Shhh......," the woman hissed from the floor. Sebastian stumbled back as he saw her.

She sat on a bench, facing the wall, and rocked back and forth. Her slender back looked delicate and soft, but he could see the drooping gray flesh in the profile of her face.

"You'll wake my daughter," she hissed with a rasping voice that felt like furry legs scuttling through his ears.

He backed into the earthen wall, not allowing his eyes to flick away for even a moment. Though she appeared helpless, something malevolent lurked beneath her wasted body.

"I've brought something for you," he said, ignoring the thumping of his heart.

She stood in a jerky spasm and picked up a spider-webbed mirror. She watched him through the broken glass, but he did not look into the reflection.

"Your potion." He took the belladonna berries from the pouch and dropped them into the jar. Withdrawing his blade, he sliced along his forearm and allowed his blood to drip into the container.

The Lourdes drew hungry breaths as she watched. Her long gray fingers fluttered along her vanity table. They settled on a long knitting needle.

Sebastian moved to the hole and sprinted up the roots. The Lourdes screeched in agony behind him. He placed the jar on the ground, just beyond the reach of the willow branches, and returned to the burrow.

"I will bring it back to you on one condition."

She turned and glared at him. Her flinty black eyes held hatred and longing. She licked the scaly flesh of her lips. Her face was a pool of gray tissue that drooped and pooled. Though she looked ancient and decrepit, her eyes made Sebastian uneasy. Dark black holes filled with wickedness and knowing. He could feel her gaze surpassing his body with those eyes and reaching into the mysteries of his soul.

She tilted her ruined face back and let out a long gritty laugh. The laugh grew into a howl and echoed on and on, even after she'd closed her mouth and turned away from him.

"Those who do not learn from the past are destined to repeat it," she spit, taunting him with her words. "The dead are dead, whether they walk again or not."

"What do you care?" he challenged. "I have what you want. You obviously know what I want, so give it to me."

She picked up the knitting needle and plunged it into her hand. Blood, red but nearly black, spurted out and ran over her moldy pink dress.

"I am dead, dead and decayed, rotted and ruined. The worms dance on my grave, pitter pat they go, how do they dance with no legs?" She cackled again.

"If you're not interested…" Sebastian shrugged. He turned as if preparing to leave.

"Stop," she growled and Sebastian froze, suddenly convinced that the Lourdes had somehow scurried up behind him and was about to plunge the sewing needle into his back.

"Bring me the potion."

"No."

The Lourdes shrieked and clawed at the walls with her pointed nails. She ripped away dirt and roots and bugs.

Sebastian waited.

"In the corner, there's a chest. Bring it to me."

He moved deeper into the hovel, turning back again and again to ensure she did not follow. He found the trunk and swiped the cobwebs away as he dragged it across the room to the Lourdes.

He wrinkled his nose as he neared her. The smell of decomposition was heavy and pungent.

She fumbled open the metal clasp and sifted through the contents. Finally she emerged with a tattered leather-bound journal. She flung it on the floor at his feet.

He picked it up and flipped through it quickly. Pages of directions and diagrams. He saw lists of ingredients. Near the end of the book, a picture fluttered out. A black-and-white photograph of a young girl wearing a pale dress with ruffled sleeves. Big dark eyes stared at the photographer, and the curve of a smile played on her lips.

The Lourdes gasped at the picture and lunged toward Sebastian. He darted away and ran out of the lair, clutching the book in his hand. As he left the willow, he stared at the jar and almost stooped to take it with him. Then he heard the woman's maniacal laughter and fled for the woods.

****

"She said that Ira has the amulet," Abby told Sebastian.

They sat in the kitchen, eating the Thai takeout that Abby picked up on her way home. Oliver had returned to Ula to tell the witches about their discoveries.

"And she thinks the amulet holds Kanti's soul?"

"She didn't say that, but I think so, yes. I think about the relic that had encased part of Devin's spirit."

"The lighter?"

"Exactly—why couldn't Kanti have created something similar?"

"Well it makes sense," Sebastian admitted. "Obviously the Vepars are getting more powerful through her, so they must have a link."

"I think so too."

Abby drank the last of the Tom Kha Gai soup from the bowl.

"So good," she sighed. "Do anything other than fix the furnace today?"

Sebastian shrugged and shook his head.

"Nope, pretty uneventful day. Found some recipes for juicing and smoothies online for you."

"For me?"

"Yeah, recipes to help support you and the baby. I talked with Helena about it and she agrees. We want to make sure you're getting super nutrient-dense food for that little powerhouse you're growing."

Abby smiled.

"That would be good. I have been exhausted lately. I'm taking the supplements from the vitamin store, but I'm starting to think this baby of ours is sucking me dry."

****

Abby laced up her boots. Waterproof and durable, they went above her knees. She put on her coat, zipped it high and then added a scarf and the red winter hat that Helena had knitted for her. She trudged along the frozen shoreline, savoring the cold air gusting off the lake.

When Abby had woken that morning, Sebastian had gone to town for "baby fodder," according to his note.

The snow had stopped after days of falling. The drifts were deep and soft and she moved slowly, trying not to sink so deep that the snow piled into her boots. As she traveled further away from the house, she noticed a crow following beside her in the trees. After several minutes, he was joined by a second crow and then a third until five of the birds trilled and warbled beside her.

"Well good morning to you too," she told them.

One of the crows flew from the tree, swooping close. She stopped and watched as the other birds did the same. One by one they flew down, circled around her, and returned to the tree.

She sensed a warmness in her belly and reached beneath her coat, pressing her hand on her stomach. She felt a tiny flutter. The birds swooped in unison, surrounding her. Though they dove and weaved close to her head, Abby felt no fear. Instead, she felt a connection with the birds.

She held her arms out to either side and two of the crows landed on her outstretched arms. They were heavy, but she held them easily. They clucked and talked, watching her with their beady black eyes. After several moments, they flew off. She continued her walk and the birds kept pace. Sometimes they merely flew from tree to tree and other times they sailed close, their oily black wings iridescent in the sun.

After a half hour of walking, Abby returned to the shed. She wanted a hammer and nails to hang Lydie's drawing. She fumbled through drawers and laughed at the array of tools that Sebastian had assembled. Not an organized man, he had put light bulbs with grass seed. She opened a drawer in his workbench and spotted a box of nails. She pulled it out, but a photo clung to the bottom of the box. Peeling it off, she looked at a young Sebastian pushing his sister Claire on a swing. The photo was taken from behind. Sebastian's black curls blew in a breeze, and beyond the swing set a beach gave way to a glittering lake. Abby could see Claire's legs extended in the air as she swung forward, her pink-painted toenails showing above her head.

Abby's hand trembled as she reached into the drawer. More pictures lay scattered in the cavity and then her fingers brushed something larger. She pulled a shabby leather journal from the drawer and set it on the table. She stared at the threadbare cover. A faint symbol was sunken into it. The triple goddess, which revealed three moons representing the mother, the maiden and the crone, looked back at her. It was not an unusual symbol necessarily; however, Abby had first laid eyes on the symbol far in the forest, carved into a tree as she searched for a dark witch.

"The journal could have come from anywhere," she said out loud.

But she knew. She didn't want to touch it, but she had to. Flipping open the journal, she frowned at the tiny, cramped writing. Words jumped out from the pages—death, immortality...resurrection. She tried not to see the images, crude drawings of a figure, a girl, with symbols scrawled along her torso, legs and arms.

The sound of an engine pulled Abby from the pages. She clapped the journal closed and shoved it, and the pictures, back into the drawer. Through the window, she watched Sebastian park his car and climb out. He brushed a hand through his dark curls and then leaned down to grab the groceries. She started out of the shed, ready to confront him, but then another engine sounded and she looked down the long, wooded driveway.

Oliver's VW Bus pulled next to Sebastian's car. Oliver waved wildly from behind the wheel, grinning. The other witches of Ula sat in the back. Victor and Kendra arrived next, parking alongside Oliver.

"We're here to dig a grave," Victor announced triumphantly, as he stepped from his car.

****

Lydie and Julian, the fire elements, and Abby and Elda, water elements, stood facing one another through a large expanse of trees. Sebastian, with the aid of Julian, had meticulously sectioned off the area they believed the map portrayed. Lydie and Julian focused on melting the snow and thawing the earth. Elda and Abby directed the water toward the lake. As the snow disappeared and the ground softened, Oliver and Faustine sifted the mud. They worked with Kendra, Victor and Helena, air elements, to transfer the dirt into piles at the periphery of the space. Sebastian walked along the edge, patrolling the piles of dirt in case they missed a fragment of bone or some other clue as to Kanti's whereabouts.

The morning sun offered little warmth, but worked wonders on morale. Digging up the body of an angry spirit was unnerving enough without an overcast day to contend with. As they searched, Abby glanced at the faces around her. Everyone, save Oliver, held a look of grim determination. Even Lydie stared intensely toward the ground in fearful anticipation. Oliver, always clinging to the silver lining, occasionally plunked mud onto Lydie's head. She shot a fireball in his direction. It narrowly missed his right ear and he howled as if she had burned him.

Elda and Helena both smiled and Julian offered his past student a stern look, but Abby appreciated the lighter mood that Oliver brought to the gathering. Sebastian hardly seemed present at all. He moved along the perimeter of accumulating mud, at times disappearing into the trees. He held no expression at all, but when he caught her looking, he offered Abby a distracted smile.

The hole in the ground grew deeper and wider as the witches worked. Finally, eight feet in, Faustine called them to a stop.

"She's not here," he told them, wiping sweat from his brow.

"Maybe just a little further," Helena countered, though she looked completely exhausted.

"No," Julian agreed. "One of us would have sensed her by now. Faustine is right, she's not here."

"Hold on." Oliver jumped into the hole and placed his palms against the mud walls. "I do feel something here." He grabbed a handful of dirt and sifted it through his fingers. "Something decayed in this ground, and it's not animal."

"There could have been other bodies buried here," Victor cut in. "How do we know this whole area wasn't populated at some point?"

"They dug her up and moved her, right?" Helena said, sitting on the ground with a huff. "I feel her too—she was here."

Abby searched for the sensation that Helena described, but felt only the rapid beating of her heart. A wave of dizziness washed through and she too sat down on the soggy earth.

Sebastian looked thoughtful and then walked to a towering oak tree. He put his hands on the wide trunk.

Abby felt a tremble in the earth and scrambled to her feet. All of the witches looked alarmed, their gazes shifting to Sebastian. The tree that he touched began to quake. It split down the middle, groaning as its two halves ripped apart. The earth beneath it opened and revealed an intricate network of enormous roots. There, intertwined within the roots, Abby saw the dull gleam of a rib cage. Sebastian reached into the roots and pulled out a mud-caked skull.

CHAPTER 24

They excavated the bones slowly and methodically. Abby imagined that anthropologists on an archaeological dig might have been impressed with their technique. They carefully wrapped each bone in newspaper and bundled them in cardboard boxes. When they completed the task and Faustine sealed the final box, they loaded into several cars and Oliver's van to return to Ula.

Though Abby wanted to crawl into her own bed and sleep, Julian and Faustine insisted that all of the witches return to the island. The possibility that disturbing Kanti's bones had potentially upset the vengeful spirit spooked Sebastian, and he agreed that they should go to the coven.

"Do you think she led us there?" Abby asked Sebastian, when they retired for the night at the castle.

"I think something did. Was it her? Or some divine power that wants us to get rid of her, I don't know."

He slipped his T-shirt over his head and then shrugged off his jeans. She admired the smooth tapering of his chest down to his narrow waist.

He noticed her watching and pulled her to him, kissing her slowly. She reached her arms around his neck and held him tight against her body. She hungered for him. Perhaps a consequence of her pregnancy, she didn't know, but she thought about Sebastian naked more than she cared to admit.

He stripped off her sweater and kissed her shoulders and neck. With a gentle push, she fell back onto the bed. He unbuttoned her jeans and slid them down, kissing her calves and thighs. He moved up to her stomach and she cupped his head in her hands, crushing his soft black curls. He moved on top of her and she searched his eyes. She saw only light reflected back to her; no darkness lurked in the swirling prisms. She almost asked him about the journal and Victor's drawings. She wanted to, but as he kissed her and murmured into her neck, she wanted one more night to not think about what those things meant.

After Sebastian fell asleep, snoring quietly beside her, Abby slipped from the bed.

She left their room and went to the library. The fire crackled as it did all hours of the day and night at Ula. Victor sat alone, watching the flames. On the floor beside him, she noticed one of the boxes of bones.

She closed the door softly, but he didn't hear her. His dark eyes stared fixedly at some vision that she could not see. After several minutes, she moved closer and he stirred, turning to her with a glassy expression.

"Mesmerizing," he said, indicating the restless blaze.

"Did you sense anything amiss? With Sebastian?"

Victor stared at her bewildered for another moment and then his eyes began to clear. He climbed to his feet and took a chair closer to her.

"I think the stunt with the tree was pretty phenomenal. Who or what communicated where those bones were? And what kind of energy opened up that tree?"

"Elda thinks the trauma of several months has triggered a dormant energy in him. She thinks he's a witch, after all."

"Maybe," Victor said. "And then again maybe not. What if it's not his power at all that we're witnessing, but something acting through him?"

Abby grimaced. She had thought something similar, but feared speaking it out loud. She wanted to tell Victor about the journal, to confide her secret to just one other person, but she couldn't. She already felt that she betrayed Sebastian with her thoughts. She couldn't stand to cast any more suspicion on him until he had been given a chance to explain.

"Have you had any more dreams of him with Dafne?"

"No, but I've been pulling long hours. My sleep is pretty hard and fast, not much room for dreaming."

"Do you think I should tell Elda or Faustine?"

Victor shook his head.

"I don't think you should alarm them until we have a better idea of what's happening. You don't want to put him on the defense."

"No I don't, not at all, but I also don't want to wait until it's too late. What if they could help him? What if they could prevent something catastrophic?"

"Wait a little longer," Victor advised. "Let's see what we discover through Kanti's bones."

Abby returned to bed, but she slept fitfully. Nightmares plagued her. Again and again, she stood at the edge of a gaping hole and stared at the crumpled body of Sebastian clutching a maggot-riddled skull.

****

"Hello my future wife," Sebastian said, grinning.

He walked into Lydie's dream room. Sweat shone on his face and neck and spotted his gray T-shirt.

Abby sat on a fluffy mushroom and petted the fat cat Kissy, who glared at Sebastian when he stole Abby's attention.

Lydie swung from a swing suspended far above the floor. Oliver and Victor sat on the top of the indoor sand dune, where they argued about whether the Internet would ultimately destroy humanity.

"Connection," Victor said simply. "The Internet has liberated the world. I can talk to a mother of five in Pakistan about her hopes for her daughters' futures or play World of Warcraft with a kid from Russia."

"Or download plans to make a bomb or buy an arsenal of semi-automatic weapons or join a child porn ring."

"Or watch videos of kitties," Lydie called out.

"That sounds like a conversation I don't want to join," Sebastian told her, leaning down and kissing Abby.

"Agreed," she said. "Any progress?"

She referred to Sebastian's training with Faustine and Julian. Though isolating a specific element of power had thus far proved impossible, they had hoped to channel some of the amazing energy he'd exhibited the day before.

"Yeah, a bit. Mostly I moved some heavy rocks that should have been impossible to lift."

"Ooh, my Hercules," she teased, squeezing his bicep.

"I'm going to run up and take a shower, and Bridget wanted me to tell everyone that lunch is ready. Chicken Tikka Masala."

"Oh yum, that's my favorite."

"I know." He winked. "I told her you've been craving good Indian food."

****

"Why won't he come here?" Faustine asked, clearly irritated.

"There are a lot of reasons," Victor began, glancing at the faces of Elda, Abby and Sebastian like they might be nodding in agreement.

They sat in the dungeon room known as The Circle or the oratory. Books of Shadows lined a high shelf and Abby tried to study the names etched into the leather spines. Great swaths of color painted the stone floor as the noontime light shone through the intricate stained-glass windows that bordered the room.

"Dante is not comfortable with covens. And," he continued quickly, as Faustine started to interrupt him, "he's not sure that your protective enchantments won't hinder the spell."

"But you performed this magic at Sorciére," Faustine countered.

Victor frowned as if he hadn't thought of that.

"Look, Faustine, the bottom line is that he said he won't. He has his reasons and I respect that."

"How do we know this magic is safe?" Elda asked. She sat near a desk scattered with stones, crystals and notebooks.

"He's been working with the spell for over a year. I've done it ten times at least. It's safe."

"Safe from what?" Abby asked. "I mean we basically astral traveled, right?" She remembered the experience from the All Hallow's Ball. After taking a sip from Dante's glass, she opened her eyes to discover that she and the other witches had been transported to the ocean floor in the Atlantic. She remembered how real it felt. Unlike astral traveling, where most sensation was muted, she felt the water and the cold as if she genuinely sat on the ocean floor.

"Yes, basically. I believe it's a form of astral projection, but it transports several of us together and to a very particular place."

"Have you ever used other bones? Or only the fish?" Sebastian asked. Abby had told him in detail about the journey after they were reunited.

"He's tried with other bones," Victor admitted. "The fish with wings is special, obviously. Dante has tried to carbon date the bones, but they appear to exceed the timeline that we can work with."

"So that makes them?" Sebastian asked.

"More than fifty thousand years old; how much more, I couldn't say."

"What's happened with other bones you've used?" Abby asked.

"Something similar. All of the witches participating project to a certain location. We used human bones that Dante snagged from a research center once. We traveled to a hillside in Ireland—at least we think it was Ireland."

"So you really don't know where the bones take you?" Faustine asked. "Or why?"

"They reveal secrets," Victor said simply. "In the Atlantic they took us to a shipwreck. In Ireland, there was a very intriguing circle of stones."

"I'm not sure why we are confident that this is the ideal magic to perform with Kanti's bones," Elda said, and Faustine nodded with her.

"Galla could not make a connection when she touched the bones. You've consulted with the other witches of Sorciére. You've considered your own library of information and you are no closer to understanding the significance of the bones. I am telling you that it will work. How do I know that? Because I'm a witch. As are you. This isn't a hair-brained scheme; I know that this is the next step." Victor spoke with conviction and a little bit of annoyance.

Abby knew that Victor preferred not to work with covens because elder witches, such as Faustine and Elda, rarely put their faith in younger generations. They had grown accustomed to believing that the old ways were right and that all new magic was suspect.

"It's decided then," Sebastian cut in. "Chicago, here we come."

****

"Home, I have missed you," Victor said, when the elevator opened into the spacious loft that he shared with his friends in Chicago.

"Espresso?" Kendra asked, immediately shuffling out of her coat and boots.

Oliver laughed.

"Bit of a caffeine junkie, eh?"

"That's putting it mildly," Kendra told him over her shoulder as she beelined for the kitchen.

Oliver, Abby, Sebastian and Julian had accompanied Victor and Kendra to Chicago. Though Elda encouraged Faustine to go, he wanted to continue sifting through the documents of the Asemaa and believed that Julian would be a better choice for the journey. Abby wondered if he secretly wanted to search for other spells to use on Kanti's bones.

"Greetings, friends in the north," Ezra told them. She wore black yoga pants and a red Chicago Bulls sweatshirt. At barely five feet tall, she should have seemed diminutive, but she exuded a toughness that reminded Abby of a guard dog. Her short hair, dyed turquoise, hung lopsided across her forehead.

"Julian," the older witch told her, extending his hand.

"Ezra," she offered her own.

Julian tilted her arm, looking at a tattoo on her wrist.

"Ganesh," he commented.

"Remover of obstacles," she replied. "Tattoos are to me what espresso is to Kendra."

Abby glanced at the tattoo of the decorated elephant's head.

"Who's Ganesh?" Oliver asked, leaning over to see the tattoo.

"The Hindu god with an elephant's head," Sebastian said, surprising them all. "Why does everyone look at me like that?" he asked, irritated. "I haven't lived my entire life in a cardboard box."

"Nice to see you again, Sebastian," Ezra told him, winking.

"I was into Hindu mythology for a while in my younger years. My mom loved spiritual icons. She had three figures of Ganesh on our fireplace mantel."

Abby grabbed his hand and squeezed. She loved learning new things about Sebastian. In those moments, she knew they had decades of discovering each other ahead, and it made her excited for the rest of their lives.

He grinned at her and shrugged.

"How's your mom, Abby?" Ezra asked.

"No news is good news, I guess. I've been so busy, I haven't had a chance to check in, but Helena has been reaching out to her telepathically and says she seems well."

Dante and Marcus sat on barstools at the kitchen counter. They introduced themselves to Julian and Sebastian. They had already met Abby and Oliver.

"You look familiar," Sebastian told Marcus, trying to place him.

The witch tucked a strand of wavy copper hair behind his ear and nodded.

"I'm amazed that you remember. It was the All Hallow's Ball. I met you by the wishing fountain, but figured after everything that happened..." Marcus trailed off. His silence referred to Sebastian's memory loss at the hands of the witch Dafne. Had it been up to her, he never would have retrieved his memories.

"Okay, yeah," Sebastian agreed. "I think you were doing back handsprings around the room."

"Show-off ," Dante teased, kissing his ear.

Marcus swatted him away playfully.

"The world looks more right when I'm upside down."

Sebastian grinned.

"That makes perfect sense to me."

"Anyway, we've set up the meditation room," Ezra told Victor. "Is everyone participating?"

"I'm not a witch," Sebastian confessed, as if that excluded him.

"You're something," Dante said, eyeing him with interest.

"He's in," Julian added. "It's worth trying," he told Sebastian. "Abby is going to sit out so that she can be present with our bodies."

"Any other reason?" Dante asked, his eyes twinkling.

Abby saw his gaze flick toward her stomach, but he didn't say more. She vaguely remembered Victor mentioning that Dante could read minds. She wondered if he was reading hers or the baby's.

"Actually, there is," she confessed. "I'm pregnant."

"Wow, that's wonderful!" Marcus stood and gave her a long hug. Ezra slapped her on the back in her own, slightly less feminine form of congratulations.

They retreated to the meditation room, a large square space, enclosed with long colorful tapestries that hung from beams beneath the ceiling. The windows were covered by sheer linen drapes. Round, brightly patterned meditation cushions were arranged in a circle around an altar of flickering candles.

Dante took out a small silver pouch and set it on the floor.

Kendra handed out empty wineglasses . Dante picked up his own glass and filled it with amber liquid from a carafe.

"What is it?" Julian asked.

"Apple cider," Dante told him. "We just need a carrier. Feels like a cider time of year."

Dante took the canvas bag that Julian had brought from Ula. He did not look in the bag, but closed his eyes and felt among the bones with both of his hands. Finally, he removed two shards of bone the size of silver dollars. Holding the bones in his palm, he brought them close to his face and whispered into his hand. Dropping the bones in his glass, he opened the silver pouch and poured a sprinkling of green powder into his goblet.

Julian leaned forward with interest, as if he hoped to hear Dante's incantation. Dante seemed not to notice, but Abby thought he drew his hand a bit closer to his face. The witches passed their glasses to Dante and he filled each with a sip of the fizzing cider.

Abby took a cushion and settled outside of the group, but close to Sebastian. He held his glass up to her and then tilted his head back and drank.

CHAPTER 25

Sebastian felt an immediate buzz throughout his body. His skin prickled and he started to turn to Abby, but already his consciousness had been ripped from the meditation room.

He felt blindly with his hands. Darkness encased him. A black wall of dirt pressed against his face and his back. It surrounded his legs and arms. He couldn't breathe. He clawed at the dirt and tried to kick his legs. The wall of earth pressed in on him from every direction. Dirt pushed into his eyes and his nose. He started to scream and the dirt moved into his mouth.

****

Abby watched the witches drink and tried to remember the sensation as the potion took hold, but she only recalled spinning very fast. She watched their slack faces and wondered where Kanti's bones had taken them.

Sebastian was the first to move. He began to moan and suddenly tumbled from his cushion. He kicked and tore at the air. His screams echoed through the vacuous room. Abby ran to him and shook his shoulders.

"Sebastian, wake up," she shrieked, panicked. His eyes did not open. She slapped his face, but her touch did not register. He continued to cry out and writhe on the floor.

Abby ran to the kitchen and got a glass of cold water. She hurried back and threw it in Sebastian's face. It did not rouse him.

The others had begun to move as well, though no one had awoken. Kendra lay on her side, whimpering, in the fetal position. Her eyes clenched tight. Julian shook his head from left to right. He struck out at the air and mumbled incoherently. Dante did not struggle, but a stream of white foam had formed on his lips and began to ooze from his mouth.

"Marcus," Abby screamed. The witch, who was also Dante's lover, had been working on an addiction pamphlet for an awareness group and chosen not to participate.

She ran through the loft screaming his name. Finally, bewildered, he stepped from a room, headphones over his ears. At the look on her face, he ripped them off.

"What? What's happening?"

"I don't know, hurry."

They rushed back to the meditation room. Dante continued to foam, and with horror, Abby saw that it had a pinkish hue—blood.

Marcus bent down and pressed his hands on either side of Dante's face. "He's burning up."

Abby touched Sebastian's face. He felt hot as well.

"Okay, calm down," she said mostly to herself. "We can do this. Marcus, is there any way to break the spell?"

Marcus looked up at her frantically.

"We've never had to."

Abby closed her eyes. She raked through her mind to her study at Ula. Elda had taught her an incantation to pull a witch from their astral travel. Abby didn't know if Dante's magic was astral travel, but it had to be similar.

"I need a hook," Abby told him, already running back toward the kitchen.

Marcus followed, though she knew he did not want to leave Dante.

"A fishhook?" he asked, his eyes darting in every direction as if one might materialize before him.

"Yes, or an object shaped like one. Something I can use to pull their consciousness back."

"Ezra," Marcus bellowed, eyes lighting up. He sprinted across the loft and Abby continued to search through kitchen drawers and cupboards. She needed salt and water. She found a bottle of sea salt and filled a clear glass bowl with water.

Returning to the room, she sat the bowl in the center of the circle of witches. They continued to move and cry out, but still no one woke. Abby walked a circle outside of the group, sprinkling salt on the floor. Along one of the window ledges, rocks and crystals were arranged on a swath of black cloth. She grabbed a hunk of obsidian.

"Marcus, I need string or yarn," she shouted, not bothering to quiet her voice. Instead, she hoped it might startle one of them awake, but all of their eyes remained closed.

Marcus dashed back into the room holding an apple-shaped pincushion and a sewing box jumbled with items. Abby picked through the box. She found a small roll of green thread.

"Here." She handed it to Marcus. "Tie a piece of string to their ring finger on their right hand. Leave the string long, pull it into the center of the circle and leave it on the floor."

Marcus nodded. He went to Dante first, and Abby saw the desperation on his face as picked up Dante's limp hand.

Abby continued searching through the box. She found needles, safety pins, buttons and jewelry pliers, but no hook. She took out one of the safety pins and, using the pliers, carefully bent the pointed end into a hook. It was rustic, but she thought it would work.

She helped Marcus finish tying the thread and drew the ends of the string toward the center bowl. She tied all the ends around the heavy piece of obsidian that she had plucked from the window ledge and then rested it in the water.

"What can I do?" Marcus asked. He squatted close to Dante, brushing hair back from his face. "Victor looks okay," he said suddenly. "He's the only one not moaning."

Abby looked at Victor, who had slumped forward, but otherwise sat very still. His body did not tremble. Abby went to him and touched his neck.

"He's not hot."

She considered trying to wake him, but shook her head.

"It doesn't matter. We need to do this, now. Join me in the center. I'm going to reach into the astral plane and try to hook them with this." She held up the crude hook. "I need you to sit with me and channel your energy into the water. I'll need all of the power we can conjure."

They sat on opposite sides of the bowl. Abby submerged her hand in the water and grabbed the rock. She felt an immediate sense of ease coupled with a buzzing energy. The blue light, nestled at the base of her spine, came to life.

She closed her eyes and envisioned the water pouring into her body, awakening each cell. The weight of her body grew lighter until she began to feel that she could detach and float away. She focused that lightness into the green string. Her consciousness drifted out beyond the realms of this world. She soared through darkness and starlight. In her body, she lifted the hand with the hook. She did not have an astral body. Only a shimmering geyser of light that encompassed everything and nothing. When she encountered that same light before her, she knew she had found one of her friends. In her body, the hook slipped forward and caught the green string that connected to Sebastian's finger. She felt his light resist her, but then suddenly as if something had snapped, the light drove toward her in a rush. The impact nearly sent her back into her own body, but she fought the urge to get sucked back into the meditation room.

Harnessing the pulsing blue light, she continued. Again and again, she encountered the magnificent light that belonged to one of the other witches. Each time, their energy initially denied her, but then some tether broke and they returned to their bodies.

The last witch that Abby had to pull back was Victor. Though neither of them had bodies in her space, she recognized his energy. Unlike the others,

Victor did not resist her. Instead, his energy pulled her. She felt the blue light within her growing dim as her light was absorbed in his.

In her body, she waved the hand with the hook madly and clutched the obsidian. She started to feel that her very essence would be consumed by Victor's light. That once he took her completely into himself, her soul would leave her body and be stuck forever in an astral darkness.

"What's happening?" Sebastian's familiar voice echoed to her from the physical world.

Suddenly another light appeared behind her. A friendly energy that drew her forcefully back. She exploded into her body and started to fall backwards. Sebastian caught her. Slowly her eyes focused on the room. She pressed her hand against her chest and tried to slow and lengthen her short, rapid breaths.

"It's okay," he told her, pulling her fully against him. She turned and buried her face in his neck.

She still felt the terror as Victor's light had begun to absorb her own. Her whole body shook with the tension of trying to escape that overwhelming pull.

She looked into Sebastian's face.

"Are you okay?" She searched his eyes and saw his panic subsiding.

"I was buried alive," he told her. "I thought I had died."

****

Lydie slipped on her cloak and pulled the hood over her face. She carried her satchel down to the lagoon and climbed into a rowboat.

"Wooden oars deft and true
Guide me without guiding you
Swift and strong
We'll move with grace
Now take me to the open space."

She spoke the incantation that Max had taught her to make the boat row on its own. She touched the oars lightly with her fingertips and allowed some of her energy to move into the wood. The boat jerked and then glided smoothly into the lagoon. She turned and waved at the castle, though she doubted that any of the witches watched her leave.

Despite the frosty day, the sun shone brightly in a cloudless blue sky. Oliver and Julian had accompanied Abby and Sebastian to Chicago. Lydie had not been invited. She knew why. She was twelve years old, a child in their eyes. She wondered if they would ever see her as more.

As the boat slid beneath the rock face and into the dark tunnel that left the island, Lydie lit a ball of fire in her palms. It bobbed and swayed with the rocking of the boat. The light cast away the shadows and she allowed the breath that she had been holding to release in a rush. She had never liked the dark shaft through the cliff. It spooked her as a small child. She remembered her father holding her tight and pointing out the tiny bats that lined the ceiling of the cave.

"Bats above and water below," her mother had joked, looking uneasy as well.

Lydie knew that her parents always felt out of sorts at Ula. They loved the witches, but the island itself made them claustrophobic. Whenever they returned home from a visit, her parents insisted they run wild through the woods. Barefoot, Lydie often naked, they weaved through the forest, springing over logs and scurrying up trees like squirrels.

Lydie trailed her fingers in the icy water. She could have conjured her fire energy to stay warm, but she rather enjoyed the bite of the cold. It cleared her mind. As long as she focused on the sting in her fingertips, she didn't have to think about Max, Dafne, her parents and more—so much more.

She pulled her personal Book of Shadows out of her bag. Helena had helped her make the leather-bound book several years before. It included her journal, her experiments with magic and, recently, her dream of the future. Lydie liked words, but she loved pictures.

She flipped to an empty page and took out her charcoal pencil. She drew a house nestled high in a tree—similar to the cabin that the Ula witches had built in her dream room. Tiny rocking chairs sat on the wraparound porch. A swing hung from a branch, more than a hundred feet in the air. She started to draw a spiral staircase wrapping around the huge trunk and then erased it. Too easy for enemies to get in that way. Instead, she created a rope ladder that could be easily pulled in. Birds, chipmunks and raccoons filled the branches and peeked out from thickets of dense leaves. In a large window, she sketched the profile of a man. She imagined a hybrid of Oliver and Sebastian, but with wild reddish hair like her father had.

She laid her pencil down and studied the drawing. She could do it. She could have that life. She wouldn't be afraid. She would marry a powerful witch and together they would be safe.

She stared out at the choppy waves of Lake Superior. The Coven of Ula did not lie close to any shore. Only water greeted her as she gazed at the horizon.

She leaned over the side and peered into the lake. A speck of black caught her eye, but it disappeared under the boat before she could see it clearly. She conjured a flame and encased it in a bubble shield. Moving to the other side of the boat, she dropped the fire into the water. It illuminated the darkness and she screamed, reeling back into the boat. Dafne, her black hair fanning out, had been staring back at her. She moved back to the side and gripped the boat edge, once again looking into the depths. Lydie saw only her reflection. Any trace of Dafne had vanished.

CHAPTER 26

The chaos in the room made Abby's head spin. Dante had awakened, but began to choke on the spit and blood in his mouth and lungs. Marcus rolled him onto his side, where he heaved onto the floor.

Julian, still disoriented, went immediately to Dante's aid. He pulled open his eyelids and pressed along his chest and throat. Finally, he pushed Marcus out of the way and lifted Dante up, thrusting his fist into Dante's belly. Dante began to choke and sputter, gasping for air. In a whoosh, he threw up a stream of saliva and dirt. The dirt, turned to mud, poured out of his mouth as Julian carefully lowered him to the ground.

"Get him a glass of water," Julian barked at Marcus, who fled the room looking terrified at what Dante's body had surrendered.

Sebastian looked shocked.

"What is it, what's happened?" Kendra asked, struggling to her feet and swaying woozily. She tried to maintain her balance, but pitched to the side and landed on her elbow with an audible crack. She screamed in pain. Ezra, who watched the fall with a dreamy far-off expression, opened her eyes wide at Kendra's cry. Ezra did not try to stand, but crawled to her friend on hands and knees.

Oliver watched the scene with his own matching expression of bewilderment. He shook his head as if to rid his ears of water. His eyes came to rest on Abby.

"What happened?" he asked, as if she had an answer. In the unfolding confusion, she could not find her voice, but just stared back at him helplessly.

Marcus rushed back into the room as Dante vomited another gush of blood and dirt.

Julian held Dante across his legs. He pressed his fingers to his neck. Dante's skin had begun to take on a grayish hue.

Marcus tried to hold the water to Dante's mouth, but he seemed to be losing consciousness.

"What's wrong with him?" Ezra exclaimed. She had made it to Kendra and they sat on the floor, arms wrapped around each other, both looking scared and disoriented.

"Abby, we need your blood," Julian said.

Abby looked at him, trying to understand what he was saying.

"Elda said there are vital healing compounds in your blood. We need some of it. Now!" His sharp tone startled her out of her reverie, and she struggled to standing with Sebastian's help.

"It's okay," she told him, seeing the concern in his eyes. "Julian's right. It helped Helena—we have to try."

"Victor," Julian shouted. Victor still sat on his small meditation cushion. His eyes were open and a tiny smile played on his lips, but he didn't appear to be present in the room.

"Victor?" Oliver snapped, moving to Victor and shaking him roughly. "Snap out of it."

When Victor still did not reply, Julian turned to Ezra and Kendra.

"We need medical supplies to do a blood transfusion. Where can we get those?"

"Josh," Ezra replied quickly. She held on to Kendra's hand until she got her feet firmly beneath her. "Josh helps with our medical clinic in the city."

"There's no time to waste," Julian said.

"I'll help," Oliver said, following Ezra from the room.

Dante had stopped throwing up, but his breath came in short rasping bursts.

Without thinking, Abby moved toward him and squatted down. She put her hands on Dante's back. His energy thrummed beneath her fingers. As she drew her hands down his back, she noticed a slowing to the energy. She pressed her hands into his back.

"We need to flip him over," she told Julian.

They carefully rolled him onto his back. His eyelids fluttered and then closed.

Abby drew her hands to his stomach. She lifted his shirt and laid her palms flat on his abdomen, then closed her eyes and tried to feel into his body with her mind. She traveled through the waves of energy and found the slow-moving vibration. A dark mass seemed to have lodged itself just below his diaphragm. She massaged slowly in a circle. Though she did not feel a growth in his body, she knew that something toxic had taken hold of him in that place. She felt her hands growing warm and then hot as she touched him. The dense energy started to loosen. She guided it down toward his feet, feeling that if she offered it an escape route, it would take it, and flee his body.

Julian made a similar sweeping motion over Dante's body toward his feet. Abby felt the cells begin to move faster as the darkness dissipated and slipped away.

"Camphor oil? Or charcoal?" Julian asked Kendra.

She held her injured elbow and nodded.

"Marcus," Kendra said, beginning to get color back to her face. "In my medicine cabinet there's a blue bottle of camphor. It's on the bottom shelf next to the oil blends."

"Got it," he said and hurried from the room.

"And cotton rags or an old T-shirt," Julian called after him.

"You've got the touch," he told Abby and smiled.

Abby forced a smile back, but her whole body trembled with the effort. As Dante's vibration increased, she felt her own energy wane.

"Not much longer now," Julian assured her, sensing her fatigue.

Marcus returned with the camphor oil. Julian held the bottle in both his hands. He closed his eyes and Abby noticed that his lips moved, almost imperceptibly. He uncapped the oil and doused the T-shirt, carefully wrapping it around Dante's feet.

"What will it do?" Marcus asked.

"Pull the toxins out and bind them to the oil."

"Toxins?" Kendra asked.

"It's toxic, that's for sure," Abby agreed.

Finally she felt the heaviness move out of Dante's body. As she smoothed her hands over his legs, a sudden tingling drew up her arms. The grayness began to drain from his body and his face.

"It's gone," she sighed, relieved.

Sebastian stood behind her, rubbing her shoulders. She leaned back against his legs and took one of his hands.

"We still need the transfusion," Julian said.

Abby felt Sebastian bristle behind her.

"I know you're exhausted, Abby, the hardest part is over. Do you have a bath here?" Julian directed his question at Kendra.

"Is it really necessary?" Sebastian asked.

"Yes. He was throwing up blood. Something is damaged in there. From what I understand, her blood will heal just about anything."

Kendra watched her with interest.

"It's okay, I want to," Abby assured them.

"There's a bath," Kendra answered. "Marcus designed it. He's a water element too. It will be perfect."

****

"What can I bring you?" Sebastian asked as Abby slipped beneath the hot water.

She closed her eyes and moaned as the water moved over her aching body.

"Just sit with me?"

"Of course."

He perched on the edge of the tub, moving behind her so that he could lean down and gently massage her scalp.

"What happened?" she asked.

A part of her wanted to sit in silence and allow the water to rejuvenate her, but she wanted Sebastian's story while they were alone.

"I think she was buried alive—Kanti," he said tensely. "There was dirt everywhere. I could feel it suffocating me. I felt like I was ripping off my fingernails clawing at the dirt. It was so heavy and dark. I don't think I've ever been so scared."

She reached up and rubbed his leg.

"You shouldn't have done it."

"It was the same for Dante," Sebastian told her. "I'm sure of it. You saw the mud he was coughing up. How is that possible? We were sitting here in the loft. How did that mud get inside of him?"

"There was something else inside of him too," Abby said, shuddering. She thought of that dark energy pulsing in Dante's abdomen.

"I saw it. I watched you push it out of him. Was it her? Kanti's spirit?"

Abby shook her head.

"I don't think so, but honestly, I don't have a clue. I feel like I need another hundred years in this life before I'll have a context for ninety-nine percent of the stuff that's been happening lately."

"How did you bring us back?" Sebastian asked. "I was dying, I was buried alive, and then suddenly I felt you. Your light surrounded me and pulled me out."

"Elda taught me. After I saw you in the Pool of Truth, she wanted me to learn how to draw people back from their astral travel. I wasn't sure if it would work."

"But it did."

"Yes, but something strange happened." She paused and ducked beneath the water for a moment, gathering herself for the memory. When she emerged, water poured down her face in rivulets.

"When I tried to get Victor, I felt him pulling me. It terrified me. It wasn't just the sense that I was being drawn toward where he was, but that his energy intended to absorb mine completely."

Sebastian moved around the edge of the bathtub to face her.

"Did it seem intentional? Like he did it on purpose?"

Abby bit her lip and considered.

"In the moment, yes, but now, I'm not so sure. You saw how out of it he was in there."

"Not just out of it," Sebastian added. "Creepy. He was smiling, he looked happy. He obviously didn't get buried alive."

"None of the other witches were with you underground? When we used that magic at Sorciére, all of us traveled to the same place. Why did it work differently?"

"I'm still coming to terms with the experience. I may need a few days before any theories start popping up. I feel brain-fried."

"You and me both."

"Are you sure about this transfusion? You're exhausted and the baby..."

"She's okay. It's weird, but I think I felt her when Victor's energy was pulling me. I experienced this powerful, serene presence. I think it was our daughter."

Sebastian smiled and scooted onto the floor. He rested his chin on the edge of the bathtub.

"You give me hope, Abby."

****

Oliver and Ezra unloaded the equipment from the van.

"Thanks Josh, you're a lifesaver ," Ezra told the man behind the wheel. He smiled and touched his fingers to his ball cap.

"You and me both," he told her. "Literally."

"Thanks man," Oliver added.

They had not been introduced, but there was little time for niceties.

Oliver and Ezra pushed the cart, loaded with medical supplies, back into the building and onto the elevator.

"Does he know you're a witch?" Oliver asked her.

"No. He's a don't-ask-don't-tell kind of guy. I implied that we're trust fund babies when we first got the clinic started. We have lots of money and want to do good with it, that kind of thing. He might notice that patients have pretty miraculous turnarounds on days when we visit the clinic, but the human brain is great at rationalizing."

"Yeah," Oliver agreed. "It's easier to believe the lies sometimes."

"Pretty much. What we believe is what we see, after all."

"Where did you go?" Oliver asked. "During the spell."

Ezra frowned and watched the floor numbers lighting above them.

"I was in a dungeon. Maybe a Vepar's lair. I've never been in one, so it's hard to say for sure."

"Did you see Dafne?" he asked, hopeful.

"No, I didn't see anyone. I walked out though. It wasn't like the magic we've done before. Usually all of the witches who drink the potion are there together. I was alone and scared. I kept walking because I felt like something was stalking me in the tunnels. I wanted to run, but everything felt really heavy. I finally saw light and ran out of the tunnel only to find myself on the edge of a cliff. The only escape was down, but it had to be a thousand feet onto jagged rocks."

The elevator dinged as they reached the top floor. Ezra pushed the cart and Oliver followed.

"What about you?" she asked.

"Woods, but something was chasing me too. I was running away and branches kept scraping my face. My head told me to turn and fight, but my body kept running."

"Oh thank God," Ezra said, as they moved into the meditation room. "His color is coming back."

"Thanks to Abby," Kendra told her.

"Where's Victor?" Oliver asked.

"Julian is with him. Giving him some kind of tea. He thinks it will bring him back."

"He's still astral traveling?" Ezra asked, surprised.

"Not exactly. He's conscious, but, I don't know, somethings not right."

"Oliver, can you sling Kendra's arm?" Ezra asked, handing him a roll of gauze.

Sebastian drew back the curtains to the room and walked in.

"Abby is getting dressed," he told them.

"Tell her to find somewhere comfortable to sit. It shouldn't take more than twenty minutes to draw her blood."

Abby settled on the couch and watched as Ezra hung a clear blood bag from a metal frame. She connected a tube between the bag and a large needle. Abby cringed and looked toward Sebastian instead.

Ezra wrapped a rubbery band around her upper arm and pulled it tight.

"Can you flex your hand for me a couple of times?"

Abby opened and closed her fingers. Sebastian watched her closely, holding her other hand firmly.

"Little poke," Ezra told her as she slid the needle in.

It hurt, though not terribly. She preferred Bridget's stone method—even if it was more placebo than actual numbing.

Abby could see Julian in the kitchen. He stood next to Victor, who sat hunched on a stool. Julian kept lifting a blue coffee mug to Victor's lips and encouraging him to drink.

"Easy as Sunday morning," Ezra said, several minutes later.

Abby glanced up, surprised to see the bag nearly half full.

"You've got some powerful blood flow," Ezra told her, sliding the needle out of her arm. She pressed a cotton ball against Abby's skin and taped it down.

Sebastian kissed her hand.

"How do you feel?" he asked.

"Fine," she said honestly. "Not woozy or anything."

"Witch gifts," Ezra told her with a wink.

"How'd you learn to do that?" Sebastian asked.

"I used to be a nurse," she admitted. "I still am, I guess. Just better at it now."

"Oliver, could you and Marcus carry Dante into Victor's room? It's close so it will be easy for us to monitor him there."

Oliver and Marcus lifted Dante and gently moved him to Victor's bed.

"He's going to be okay," Oliver reassured him.

Marcus looked pale and waxy. Little worry lines stood out around his mouth.

"I panicked," he sighed. "He was spitting up blood and we couldn't wake anyone up. I completely panicked."

Oliver cocked his head and looked amused.

"And? We all panic, man. Especially when people we love are foaming at the mouth. When I was a younger witch, just discovering my powers, my dog Tex got run over by a car. I flipped out. I put him in the car and raced across town to the vet only to find out they were closed. He died before we got there. I kept thinking afterward, 'you're like a superhero, you idiot—you could have saved him yourself.' I told Elda that story at Ula once, and she reminded me that everything happens for a reason. I used to think that saying was hokey, now I know it's the truth. Every moment guides us; we're not always meant to save the day."

Marcus looked down at Dante. He leaned forward and kissed his forehead.

"I appreciate that, Oliver," he told him. "I'll just stay in here with him."

"We're ready for the magic blood in here," Oliver called to Ezra.

****

"He's doing much better," Ezra said, leaving Victor's room. She had been checking Dante every half hour since the infusion. "Not yet awake, but heart rate and blood pressure are good."

"I'm still trying to figure out what happened," Victor complained, rubbing his temples. "I have a splitting headache and Kendra's pain potions haven't touched it."

Julian handed him another cup of steaming, rank-smelling tea.

"Ugh, another one?" he asked. "Are you trying to kill me?"

"Just the opposite actually," Julian replied curtly.

"What's in that concoction you've got there, Julian?" Oliver asked, wrinkling his nose as the smell wafted his way.

"Sebastian's tried it," Julian said, smiling.

"Don't remind me," Sebastian grimaced.

"When?" Abby asked, nestling deeper into the crook of Sebastian's side.

They all sat on couches and chairs in the loft trying to piece together what had happened during Dante's spell.

"It helps with memory retrieval," Julian said, "but more so, it helps right the mind when something has wreaked havoc in there."

"In France," Sebastian answered Abby's question, kissing the top of her head.

"Maybe I should have some too," Kendra commented, closing her eyes. "I can't get those visions out of my head."

"Talking will help," Julian told her. "Now that Victor has joined us, I think it's time to tell our stories."

"What about Dante?" Victor asked.

"I think it best if we not wait," Julian said. "I will begin. I was in a Vepar's lair. I recognized it by the smell, which was interesting because generally in astral travel there is no sense of smell. I'm not sure exactly what this magic is of Dante's, but I think it's important that we study it further."

Victor inhaled sharply, but did not speak.

Abby glanced at him, but his face betrayed nothing of his thoughts.

"I was standing outside a great wooden door. I could hear whimpering on the other side. I, Julian, wanted to help the person behind that door, but I had no control over my body. I turned and walked deeper into the earth. I came into a room with a blazing fire. I don't know how the smoke was escaping, but the fire danced with orange and purple and green flames. I stood there and stared at it until I was pulled back into my body. I felt fear. I don't know why, but I wanted to leave that place; however, nothing I did brought me back. I felt the tug as Abby reached into the astral plane and pulled me home to my body. I could have screamed for joy when I opened my eyes and I was back in that room."

"Me too," Sebastian agreed. "I'm pretty sure I ended up in the same place as Dante, buried alive."

He described his experience of trying to claw his way out. The other witches looked at him in horror, obviously connecting his experience and Dante's.

Ezra followed.

"I believe that I was in a lair too, but instead of going down, I followed a tunnel that took me out to a cliff. Something followed me, I could feel it, but I never saw anything."

Oliver described a similar feeling as he raced through woods to escape something that stalked him.

"Was there snow?" Julian asked.

"No, I hadn't thought about that. It was summer. Lots of green. I couldn't see far ahead because the woods were dense."

"Could you have been in another place?" Abby asked. "Somewhere warm? Down south maybe?"

"I don't think so," Oliver admitted. "It felt like Michigan. The freshwater lake smell and the same species of trees and plants."

"Me too," Ezra added. "I'm pretty sure I was looking down on Lake Superior."

Julian frowned.

"So the magic transported us to a different time, that's the only explanation."

"To one of Kanti's experiences," Sebastian added.

"What makes you say that?" Oliver asked.

"A feeling. I wasn't alone in my terror. It was like I felt it double, through me and through the person who had actually been buried alive—and I believe that was Kanti."

"And you think the lair you were in was on Lake Superior. You've been there, then?" Julian asked Ezra.

She nodded.

"I used to hike there and camp by myself. I liked the quiet. The cliffs are spectacular. I remember them well."

"So the Vepars have a lair on Lake Superior?" Abby worried.

"It would make sense," Oliver noted. He balled his hands in his lap. "It was so easy for them to attack us."

"But they didn't return to that lair with Lydie. Why not?" Abby asked. "If they had a cave on the mainland, why travel into the lower peninsula?"

"Because they were luring us into a trap," Julian reminded her. "They're protecting the lair on Lake Superior. That's why we don't know about it. If they're being hunted, they go somewhere else."

"What do you remember?" Ezra asked Victor, who continued to sip his tea with a look of utter disgust.

"Nothing." He shrugged. "I remember taking a drink of cider and then waking up in the kitchen."

Abby watched him carefully. She thought back to the sense that he'd tried to consume her in that astral space. Maybe it wasn't him at all, but Kanti who tried to absorb her light.

"I was in a cabin," Kendra recounted. "There was fire all around the cabin. Smoke was pouring through a crack around the door and into the windows, which were just holes, no glass. The room smelled like blood. There was bloody straw on the floor. When I looked at my own body, it wasn't my body, but another woman's hands and legs. They were streaked with blood."

A tremor moved through her and she wrapped her uninjured arm across her chest.

Victor sat next to her. He placed his cup on the coffee table and put an arm around her shoulders.

"I agree with Sebastian," Kendra continued. "I think I was in Kanti's body, in her memories."

"I don't think this was a mistake," Julian said finally after several minutes of silence. "I'm not sure what happened to all of us, but that lair on Lake Superior is new information. It narrows down our search."

"You think they took Dafne there?" Abby asked.

Julian nodded.

"I do. I think she may have even been the one I heard behind that door."

"That's a pretty big assumption," Sebastian interrupted. "Look, I don't want to be the naysayer here, but we've made a lot of mistakes going after Tobias. Kanti seems to have the power. How do we know she didn't just show us exactly what she wanted so that we'd walk right into another of her killing grounds?"

"That would mean your experience was in the present moment, not the past," Ezra pointed out to Julian.

"True, but that's my sense. Unfortunately, none of us have more to go on than that."

Abby noticed that Victor looked pointedly away when she glanced at him.

"He's awake," Marcus exclaimed from the other room. "Dante's awake!"

****

"Thank you," Dante whispered to Abby as she accompanied Julian into Victor's room. His voice sounded hoarse and the effort of speaking seemed to exhaust him.

"I'm just so happy I could help," she told him.

She sat in a chair near the end of the bed. Marcus sat on the bed next to Dante, holding his hand.

"Do you remember anything?" Julian asked, taking a chair near Abby.

Dante closed his eyes and nodded.

"I was in a hole and someone was shoveling dirt on top of me. I tried to climb out, but my body wouldn't obey my thoughts. I was getting buried alive. I was shoving it away, but it came in droves. It filled my mouth. I had to swallow it or suffocate."

Dante lifted a trembling hand to his throat.

"It was real, wasn't it?"

Julian sighed and looked away.

"Yes. There's no other explanation."

"Do you have any idea who was burying you?" Abby asked, glancing toward the sitting area where the other witches remained.

Victor had nearly accompanied them to speak with Dante, but Julian encouraged him to relax and focus on gathering his thoughts.

"I thought I heard a voice," Dante started. His gaze shifted to Abby, but he quickly stared at the floor when she met his eyes.

"Whose?" she asked, not sure that she wanted to hear the answer. "Sebastian. I thought I heard Sebastian."

CHAPTER 27

"I think I saw Dafne in the lake," Lydie told Elda.
The witch stood in the healing room carefully stripping the linen from the beds. She stood and turned to Lydie, surprised.
"In the lagoon?" She started to walk out of the room, but Lydie stopped her.
"No, in the big lake. I took the rowboat out."
Elda put a hand to the pendant around her neck.
"Just now?"
"Yes. I didn't imagine it."
"She didn't try to speak with you?"
"No, she swam under my boat, but there was something different about her eyes. They didn't look like Dafne's eyes."
Elda frowned.
"I think that she's being possessed."

****

"Oliver and Ezra went for takeout," Victor told them.
Julian and Abby had left Dante to sleep and Marcus to continue his vigil.
"Salads okay with you guys?" Kendra asked.
"Sure," Abby said, though food was the furthest thing from her mind.
Julian held a similar expression of unease.
"Sebastian?" Abby asked, scanning the loft.
"Went to the roof," Kendra told her. "He said he needed some fresh air."
"Shall we?" Julian asked her.
Abby bit her lip and nodded. She preferred to talk to Sebastian alone. If he reacted defensively, Julian might misinterpret his behavior and assume that he had something to hide.
Their footsteps echoed in the cold stairwell as they walked to the upper floor. Abby had put on her jacket and gloves, but still shivered beneath her layers.
"Take a deep breath, Abby," Julian told her, pausing.

She tried, but the chilly air constricted her lungs.

Julian touched two fingers lightly to her chest.

"Keep pulling the air in. Envision it moving through a wall of fire as it passes across your lips."

She tried again, picturing the fire, and the inhalation came easier.

"Now imagine that each breath moves through your whole body, from the top of your head, out to your fingertips and down to your toes. Feel it warming every cell."

She breathed, and a warm glow spun through her body until she no longer felt cold at all.

"Better?" he asked.

"Much."

"Is there anything you want to tell me about Sebastian before we go up there?"

"I'm not sure what you mean."

He sighed.

"You young witches exasperate me. You're all so stubborn, so intent on keeping your secrets."

Abby stepped back, surprised by Julian's frustrated tone.

He watched her intently, but she held her silence.

"Everything comes out, you know? In time, the truth is revealed and the longer you hold it back, the more deception you weave into the fabric of your life. Deception is an energy like all other things. It lives and breathes inside of us. Is that what you want in your body?"

He was referring to her child, and Abby put a hand protectively over her stomach.

"Of course that's not what I want," she told him angrily. "But I also don't want to cast suspicion on the person I love when one of you old witches already tried to destroy him for that very thing."

Julian smiled and shook his head.

"Like a tempest, you are. Forgive me? I was not trying to create a rainstorm. Just so we're clear, I can sense that you're hiding something and it puts me on edge. I've had a lot of pain in this life. At this point, I've got nothing to lose, but all of you," he waved his hand toward her stomach, "you have everything."

Above them the door opened and they heard footsteps pounding on the stairs. Sebastian came into view. His black curls dripped and his face looked red and chapped.

"It's pouring rain out there," he exclaimed.

****

"Brrr, it's cold," the woman moaned, wrapping her scarf further up her neck so that it covered her chin and mouth.

"It's a winter paradise," the man corrected her, awkwardly lifting a snowshoe and knocking it against a tree to remove some of the snow that had caked on and begun to slow him down.

"You said hot cocoa and roaring fires when you sold me on this vacation, Jeremy. So far it's mostly been icicles and mittens."

He laughed and flicked his snowshoe at her. A glob of snow hit her in the forehead. She wiped it away furiously and tried to hobble across the snowy cliffs toward him.

"Be careful," he reminded her.

They hiked along the craggy cliffs of the Lake Superior shoreline. In winter, the dark rock was mostly covered by snow and ice.

"I wouldn't have to be careful if you'd taken me somewhere civilized, like Florida or Hawaii."

"Oh, come on, girlie, what's life if we always live in the comfy spaces? This is an adventure." He held his arms out to either side and grinned.

The woman smiled, reminded of why she had fallen for Jeremy in the first place. If nothing else, he did remind her that she was alive.

She took a breath and savored the expansive view of Lake Superior that stretched out behind him. The dark waters tossed and churned. The sun lit the day, but brought no warmth.

She walked to Jeremy, laboriously, and hugged him.

"You feel like an abominable snowman," he told her, squeezing her tight.

The snow sparkled beneath the afternoon sun. As a shadow blotted out the shimmering snow, she looked up. Expecting a bird, she shoved Jeremy away and screamed as a wolfish creature with bat-like wings rose up from the cliff.

Jeremy twisted around.

"Run," he shouted, trying to do the same, but tripping over his snowshoes.

She ran. She wanted to stop and help him. She should have stopped to help him, but sheer terror drove her away.

She tripped and fell. Crying and swearing, she fumbled at the latches on her snowshoes and yanked them off. She stood in her hiking boots and dared a glance back. Hunched over Jeremy's body, the creature's head rose and fell as it consumed the man she had only just begun to love. She tried not to see the glittering snow streaked with red.

She turned and ran into the forest.

****

"It's concerning," Faustine agreed after Julian recounted the experience in Chicago with the bone magic.

"I feel like it implies our worst fears," Elda said. "That Sebastian is being seduced by this dark spirit. However, I don't sense that energy in him."

"Nor do I," Helena added.

Julian shook his head, but did not offer his opinion.

"It is true that I don't perceive it in him," Faustine murmured. "But do you think Dafne fell for a man whom she sensed desired great power? I don't believe that Tobias had it in him either. I think something put it there. I think one morning he was the Tobias he had always been and the next morning, he was something else."

"With no predisposition to evil? He killed all of her friends, Faustine, all of their friends," Helena argued. "He burned them alive. Is there any entity strong enough to strip someone of their very soul?"

"I tend to agree with Helena," Julian commented. "It seems to me that Tobias hungered for power as did Ira, or Alva, as we know him now."

"What makes you say that?" Faustine asked.

"Mostly the journals of the Asemaa. There are a handful of comments about Tobias—the man. He was a fisherman, but never satisfied with that life. Some of the Trager people spoke of him as a dreamer, a man who desired a better life than the one he'd been given. Perhaps in Dafne, he saw an opportunity. She was a witch, a talented, powerful witch, but then along comes Alva, with a better offer."

"So, Alva knew he was next in line? And groomed him?"

"Well, that I don't know," Julian admitted.

"Should we be worried about Abby?" Helena asked.

"Of course," Faustine said, incensed. "We should be worried about Abby, Sebastian, Lydie, Oliver and ourselves for that matter. Nothing we do seems to take us closer to the heart of this thing. Meanwhile this Kanti spirit grows stronger and continues to pursue her plan, whatever that may be."

"Dante said that Sebastian was burying him alive?" Elda asked for the third time.

"Not in those words, but yes. He said that he heard Sebastian. He thought Sebastian was shoveling the dirt on top of him."

"But Sebastian described being buried alive as well?" Helena asked though she knew the answer.

They had been discussing the experience in Chicago for more than an hour. Julian had confided what occurred as soon as he returned to Ula.

"Could Sebastian have been digging him out?" Helena asked.

"I doubt it," Julian admitted. "He felt trapped. He couldn't see, couldn't move, couldn't breathe."

"And another thing, Abby described Sebastian as thrashing and yelling. The only person who didn't appear to react with fear and panic was Victor."

****

Julian and Oliver picked along the rocky shoreline. They both wore black nylon suits that Helena had made for them. Thick enough that a Vepar's fangs or the skin-walker's claws would struggle to break through. They were also designed for intense cold. Though both witches could increase their body heat by focusing their element, if they were injured, they might not be conscious.

"Where was the couple attacked?" Oliver asked, reaching behind him for the second time to check his bow. His arrows were tipped with Julian's powder. In each pocket, he held a vial of venom antidote.

"About a mile further," Julian answered, cocking his head and nodding. "Faustine is sending me a map of the cliffs up there. He's found some sea caves that he finds promising."

"Why would they attack and risk exposing themselves?"

"I've been wondering that myself," Julian admitted. "I have a couple of theories. One, in the animal form, they have less control."

"They took Sebastian from a cabin at night, Lydie from Ula. They didn't kill either of them. That seems like an awful lot of control."

"Which makes sense in the beginning when it is new and they are careful, but what happens when you spend more and more time in the psyche of a creature? Not just a monster, as the Vepars already are, but an animal with a prehistoric brain and powerful instincts to kill and eat. At what point does the animal begin to take over the higher mind?"

Oliver nodded, remembering the wolfish thing that Tobias had become. "Other theories?"

"That they're calling us to them. They know that we will respond. It's our duty as witches and, in this case, it's personal."

"That was my first thought."

"Unfortunately, we all tend to agree on that point. This Kanti has been far too premeditated to suddenly let her creatures wreak havoc and expose her. It's more likely that they have orchestrated this attack to call our attention to it."

"I'm suddenly feeling a bit unprepared," Oliver grumbled.

"There they are," Julian said, stopping.

He pointed to a black crevice in the cliffs ahead.

They took their time, pausing often to watch the cave, but nothing emerged.

As the sun sunk on the horizon, Oliver removed an arrow and cocked in in his bow. Julian wore a belt of steel stakes, and he drew two daggers from sheaths around his ankles.

They stayed close to the rock wall as they drew toward the opening. A screech from deep in the tunnel stopped them both.

"Skin-walker," Julian murmured.

"I remember the sound, vividly," Oliver agreed.

They ducked into the opening. As witches, they could see easily in the darkness, but it took a moment for their eyes to adjust. As they walked deeper into the cave, Oliver slowed his breath. Claustrophobia had never been a problem before, but after his last experience in a Vepar's lair, the underground world felt more oppressive. He shook away visions of the dead soldiers the Vepars had created, though calling them soldiers gave them too much credit. They were barely animated, dead things given a puff of breath that they exhausted quickly.

The screeching came again, but further now.

"It's moving away from us," Oliver whispered, stating the obvious.

"Shh."

The pathway sloped down. It grew narrower.

Oliver shifted, crouching lower as they moved. He returned the arrow to its sheaf and took out a knife.

Now the screeching grew louder, deafening. They were getting close, but the tunnel seemed to be shrinking more and more.

Ahead Oliver could see something dark wriggling in the black. It shrunk away from them, fixing them in its gaze with shining red eyes.

"Is it a skin-walker?" Oliver asked, unsure about the creature before them. Tobias had been larger, terrifying and more...human. This thing seemed like a giant angry bat, more scared than lethal.

"It's a decoy," Julian said suddenly. He turned and began to run out of the tunnel.

CHAPTER 28

"Now this is raspberry leaf tea," Helena announced, holding up a bowl of herbs. "It helps tone the uterus in preparation for birth and may even speed the birth along."

Abby and Sebastian sat at their kitchen counter, where Helena had arranged a menagerie of herbs, supplements and tinctures to aid in Abby's pregnancy.

"Is her uterus trying to get a date?" Sebastian joked. Abby rolled her eyes and Helena bent over laughing.

"You and Oliver could be brothers with those terrible jokes, you know?" Helena teased.

Sebastian grimaced and waved toward a bowl of sparkling ginger.

"Candy's on the menu?"

"Not candy, candied ginger. Helps with nausea. Though you can opt for straight ginger instead, or ginger tea."

"Did someone say candy?" Lydie asked, padding into the kitchen in her slippers. She held Baboon in her arms. "I thought we were watching movies and eating popcorn tonight?"

She eyed the contents on the counter.

"We're almost done, honey," Helena told her. "Go pick out a movie, we'll be there in ten minutes, tops."

"Please, no more Annie, either," Sebastian called behind her. "If I have to hear 'It's a Hard Knock Life' one more time, I may knock myself out."

"Oh I love Annie," Helena murmured. "I used to have a TV you know, at Ula? But then Faustine got the flu and we had several electrical explosions in the castle. Ended my movie era."

"His flu caused electrical explosions?" Abby asked, impressed.

"Yep, he has quite the electromagnetic field, a force to be reckoned with, surely."

"Maybe we should finish this tomorrow," Abby yawned. "Lydie will be peeved if I zonk out before the opening music."

"Sure honey, you're the queen of this household." Helena winked. She put lids on several of the containers.

"The queen, I like that," Sebastian added, pulling one of Abby's long curls and watching it swing back and forth.

"This hair is getting out of control," Abby started, reaching her hands back and attempting to gather it into a ponytail. "It was already growing fast, but since I started taking the prenatal supplements, I swear it's three inches longer."

"You're a mama lioness," Helena growled.

"Heck yeah, much sexier than a hippo." Sebastian laughed.

Abby leaned over and tried to bite him.

"Better not cross me then," she told him when he danced away.

"Popcorn and black bean brownies?" he asked. "Made special for the occasion."

"Yay movie time." Helena jumped up and down and laughed.

"What'd you find for a movie, Lydie?" Abby called toward the living room.

"Avatar?"

"Yes!" Sebastian yelled, his head in the oven. He came up with the pan of brownies.

"What's Avatar?" Helena asked.

"Only the best movie of all time," Sebastian began.

Abby grinned and walked into the living room. Sebastian might spend five minutes describing the ethical implications of the movie in comparison to their own society. She joined Lydie on the couch.

****

Dafne raced through the woods. Branches ripped at her face and hair. After months of captivity, her legs had no strength. Bones and skin with little muscle to propel her forward and away from the devil that chased her. She fell and skidded in the snow.

It took her. She had no strength to fight the spirit. Even if she wasn't weak in body, she was weak in her soul. Bone tired, weary to the core of her being. She considered surrendering to the being, allowing Kanti to take over completely. Dafne could slip into oblivion. She could wake after it was over, but she knew that this was her last chance. Soon the being would strip the last of her energy. She would die and Kanti would go on.

She drifted into the background. She felt the darkness of Kanti's presence, pushing her further into the recesses of herself. She struggled to keep contact with her body, to see through eyes that she no longer controlled.

Kanti turned back toward the house. Dafne heard the distant sound of voices. She knew that retaking her body had alerted Abby and the others.

As if looking through smudged binoculars, she saw them. Abby, Sebastian, Lydie and Helena. They stood on the porch looking into the moonlit woods, searching for the noise that awoke them. They felt the presence of something, but they could not name it.

The sight of Lydie and Helena made Dafne's heart ache. She wanted to seize her body and run to them. She wanted to fling herself into Helena's arms and beg mercy from the witches, the friends, that she'd betrayed. Kanti felt her rallying and stopped in the forest. Dafne felt a wave of black push her further from her body. She started to fall into the void—the place that she disappeared into when Kanti possessed her. A place where she had no consciousness, no memory of what transpired. She clung to the edge of awareness. She retreated so that Kanti could not sense her.

Kanti darted through the shadows. She conjured a fire and held it in her palm. She put the fire to her mouth and swallowed. The rush of flame and power poured through her. She took out the dragon dagger and removed the blade from the sheath.

****

"Answer your damn phone," Oliver spat, dialing Abby's number for the fifth time. "What is the point of these useless things if no one ever answers them?"

"They may be fine," Julian told him, staring through the windshield as the trees raced by. His eyes darted everywhere. He was not only wary of creatures on the ground, but also those in the sky.

"You don't think so though, why? Why, Julian?" Oliver demanded, starting to throw his phone and then taking a deep breath before setting it on the dashboard.

Julian glanced at him.

"Sebastian has been experiencing some things. A pull toward dark pursuits. Eventually this curse is meant to move from the abstract into the tangible. That skin-walker we just encountered was placed there to draw us away from something. What this spirit wants is not at Ula—she wants Sebastian and Abby."

"And Lydie and Helena are with them right now." Oliver slammed his hand on the dashboard. "No, it's okay," he spoke out loud. "Helena is a powerful witch, they're all powerful. It's going to be okay, right?"

Julian said nothing.

****

Abby stood in the snow, disoriented, but alert. Sebastian had woken her. The movie had nearly ended and she had dozed on the couch. It was Lydie who sensed something off and then Helena who heard a sound in the woods, a familiar screech.

They stood on the porch. Abby's eyes raked across the trees and the lake. Her ears perked for any sounds that didn't belong. At first, the four of them stood motionless, listening, and then Lydie lifted her face to the night.

"I smell something...animal," she whispered, and Abby glanced at her.

Abby expected Lydie to appear the way that Abby felt, terrified, but Lydie looked determined and angry. Helena opened the door of the house and slipped inside. She returned with pouches of Julian's powder and a shotgun.

"Abby," Sebastian started and she could see the fear in his eyes, fear for her safety.

"No," she told him. "I have to stay and fight, Sebastian—it's the only chance we have."

The hairs on the back of her neck stood on end. The baby shifted within her. The ball of blue energy had begun to expand at the base of her spine. She was ready to fight.

Sebastian started to argue, but he stopped as she drew her hands in front of her and the energy began to glow in her fingers.

"How did they get in?" Helena asked. "We placed a dozen spells at least."

"Someone on the inside," Abby answered, reluctantly.

She turned to Sebastian.

"If Claire is about to walk out of those woods, this is the time to tell us," she said.

Sebastian looked at her, surprised.

"We don't have time to have this conversation, so I'm only going to say this once. If you love me, trust me. From this moment, until the night ends, I need you to trust me," he told her. "They didn't get in through me."

Abby looked into his face and nodded.

Lydie looked back and forth between them.

"I think they're here," Lydie whispered, raising a shaky finger toward the trees.

****

Kanti stepped from the woods. Although she inhabited Dafne's body, her spirit molded Dafne so that she looked like a hybrid of the two. Skinny and pale, with black hair and black eyes shining, she moved from the darkness of the trees into the open. Abby could see the girl from her dreams in the woman before her. Shoulders squared and held high, she marched toward them without fear. Abby glimpsed the glint of the dagger.

"It's Dafne," Lydie squeaked, though she sounded unsure.

It was Dafne and it was not.

"It's Kanti," Abby said.

In the moonlit earth, Abby saw the shadow of a flying creature. The skin-walkers. Tobias and Alva and more. Five or six in all flew over them.

One of the skin-walkers dove. It seemed to hit a force field above the house that blasted it away.

"Some of the protective spells are holding," Helena whispered.

Kanti lifted the dagger and began to slice through the air. She drew the blade in a dizzying pattern.

"She has access to Dafne's magic," Helena moaned. "She's undoing the spells."

Abby watched the emptiness in front of Kanti grow solid, waver and then disappear.

"It's broken," Lydie said.

Sebastian started to walk forward. Abby reached for his hand, but he brushed her aside. He stepped from the porch slowly, almost catatonically. The man who had stood by her only moments before seemed to transform before her. He looked vacant, empty.

"What's he doing?" Lydie asked, turning to Abby desperately.

"We have to stop him," Helena said and she lifted her arms into the air, creating a cyclone of wind and snow.

"No," Abby commanded.

Helena paused and before she could fling the vortex of wind, one of the flying Vepars fell upon her. Lydie conjured a ball of fire and threw it at the beast, but it had already ripped away from Helena with a hunk of her hair in its mouth, but nothing else.

Helena barely seemed to notice. She reached into her cloak and grabbed a pouch of Julian's powder. She created another wind tunnel and threw the powder, driving it toward the skin-walker. It nearly reached him, but the wolfish-bat thing disappeared into the darkness of the sky.

"Oh thank God," Abby breathed as Oliver's van careened down the snowy driveway. It skidded to a stop. Oliver and Julian leapt out.

"We made it. I can't believe we made it," Julian murmured, running for the porch behind Oliver.

"Where is Sebastian?" Oliver asked.

Lydie pointed toward Sebastian, walking toward Kanti in the distance.

"Dafne?" Oliver started and Helena grabbed the sleeve of his coat.

"No, it's..."

"Kanti," Abby finished.

Oliver unstrapped his bow and cocked an arrow. He aimed for Sebastian's back. Abby saw him from the corner of her eye and lunged at him, knocking the bow from his hand. It skidded across the snow.

"We're going to let him go and join them?" Oliver raged, incredulous.

"Would you put an arrow between his shoulder blades?" Julian asked, staring Oliver down.

Oliver glared at him and picked up his bow and arrow. He did not take aim again.

Abby watched Sebastian walk to Kanti. She smiled up at him with Dafne's mouth. He did not return her smile, but stood obediently as she removed a long silver chain from her neck. In the moonlight, Abby saw a golden amulet with a pulsing red stone in its center. Sebastian kneeled and she placed the amulet around his neck.

CHAPTER 29

"No, no, no," Abby murmured the word over and over, not wanting to believe what unfolded before her. Her Sebastian would not—could not—choose hatred over love. She wanted to run to him, to drag him bodily away from the dark witch who had taken Dafne and now Sebastian as well. Her feet stayed rooted. She knew if she tried, Oliver and Julian would stop her. She wanted to crumble into a ball of despair, but she had to stand and fight.

Two more of the skin-walkers attacked. The first went for Oliver. He squatted, pulled his bow from his back and launched an arrow at the beast. It twisted away and he missed. The second snatched the bag at Julian's feet. Julian threw a cloud of dust into the creature's face. It rose away, the bag clutched in its talons, and then twitched and released its grasp. The Vepar flew wildly into the trees, screeching and shaking its head.

Kanti did not move. She did not turn to watch the Vepar as it disappeared into the trees. Her eyes were trained on Abby. Abby stared back at her, willing her gaze to rip the evil spirit from Dafne's body.

Another skin-walker dove, and another. Helena picked up the shotgun, took aim and fired. She missed and another of the creatures plunged and sunk its claws into her back. Julian took hold of the monster's wings and ripped it away. It turned, biting and clawing, and Julian released it before it could sink its venomous teeth into his hands. Lydie conjured a stream of fire that hit the monster in the face. It flew and then plummeted, shrieking, into the snow at the edge of the woods. The moment the fire extinguished, the beast transformed. It heaved and gasped until a man, a Vepar, emerged. He stood from the ground, hulking, seven feet tall, with patches of black hair on his blistering red scalp. Abby saw that most of his face had been burned. It looked raw and sticky. He glared at the porch and the witches and then broke into a run, his eyes trained on Lydie.

Abby conjured ice from the lake. It flew in daggers into the sky at the beasts that continued to circle. Several of the ice spears sunk into one of the flying creatures. It spiraled down and thudded on the deck, wriggling, already transforming back to a Vepar. Abby did not recognize the changing form, but shifted her attention back to the Vepar racing toward them. Lydie shot fire at the beast, but he dodged it, leaning down and scooping a huge rock from the ground. He flung the rock toward Lydie and she dove to the side. It crashed into the porch and splintered wood exploded. Abby drew more daggers of ice from the lake, directing them toward the Vepar. One of them sunk into his shoulder. He ripped it out and continued, but Helena, hunched and in pain, had sent a blast of wind at the Vepar. He struggled forward, but couldn't make any ground. Lydie, her face a mask of hatred, stepped to the edge of the deck. A huge orb of fire floated above her fingers. She sent it into Helena's wind. The Vepar caught fire and began to dance and howl. He fell to the snow, thrashing and then growing still. As the fire died, Lydie strode purposefully down the steps and into the yard. She leaned over the monster and drove the stake into the Vepar's stomach and up through his chest.

Oliver straddled the Vepar who had hit the porch. He shoved his metal blade through the thick breastplate and into the pouch beneath the heart. Abby heard a loud pop and saw a burst of black blood that sprayed Oliver. He wiped his arm over his face.

Kanti conjured a handful of fire; it grew and danced and lit her twisted features. She smiled and laughed and howled at the moon. Sebastian stood beside her. The amulet on his chest glowed brighter with the fire that Kanti held. As she thrust the fire toward the house, Abby conjured her own ball of ice and water. She cast it toward the maniacal witch. It collided with the fireball just before it struck the widow's walk. Kanti created another ball of fire and another, until she and Abby cast their energies back and forth with dizzying speed.

A black crow flew from the forest. It dove toward Kanti, ripping at her hair. She swatted it away, but then another appeared and another. They started to attack her, ripping at her face and hair. She howled with rage and opened her arms wide, creating a dome of fire that rose above her.

The birds flew to Abby. They landed on the porch around her, watching her with their curious dark eyes.

Kanti took hold of the amulet around Sebastian's neck. She trained her black eyes on his and pointed to Abby.

"Bring her to me!"

Abby watched, sick, as Sebastian turned toward her. His body moved as if controlled. His face held a sheet of impassivity. Abby started to retreat on the porch and she bumped into Julian, who had created a cyclone in the air. One of the Vepars was caught in its grasp.

"Go with him," Julian urged, so quietly that Abby almost missed it.

"What?" she asked, alarmed, suddenly convinced that Julian too had become a dark witch.

His light eyes bored into her, and she nodded.

When Sebastian stepped onto the porch, Oliver attacked. He launched onto Sebastian's back, trying to tear the amulet from his neck. A Vepar fell from the sky and sunk its teeth into Oliver's shoulder. Julian raced to his aide, pulling the Vepar from Oliver as Sebastian shrugged him off. He moved toward Abby, his eyes glassy and distant. He scooped her into his arms and terror seized her. What if she didn't fight back and he took her to Kanti?

And then he was running. Running faster than any human should have been able. Behind them the earth was splitting. Trees groaned and crashed. Sweat poured down Sebastian's face as he directed all of his energy, energy that he couldn't possibly have, into the earth behind him. The crows followed them, flying through the darkness of the trees overhead. Abby saw Kanti for an instant, shock and then savage fury crossing her face. A tree crashed and blocked her from Abby's view.

****

"Where's Abby?" Oliver screamed as the earth at the edge of the forest began to rumble and split. He watched trees crashing in the distance. He spun wildly in a circle and then his eyes fell upon Kanti. He followed her gaze to Sebastian. Sebastian fled into the forest with Abby in his arms. Kanti looked mad with rage. She pulled the jeweled dragon blade from her coat.

****

Beneath the dark canopy of trees, Sebastian set Abby roughly down and reached for the ground. He lifted a tarp, covered in snow, and flung it to the side. Beneath it, she saw a storm cellar door. He jerked it open and shoved her in, following close at her heels.

"I know you're freaking out right now, but I need you to run," he bellowed as she tripped down the stairs.

He held her arms to steady her.

In the cellar, Abby saw tunnels, sparsely lit, branching out in several directions.

"This one," Sebastian shouted, pushing Abby toward the tunnel to their left.

He took the lead, holding her hand and then, apparently frustrated by her slowness, he lifted her back into his arms and carried her.

She didn't speak. She wanted to. She wanted to ask him what had happened. She wanted to rip the throbbing amulet from his chest and demand an explanation, but she understood that they needed to get away and that Sebastian was making that happen. The tunnel ended at a huge wooden door. He kicked it open. On the other side, he set Abby down and dug a key from a divot in the wall. He locked the door and slipped the key into his pocket.

"Up and out," he said, hustling Abby up a set of crude wooden stairs. They emerged in darkness, deep in the forest and she shivered, scared. A hulking dark shape loomed before them. Sebastian reached for it and pulled off another tarp. A black Jeep stood beneath the cover.

"Get in," he told her, sliding behind the wheel.

Suddenly she thought of Oliver, Lydie, Helena and Julian.

"We can't leave," she told him urgently. "We have to go back and help them."

"No." He shook his head. He took the amulet from his chest, grimacing as his fingers touched it, and reached beneath his seat for a heavy metal box. He opened it, wrapped the amulet in a black cloth and shut the lid, screwing up the number combination on the front. He slid the box back beneath his feet.

"We have to get as much distance between Kanti and this amulet as we can."

He started the Jeep and drove down a rough, barely discernible trail that wound through the forest. The Jeep slid in the snow and bounced over roots and uneven ground.

Abby braced her hands on the dashboard and closed her eyes as a spasm coursed through her belly. She clutched her stomach.

Sebastian glanced at her.

"We're almost out, two more minutes and we'll hit the pavement."

When they reached the road, the tires squealed as they found solid ground. The trees formed a black dome around the yellow beam of headlights. Abby searched the trees, wondering what lay beyond the scope of their headlights.

"What the hell just happened?" she asked, finally.

Sebastian let out a huge sigh and then grinned.

He beat his hands on the wheel and turned to her in amazement.

"It worked! It fucking worked!"

"What worked? I thought...I thought..."

She started to cry then. A huge uncontrollable sob rolled through her body, and she buried her face in her hands.

She thought he had become one of them, that the prophecy had come true, that the curse had taken her beloved Sebastian.

"Oh Abby, I'm sorry. I'm so sorry," Sebastian murmured, reaching across the car and wrapping his arm around her. He pulled her against him and she pressed her face into his side.

Her body shook as she cried, but she couldn't seem to stop. In the moment, there hadn't been time to feel all of it, or any of it. The moment when she watched him cross the snow and stand by Kanti. In that instant, their whole life, the dream of their future, dissolved before her. Despair and relief poured out of her as she understood that it had been a setup. He had never left her.

****

As Oliver watched, a skin-walker landed at Kanti's feet. It transformed quickly. The creature rose up next to Kanti: Tobias. He smiled at Oliver and his sharp teeth glinted.

Beside him, Kanti's eyes flickered. Oliver saw Dafne, her face desperate, reclaim her body. Dafne turned to Tobias, unknowing beside her. She plunged the dragon blade into his chest. She snarled and screamed as she drove the blade in deeper. Tobias grabbed her shoulders, shoving her away, and stumbled back. Dafne dove for him on the ground. She took hold of the dagger a second time and pushed it further, harder. He tried to shove her away, but black blood spurted from his chest. The malice drained from his eyes and he fell backwards into the snow.

Oliver raced toward Dafne as Kanti washed back over her. He could see the struggle happening within her. Dafne re-emerged. She pulled the blade from Tobias and Oliver skidded to a stop, horror-struck, as Dafne turned the blade and drove it into her own heart.

"No!" he screamed and ran for her. He pulled the dagger from her hands and thrust it away as she collapsed beneath him.

"Dafne, no, no, just hold on," Oliver crooned. He pressed his hands into her chest, trying to stop the flow, but it was so much blood and moving so fast as it left her body. It soaked the snow beneath them.

She reached her hand to his face and took a rattling breath. Blood trickled from her mouth.

"Destroy the amulet," she whispered. And then she was gone.

CHAPTER 30

"Julian has known since the beginning," Sebastian told Abby, holding her hands tightly in his own. "I didn't want to lie to you and I'm so sorry that I did."

They sat together at Ula, in the bedroom that Abby had stayed in on her very first night in the castle, when witches and Vepars were mostly a dream that she expected to wake up from at any moment.

"I'm not going to say it's okay," she told him. It hurt that Sebastian had lied, and had been lying for months.

"After the second time I woke up in the shed, I knew that she was getting into my head. Whatever they did to me in the Vepar's lair must have given her access to my mind."

"So Faustine was right."

"Yes. I went to Julian and told him. He believed that Kanti would know I was deceiving her if you knew what was happening since she was influencing your dreams. She obviously had access to you too. Julian started to work with me to block her psychically. He also sent me home with a shielding elixir, which I added to your coffee."

"Are you serious?" She stared at him, incredulous.

"It made sense, Abby. We needed everyone to see me shifting to the dark side. She wouldn't believe it otherwise."

"What if his elixir had hurt the baby? Did you consider that?" She ripped her hands out of his.

"Julian knew about the baby. I made it clear that you and she were all that mattered, that everything we did had to be in service to you and our child. I would never have done any of it if I'd seen another way."

"How about come to me, your future wife? Include me? Include the coven so that we would create a plan together?"

"And lose access to an evil spirit hell-bent on destroying us all?"

"I get the feeling Dafne had similar thoughts when she started her web of lies. Look how that turned out?"

Sebastian frowned.

"Abby if you had felt what I have experienced, losing my parents and Claire, chasing this mysterious evil, then you would understand."

"It's not fair that you use those feelings. I know that Claire's death devastated you, but she can't be the reason that anything goes. If we're going to have a life together, you have to bury the past. You have to come into the here-and-now and make choices based in your new reality."

"Do you think that I was wrong? Tell me this, if the roles were reversed, what would you have done?" he asked, trying to temper the anger in his voice. Anger, but also shame. He felt badly and she knew it, but did that let him off the hook?

Abby bit her lip and looked away from him. She didn't know what she would have done.

"In Chicago, Julian pressured me to talk about you, as if he suspected you were being pulled toward evil, and wanted me to admit it. Why?"

"He told me about that," Sebastian admitted. "He wanted to gauge what you were thinking and feeling. It was important that you believed something was happening to me, something bad, because then Kanti would be able to sense that in you and perhaps also sense that you were hiding it from the other witches. He wanted your feelings to mirror back to Kanti what she already believed. He pushed you to see if you would get defensive."

"Which I did."

"Yeah."

"I have to admit, I feel like I've been played for a fool."

"You haven't. You're entitled to your feelings, but I swear to you, this was never meant to hurt you. I did all of this to ensure that I didn't hurt you."

Abby touched the tattered journal on the floor.

"You went to the Lourdes? Do you know how dangerous she is?"

Sebastian shuddered.

"Yes, I do and I did. It was Julian's idea, but the truth is that I wanted to go. I wanted to do whatever it took. For you, for our baby. I know how it must seem to you."

"Reckless."

"Necessary."

****

"It is bothersome that you did not tell us, Julian," Elda chastised.

"Seriously," Oliver snapped. "You've known Sebastian for what? Three months?"

Julian continued buttering his toast. After several moments of silence, he sighed and set down his knife.

"I think that I offered a thorough explanation for my secrecy."

"You don't think we deserved to know what was happening?" Helena asked, not touching her breakfast. "What if Oliver had killed Sebastian? He nearly did, you know?"

The sky beyond the breakfast window matched the mood in the room, gray and bleak.

"Faustine agrees with my choice. And the more who knew, the more likely that Kanti would have realized what was happening. It's that simple. Sebastian had to hide it from Abby. That's how far this had to go. Can you possibly deserve that information more than her? You don't see her raving about the situation."

"Yeah, well I'd bet Sebastian has had an earful from Abby," Oliver challenged. "And with good reason. You might have put her and the baby in danger with your lies."

"Or we might have saved her. Who knows what Kanti might have done if she believed that she had lost her control of Sebastian. Can't you see that everything depended on it?"

"My God, Abby thought he was trying to conjure his sister from the dead," Helena murmured, holding her hand over her heart as if it hurt to utter the words.

"Yes, an unfortunate belief, but that was Kanti's intention. She was using that promise to control Sebastian. Or so she thought."

"So why didn't it work? How did he get control back?" Oliver asked.

Julian shrugged.

"I honestly don't know. He is exhibiting powers. He has been since the Vepar's lair. Is he a witch? None of us can feel him in that capacity; maybe he is some kind of hybrid."

"Or maybe Kanti is giving him the power because she intends to exploit it," Elda sighed.

"That's what I thought originally, but he used it against her. You saw what happened, Oliver. He ripped the earth apart to get Abby to safety. If she had given it to him, why didn't she take it away the moment he turned against her?"

"And he took the amulet. Why didn't it affect him?"

"We prepared him for that. I didn't know of course that she would put it on him, entrust him with it so quickly, but I suspected that her power would be greatest through the amulet. She survives through it, after all. Like most evil, she became arrogant. She believed she had him under her control. She was not afraid to put the amulet on him, but you see we've been building a psychic shield around him for months. I even created a shirt made from hair, sage and copper fibers to protect him if the moment came that he had to put the amulet on."

"Whose hair?" Oliver asked, looking disgusted.

"Sebastian and Abby's. Their love is the ultimate protection. Of course, I performed magic on the hair to ensure that it held only their purist intentions."

"Obviously it worked," Elda admitted. "Did you have a moment at all, when he went to Kanti, where you wondered if she might take control of him, after all?"

Julian considered, but shook his head.

"Nope. He has a strong mind. Few people could have pulled this off. He met her four or five times. She appeared as Dafne. The first few times, he had no control. We retrieved those memories with Faustine's crystal. After that, we prepared. The last two times, he was fully present. He told her everything she wanted to hear. He played the tortured soul desperate to bring his sister back from the dead. He was the man who wanted to be a witch and hated how everyone else had power, except him."

"All those times he had Dafne in his grasp. We might have saved her," Helena murmured, her eyes sparkling with tears.

Oliver moved close to her, wrapping his arm around her back.

"I wanted to save Dafne," Julian said. "I believed in the end that we would. I thought once we had the amulet..."

"You'd destroy it?"

"Yes, of course. That's the next step. I thought we would have the opportunity to take Dafne and the amulet."

"Instead she killed herself," Helena sniffled.

"Sacrificed herself," Oliver corrected. "She wanted to end Kanti."

"She took Tobias down too," Julian added. "Her life was not wasted."

Helena grimaced and Elda pursed her lips. None of them agreed with Julian's choices. They all considered how it might have gone differently. Could they have saved Dafne?

"But she told you to destroy the amulet," Elda said to Oliver. "So she knew that killing herself would not kill Kanti."

Oliver closed his eyes, trying not to see Dafne as she faded from the world.

"She wanted out," Julian told them. "Who hasn't felt that way at some point?"

****

That evening, Victor and Kendra joined them at the Coven of Ula.

"We will wait until the full moon to destroy the amulet," Faustine told the witches gathered in the library.

"Are you concerned at all about keeping it here in the castle?" Kendra asked.

"Yes," Elda answered. "But we have a special room in the dungeons that shields magical items. Any power that Kanti has through the amulet will be restricted to that room."

Julian had draped the amulet over a black canvas.

Abby watched the firelight flicker off the gold setting.

"So what is it?" Oliver asked. He walked closer to the necklace, but stopped short of touching it. None of them wanted to get too close.

"It's an ouroboros," Faustine told him.

"A snake consuming itself," Julian finished. "In ancient Egypt, it symbolized everlasting life. Of course, it was more than symbolic. There was powerful magic cast within many of these amulets."

"By witches?" Lydie asked. She sat on the floor with her back resting against Helena's legs.

Abby had noticed an extra hardness in Lydie's demeanor since they had returned to Ula the night before. Oliver had confided to Abby that Lydie had cried over Dafne the entire drive to Lake Superior and then stopped abruptly at the shore.

"Yes, witches and probably some Vepars."

"What is the stone in the center?" Kendra asked.

"Red jasper," Victor told her.

She looked at him in surprise.

"Been studying minerals lately?"

He shrugged.

"I've come across it a few times during research."

"Also regularly used in Egypt," Julian added. "And also representative of eternal life, eternal youth—that sort of thing."

"How could she possibly have gotten it?" Helena asked skeptically. "Could the magic have been placed in the amulet after her death."

"Doubtful," Faustine replied. "I have never heard of a soul being transferred from one magical item to another."

"The man who took her was not ordinary," Julian interrupted. "Those journals implied that he had powers. Possibly a dark witch or even a Vepar, though that's less likely."

"Why is it less likely?" Abby asked. She shared an overstuffed chair with Sebastian. It felt good to have him crammed against her side.

"Because they're savage animals," Oliver murmured. He looked tired and sad. Abby knew that he mourned the passing of Dafne more than he could admit, even to himself.

"Because they're often impulsive and violent. This Kanti woman travelled with this man for a long time. He also impregnated her. I'm not sure that a Vepar can reproduce."

"I hope not," Oliver grumbled.

"So how do we destroy it?" Lydie asked, calling everyone's attention back to the necklace.

"We're still figuring that out," Elda admitted. "We've got to do our due diligence and make sure we perform the proper magic."

"There's an ax owned by the Sky Mother's Coven in Australia," Julian added. "They say it can destroy the most powerful, the most evil, objects in existence."

"How do we get it?" Sebastian asked.

"We go to Australia," Oliver answered.

****

Dafne, a fire witch, wanted her body consecrated to fire at the end of her life.

They had built the pyre together. It would sail through the cliff and into the lake beyond. Dafne lay on a bed of flowers picked from the floating garden.

The witches and Sebastian stood on the lagoon edge as Faustine folded Dafne's arms across her chest. He kissed her forehead. Elda pressed her hand into a stone bowl and smeared something red on the space between Dafne's eyebrows. She closed her eyes, as if warding off tears, and stepped back from the bed.

Lydie walked to the pyre and rested a glass ball of glowing fire on her funeral bed.

"By the element of fire you lived, passionate, driven and strong. Let fire light your path in the realms beyond this one. From fire you came, to fire you return."

She stepped back, closing her eyes as if she didn't want to watch as the others bid farewell.

Elda walked to Dafne next. She wove a braid of ice with her hands. It shimmered as Elda lay it around Dafne's neck.

"By the element of water you flowed, you dreamed, you loved, you changed. Let water carry you into the realms beyond this one. From water you came, to water you return."

Oliver stepped next to the pyre. His eyes glistened and his hands shook as he sprinkled sand over Dafne's body.

"By the element of earth you were grounded, you found roots, family, home. Let earth keep you steady as you travel into the realms beyond this one. From earth you came, to earth you return."

Helena went last, struggling to ebb her cries. She placed her hands on Dafne's arm and continued to cry. Faustine put a hand on her shoulder to steady her.

"By the element of air, you soared, you knew knowledge, wisdom and freedom. Let air liberate you from this realm into those beyond. From air you came, to air you return."

Helena took Dafne's hand and kissed it.

"Goodbye, beautiful friend," she whispered.

Faustine held his hands in the air and closed his eyes. The pyre pushed away from the shore.

Abby bit her lip. Tears streamed down her face as she watched the witch's black hair blow in the wind. Sebastian held her hand tight in his own.

Kendra and Victor had joined them for the death ritual. They stood further back from the other witches. Kendra's eyes mirrored the sorrow in the group, while Victor watched with an expression of curiosity. Abby knew that neither of the witches had experienced a death ritual for a witch. She too had never experienced one. When Max had been laid to rest, Abby and Sebastian had been in Trager.

Lydie did not cry. She stood resolute, her body tiny in the red cloak that she wore. Dafne's cloak. Oliver stood behind her, his face grim.

When the pyre reached the center of the lagoon, Lydie raised her arms. She conjured a ball of fire and then blew it from her hand. It sailed through the air and landed in the center of the pyre. The wood began to burn.

Helena sobbed into Bridget's shoulder. Bridget patted her back and whispered to her soothingly. Helena's cries echoed across the water.

The funeral bed blazed as it sailed from the lagoon, into a tunnel beneath the cliff, and disappeared from sight.

****

For dinner Bridget made all of Dafne's favorites. They had a spread of Greek salad, pasties and key lime pie for dessert.

"I'm going to need this recipe," Sebastian told Bridget across the table as he ate another forkful of beef pastie.

"It was Dafne's recipe, believe it or not. She never cooked, mind you." Bridget winked at him. "But apparently her mom used to make these when Dafne was a girl. In those days, you helped your mama in the kitchen, so Dafne knew how it was done and showed me."

"They're delicious," he said. "I helped my mom in the kitchen too, and my dad. They both loved to cook."

Bridget perked up and started questioning Sebastian about his parents' best dishes.

Lydie ate her food in silence.

Though Bridget and Helena had done their best to create a festive atmosphere for the celebration of Dafne's life, the truth was that her death overshadowed the experience. No amount of food, decorations or magic could lift the heavy reality of death.

"So when can we start planning the wedding?" Helena asked, reaching for Abby's hand.

Abby smiled and sighed. Wedding, baby, destroying an evil amulet—who had the time?

"Sebastian and I thought something small in the spring. Obviously we'd love to have it here at Ula, but I would want to invite my parents so..."

"We can make that work," Faustine declared.

Abby looked up, surprised. It never ceased to amaze her, the strange topics that Faustine commented on.

"Many of the witches of Ula have had family visit at some point. It's not something we make a habit of, but for special occasions..."

"A wedding here would be divine," Bridget added, nodding enthusiastically.

"In the floating garden," Lydie said, a smile finding her face. "I would like to sketch that."

"Ezra's a killer DJ," Victor offered.

Kendra nodded.

"Yeah, she DJs at a club in Chicago a couple times a month."

"Really?" Oliver asked, clearly interested.

Abby noticed an eagerness in his voice and wondered if Oliver had developed an interest in the feisty Chicago witch.

"We could throw an epic wedding reception in this castle," Victor continued.

"Let's not gloss over the 'something small' part," Abby reminded him.

By the spring she would be full-on pregnant. She had no interest in a wild party.

"No," Sebastian stopped the conversation. "I'm sorry to be the buzzkill, but we don't want a traditional reception. Actually," he turned to Faustine, "we want to invoke the elements, like during a ritual or..."

"Death ceremony," Lydie finished.

"Yes, like that. We want to invite magic into our marriage."

Elda nodded, seeming impressed.

"I have attended many ceremonies that invoke the elements," Faustine told him. "It would be our pleasure."

"What inspired you to desire that, honey?" Helena asked him.

"Lydie actually," Sebastian admitted. He smiled at Lydie. "She told me about her parents' wedding, the calling of the four directions and their elements. Her parents believed that they blessed Lydie by consecrating their marriage in that way."

"Well Lydie is definitely blessed," Helena murmured, leaning toward Lydie and petting her unruly curls.

"Okay, no wild party after," Victor chimed in. "Intimate magic ceremony worthy of witch and her super—her fiancé." Victor winked at Sebastian. "Followed by a small, tame, totally crazy party that maybe includes a DJ and cake."

"We can compromise on that," Abby agreed, looking into Sebastian's glittering blue eyes. He looked excited and for the first time in months, at ease.

****

Victor slipped into the dungeons. The witches of Ula slept. He had waited until three a.m. to leave his bed and creep downstairs.

He took the skull from the leather bag he had slipped it into. The bone felt cold against his hot skin. He walked the dark hallway and held the skull out before him. As he moved deeper into the castle, the skull gleamed and glowed. As he passed a door, it burned red for an instant.

He tried to push the door open, but it didn't budge. He pressed a palm against the wood and directed his energy into the lock. It clicked open.

He walked the dark room slowly, extending the skull toward shelves and cabinets. It glowed red again in front of a large black chest. He opened the chest.

Inside, he found a metal box. He did not know the combination, but called upon the air to move the dials to their appropriate numbers. The safe unlocked. Nestled in the folds of dark fabric, he saw the beautiful ouroboros. The golden snake consuming its tail—everlasting life. The red jasper stone shone from its center. He smoothed his finger along the jewel and a shiver passed through his body.

Carefully he lifted the amulet from the cloth and slipped it neatly into the velvet box he had brought to Ula. He tucked the box into the breast pocket of his jacket, close to his heart. He took the replica from his pocket. The gold and the stone were real enough. He had paid a jewelry maker in Chicago five thousand dollars to create the piece. It was valuable in its own right and beautiful, but costume jewelry compared to the amulet now in his possession. He placed the replica in the metal box, closed the lid and returned it to the trunk.

He moved stealthily through Ula, back to his room. Taking the amulet from the box, he slipped it over his neck and laid in bed. He fell asleep to the gentle pulsing of the stone against his chest.

AUTHOR'S NOTE

I love characters. For me that's the heart of writing and reading. I would love to hear about your experience with my characters and what other fictional characters you love. Reading has truly shaped my life and there's nothing more amazing than connecting with other readers who share passions similar to my own. I write as J.R. Erickson, though my legal name is Jacki Riegle. I live in Northern Michigan with my excavator husband and my beautiful little boy.

Don't forget to check out the next book in the Born of Shadows Series. Visit my author website www.jrericksonauthor.com for more information about upcoming book releases.

Made in the USA
Middletown, DE
08 November 2025

21077958R00130